Material WITNESS

L.A. MONDELLO

Published by: Lisa Mondello

Copyright © 2012 by Lisa Mondello

For more information on the author and her works, please see http://www.LisaMondello.blogspot.com

This book is also available in electronic formats at online retailers.

Who does she trust when she's living the real-life horror of one of her crime novels...

Bestselling crime novelist Cassie Alvarez, aka Cassie Lang, has murder on her mind when she walks into Rory's Bar underdressed and undercover to research her latest crime novel. Researching the cool, blue-eyed and dashingly handsome man at the end of the bar stirs her senses more than she wants to admit. But is this man of leather armor all he appears to be?

Playing White Knight to an innocent wasn't how Detective Jake Santos planned to spend his time undercover. But there's no way "CJ" is what she claims to be, and that nagging tightness in Jake's chest tells him he'd better take her home to safety and leave it at that. Then the barroom explodes with gunfire, leaving a trail of dead that includes a notorious Providence crime boss and an undercover FBI agent. When Cassie's name is leaked to the media as the only witness to the grisly murders, Cassie insists she only trusts Jake to protect her.

The FBI wants their star witness happy and will do anything to make sure Cassie testifies. But it is clear to Jake that the shooter isn't the only person who wants Cassie dead. Not knowing who to trust, he vows to protect Cassie at all cost despite the fact that guarding the beautiful novelist is a serious distraction.

This book is dedicated with love to my dear friend Scott Ricciuti. Check out his latest CD, *Like the Red Haunts the Wine*, at http://www.ScottRicciuti.com
Keep the music alive…

CHAPTER ONE

She was going to kill Maureen. There was no doubt about it now.

Cassie Alvarez yanked down the hem of her too-short red spandex mini-dress, trying to conceal what every man with a pulse at Rory's seemed to be ogling over. She was tired, cold and exposed, but it was no use. No matter how much she covered her bare flesh, she was all out there like the woman of the night she was pretending to be.

Damn Maureen...and damn her for listening.

It had taken Cassie all of ten seconds after seating herself at the bar to realize just how big a mistake she'd made in coming to a bar owned by one of Providence's most notorious crime bosses. When you walk through fire, you get burned. With all the stares she'd gotten just walking across the floor, she felt like burnt toast.

Definitely murder. It was her forte. The only question left was how? She'd plotted many murders in the past. She was good at it. And nothing was too harsh for what Maureen was putting her through tonight. The least Maureen could have done was come here with her since it was her idea.

Maureen's idea. But despite all the convincing, Cassie couldn't figure out exactly why she'd actually agreed. Her editor had always been good at pulling her strings. And that nauseated Cassie even more than having her thighs stuck to the barstool.

Note to self: Learn to assert yourself with your editor even if she is your best friend.

Cassie vowed to do just that right after she was finished wringing Maureen's bony little neck.

Turning her attention to her diet soda, Cassie used her red-striped straw to play with the maraschino cherry that had sunk

1

to the bottom of the glass. The bartender wiped the polished surface of the bar as he made his way closer to Cassie. She made eye contact with him when he came close enough. With her hand still holding the sweating glass, he snatched her drink and dumped the contents into a bucket behind the counter.

"Hey, I was still drinking that."

"You've been stirring it for an hour. It's nothing but melted ice and you're making a mess of my bar. Doesn't look good. Here's another one."

Before she could protest further, he had a clean glass full of ice under the soda fountain and was filling it.

"Don't worry. I don't expect you to tip me twice."

While her mouth was still dropped open, he made his way down to the other end of the bar, wiping as he went. She'd give anything to be home right now wearing her favorite Boston Bruins tee-shirt and the Brown University sweat pants that, even though they'd seen better days, Cassie refused to give up. Instead of three-and-a-half-inch stilettos, her feet would be warm in her fuzzy slippers. Instead, she was stuck in a bar watching people who'd be the inspiration for her next crime novel.

"Life mimicking art," she mumbled. "How's that for stupidity, Cass?"

She blinked her sore eyes as the haze of the neon lights on the window assaulted them. The quickest way to get out of here was to take notes and get into the head of her character. How could she write about a woman who was so devastated by circumstance, who felt trapped in a life beyond her control, if she hadn't lived it? She needed to step outside herself to break this block.

The room was thinning out now, but there were still enough people to talk to. The couple in their fifties, arguing at a table, looked too self-absorbed to do her any good. The "suit" with the combed-over shiny head, sitting alone at a table by the bathroom, looked like he was about to fall asleep in his martini.

Cassie snapped her glance away from him as he lifted his head in her direction. Better to leave this man with his troubles and not make them one of hers.

The argument from the couple grew louder. Apparently they'd both had a little too much to drink and were loud enough for Cassie to hear every intimate detail. *Someone was walking home tonight.*

And then there was the black-armored thug seated at the end of the bar, staring at *her*. Yeah she'd noticed. His interest in her was unmistakable. Their gazes locked for a lingering moment. The heat in his eyes was piercing.

Cassie glanced down at her cleavage and to her bare legs. It couldn't be the dress. There was nothing but a few scraps of fabric covering her.

Slowly, she turned to look over her shoulder, just to see if she was wrong and he was actually looking at someone else. The table behind her was empty. When she turned back, it was as if he'd caught her in a radar lock.

Terrific. "A little too eager beaver, but…" she muttered.

The guy was hunched over with his long arms draped stiffly on top of the bar with his black leather jacket encasing him like body armor. His strong jaw had a don't-fuck-with-me tightness she was sure was bred of years of hanging out in a dive like this.

Cassie wanted to feel bad for him. All of them really. What made a person come to a place like this thinking it could resolve their sorrows? She had to find out. Only then would she understand her character.

As she always did with people she encountered, Cassie began to formulate a character sketch. She couldn't quite come up with one for this guy though. He was…

Okay, so he was a good-looking thug. If she'd met him anywhere else she would have been…attracted to him. Her insides stirred violently, causing heat to rise from the pit of her stomach, up her chest and to her already warm cheeks, making them flame.

It's only research, for God's sake! She was only pretending to be a hooker to research her next crime novel. It wasn't like she was actually going to pick up the guy.

She pulled her cell phone out of her purse and began texting.

You're a dead woman, Maureen. Remind me tomorrow how much I hate you for this. Cassie pressed the send button.

A few seconds later, her phone vibrated. A quick look at the glowing screen and she saw Maureen's name. *Quit acting like a baby! You're a grown woman. Shake your girls, ask some questions, and then get back to that computer! You'll be writing in no time! M.*

"If I shake my *girls*, I'll fall out of the damned dress," Cassie said.

The bartender must have caught her muttering because he was headed in her direction again. Before he could say anything, she said, "I'm all set."

With a heaving sigh, Cassie turned her attention back to Mr. Thug with the cool leather jacket and smoky blue eyes. Might as well go for broke. Stretching one of her long legs over the other, tugging at the hem of the obscenely short dress to keep it in place, she tossed him her most seductive smile. She'd talk to him for two minutes tops and then she'd be gone. If she failed, she'd have to give back her advance.

Or come back here again.

Maureen would definitely make her come back.

Cassie shuddered at the thought. One evening out of her life in a bar with grease-lined walls and people was enough for any self-respecting woman. She was staying put until she gathered all the information she needed, and then she was hitting the pavement, back to her comfy but small apartment with locks and security in the nice section of the city.

CJ Carmen, the main character in all her crime novels, would have the stomach to dance right up to any one of these thugs and demand the information she needed. Too bad Cassie didn't have CJ's gumption.

That was the good thing about being a writer. No matter what problem she encountered in a book, she could keep working at it until she got it right. You couldn't do that in real life, and Cassie knew that painfully well. In real life, Cassie didn't have the grace and fluidity of CJ Carmen or the confidence with which she moved. She valued control in a world that was filled with so little of it.

Cassie took a deep breath and gathered all the courage she could muster. She'd created CJ Carmen. She could create a little gumption, too. If she had to take notes from someone, Mr. Smokey Blue Eyes seemed the most harmless of the bunch.

Which didn't say much for the clientele in Rory's.

* * *

He was a dead man. Jake Santos glanced at the clock over the line of liquor bottles neatly stored behind the bar and recalled the first rule of surviving undercover law enforcement. *If your informant is five minutes late, you've waited four minutes too long.* He'd been sitting there for fifteen minutes.

Ty would be pissed.

Jake couldn't say he'd blame him either. His former partner had taken a bullet for following emotion instead of the rulebook. But Angel had been insistent. This case was so close to breaking wide open that another few minutes may be worth his time.

Taking a long pull on his beer, he let his eyes crawl through the seedy bar. Scum bred scum, and Rory's was about as close to the bottom of the barrel as a person got. Most everything illegal that happened in Providence started with a handshake right here at one of these tables.

Where the hell was Angel?

He tossed a ten-dollar bill on the bar and waved to the bartender. As he turned to take one last look at the room, he saw her again. Yeah, he'd noticed the leggy brunette "lady" at the far end of the bar for the past fifteen minutes. It was kind of hard not to notice someone who looked as out of place here as his grandmother would.

He dragged his gaze from her legs and let his attention drift upward toward her painted cheeks. Her dark eyes were the most prominent feature of her round face. Her eyes—from this distance they looked sable—were bright and wide, but not as if she was supporting a habit, like most other women who took to the streets. She appeared more curious than anything as her gaze swept the thinning room, almost as if she were taking mental notes.

Jake cursed under his breath. He didn't care how much paint she had on her face, he'd bet his next paycheck she wasn't a hooker. The only thing they gave a damn about was getting money for their next fix. This one...she was looking for something and it wasn't a john. She was tugging at her slinky red dress, trying to hide her God-given assets instead of advertising them like most other "ladies," was another telltale sign she was way out of her comfort zone. No matter how much her high cheekbones were tinted with color to disguise her innocence, it was there just like a neon sign that screamed "hands off."

And her eyes were too curious. Curiosity like that was going to get her mugged, raped or dead before the night was over.

Jake took another pull from the bottle, grimacing at the warm taste of its dregs. He placed the empty bottle in the perspiration ring it had left on the polished bar. He didn't give a damn what this woman's reason was for being here. Now that Angel was a no show, Jake was pissed. After weeks of gaining his trust, Jake was sure tonight he'd get a personal introduction to Ritchie Trumbella, bringing him closer to making a case against the local crime boss that would finally lead to an arrest.

But Angel wasn't here. There were only a few locals drowning their sorrows at the bottom of a glass before staggering home. Well, them and the Painted Lady at the end of the bar who he knew was headed for trouble.

Jake groaned inwardly. He'd been fooled before. It may have been a long time ago, but his memory was long. The way she was casing the place...

Damn. He was a cop. A good one, too. And Jake knew that if he didn't get this woman out of Rory's fast, he'd end up reading her obit in the *Providence Journal* tomorrow morning.

He motioned to the bartender when he appeared in front of him. Sliding off the barstool, Jake tossed a crisp twenty-dollar bill to the finely polished surface of the bar and tipped his empty beer bottle toward the woman in red.

"Send another one down to the end, and get whatever she's having."

"Diet soda," the bartender said, stretching his wiry gray eyebrows up in a salute. His chipmunk cheeks glowed a shade darker with amusement.

"Diet…" *Jesus.* There had to be one hell of a story attached to this woman. He wasn't sure he wanted to hear it.

He pushed an errant wooden chair back into place against a table as he made his way toward the end of the bar. As he got closer, Jake noticed her eyes were impossibly dark, almost black in color. It was the kind of deep color that made a man fall into them in a drugged daze. Her mouth twitched slightly. His eyes fixed on the small beauty mark just to the side of her lips, and he wondered if she'd put it there as part of her disguise or if it was natural. He fought the sudden urge to brush his thumb along her cheek to answer his question.

"Have another?" Jake said, sliding into the stool next to her just as the bartender served the drinks and dropped the change from his twenty on the bar. Leaving the money in place, he pushed the soda the bartender just served next to the woman's already nearly full glass.

The delicate features of her face registered steep panic. If every other signal she'd given off hadn't been enough, this one just clinched it. There was no way this woman was working.

Jake's chest squeezed uncomfortably with an emotion he didn't feel very often and wished he could will away now. He almost felt bad for the girl, scared even. Did she have a clue what she'd gotten herself into by coming here? And dressed like *this*?

"Thank you," Painted Lady said softly. "But I already have a drink." She tilted her slender shoulder slightly and…she blushed with the gesture. Good Lord, when was the last time he'd seen a woman's cheeks turn color for something so minuscule? You'd think he'd just asked her to take her clothes off for a strip search.

"This your first time?"

7

"Ah, no," she stammered, averting her gaze.

Definite amateur.

"What's your name?"

Curling her fingers around the sweated glass, she took a quick sip of her soda. Those dark eyes glanced away for a second before zeroing in on him like a radar lock. The blushing woman was tossed aside like a crumpled piece of yesterday's news. A seductress on the prowl had taken her place.

Jake's insides kicked hard and then squeezed into a tight knot. He hadn't been in the company of a woman in... He couldn't recall. It had been way too long if he couldn't remember the last time he'd had sex.

It had been his choice, of course. Women his age wanted a commitment and he was damaged goods, too detached for intimacy or some such shit the department shrink had said. Who the hell needed that?

And how else could it be? A cop needed focus. He couldn't be effective in his job with his mind clouded with thoughts of someone at home. He'd seen just how distractions could destroy, not only a cop's career, but his life.

Jake focused on the woman's lips, unable to pull his eyes from the sheen of moisture settled there. With a move that seemed too natural to be deliberate, she ran her tongue over her top lip and wiped it clean.

Heat prickled his skin beneath his heavy jacket and settled like warm molasses in the center of his belly. He'd have to deal with his sexual appetite some other time. He was working and this woman was off limits with a capital "O."

"My name is CJ," she finally said.

After a moment, her penciled eyebrows lifted slowly, and she cocked her head to one side. It took a minute for Jake to realize she was waiting for him to respond.

"Jake."

"Nice to meet you, Jake." She thrust her hand out, apparently to shake his.

He nodded and gripped her tiny hand. It was silky soft and lost in his much larger one. She quickly snatched her hand away and rested it in her lap by the hem of dress. Another strange move. She was too nervous, too polite, and she was starting to lose some of the confidence that had suddenly appeared out of nowhere.

"Is that your real name? Jake?"

Lifting his beer to his lips, he asked, "Why would I lie?"

"Oh, I don't know. I can think of a hundred reasons why a man would want to hide his true identity."

"For instance?"

"You have a wife at home?"

He paused, staring at her. "Would that bother you?"

Jake had to keep himself from laughing as he took a pull from the bottle. The way CJ rose up high on her stool, he was sure she was about to say yes, which for some strange reason, made him feel good. If she were really a hooker, she wouldn't give a shit if he had a Mrs. at home. He'd be just money to her.

"That's your business. Not mine," she said.

He nodded again. "Damn right. But I'm not married."

He couldn't fathom why, but Jake wanted her to know that fact. It shouldn't have made a difference. There was no way he was going to take this woman to bed. But he didn't lie when it came to relationships. Lies were too easy to trip over. He'd learned that one the hard way early on in his career.

"Are you waiting for a friend?" she asked.

"Why do you ask?"

"Well, you don't work here. That much is clear. You weren't sitting with anyone or even talking to the bartender. I'm just wondering why someone like you would come to a place like this. What brought you here?"

His lips lifted up at the corners. "Do you always ask so many questions of people when you first meet them?"

She shrank a little in her seat. "Well, I…"

"What about you?"

"I asked you first."

He frowned "For the record. Men tend to avoid questions in places like this."

She looked startled. Then, almost as if she were storing

that tiny bit of information away for safekeeping, her face changed.

"What do men such as yourself like?"

Jake couldn't help but laugh. This whole picture was too absurd. He didn't know if he should be hauling CJ out of here to make curfew or lock her up for the worst solicitation he'd ever seen.

Why did his mind keep settling on pulling her into his arms and wiping that God-awful mask off her face so he could really look at her?

Lord, he was long overdue...

He needed a weekend off. Something to remind him he was still among the living where men and women and sex were concerned. Where he didn't worry about streetwalkers who needed rescuing.

He turned, about to give CJ an earful when a gust of cold wind pulled his attention back toward the open barroom door. The smell of cold March air freshened the dank odor of the room.

The man of the hour had arrived.

Jake fought to keep his reaction from showing as Ritchie Trumbella strolled into the bar like a king with his court. The two women draped on each of his arms looked much like CJ with their bodyhugger dresses and 4-inch stilettos. As soon as Ritchie greeted three men sitting at a table, he motioned to the women to move along. They walked to the end of the room toward the restroom while Ritchie surrounded himself with the rest of his entourage.

Damn! Where the hell was Angel tonight?

The older couple that had been arguing most of the evening quickly got up and left the bar.

Jake turned to CJ and saw that her eyes were like saucers, glued to the presence of this new man. If she didn't already know him, she was definitely intrigued. And he wanted to know why.

His gut twisted with her interest. And a sudden emotion that vaguely felt like...annoyance. Regardless of what he'd set out to do, he didn't want CJ to meet Ritchie Trumbella any more than he'd want his own sisters to meet the man. Trumbella was bad news and the sooner CJ understood that, the better off she'd be.

"Friend of yours?" he asked.

She snapped her attention back to him like a rabbit caught in a snare. "No. Yours?"

"You ask too many questions, CJ. You never know whose toes you're stepping on."

"I'll keep that in mind."

She lifted her soda to her lips again and took a sip. Then another. Jake's eyes lingered where the glass had been, then to the mark her lips had left on the sweat-lined glass.

"Who is he?" she asked, going against his warning.

How could she be here like this and not know Ritchie Trumbella? Why on earth was she here at all?

He owns Rory's."

Ritchie Trumbella owned a whole lot of other shady dealings, too. But if CJ didn't know this legitimate one, it was doubtful she knew anything at all about his non-paper dealings.

Taking her by the arm, he said, "Let's get out of here."

CJ's dark eyes grew impossibly wide and her mouth dropped open. Her slender body lifted high on the barstool and went statue stiff. For a minute, Jake thought she'd actually stopped breathing.

* * *

Cassie sat paralyzed on the barstool, blinking hard as the shock caused by the man in front of her set in. Sure, talking to Mr. Cool Leather Jacket with the smoky blue eyes was fine but that he was trying to pick her up... If she were sure she wouldn't fall off her heels, she'd fly for the door. No matter how attracted she was to this man, there was no way she was going to go that route if he'd been willing to be with a...

Death couldn't come too quick for Maureen.

"I think I've gathered enough...had enough soda," she said. The backs of her thighs were sticky from sweat and made a

11

squeaky sound as she helplessly slipped off the stool while trying to keep her dress from riding up her thighs.

Jake stood next to her, his hand still gripping her upper arm. Her body tightened with the physical contact. He smelled of leather, a hint of the beer he'd just consumed, and something else. It wasn't the cheap, heavy cologne so many men wore. He smelled musky, very male, erotically appealing.

"What are you doing?" she demanded, trying to pull free.

"It's a good idea I take you out of here."

"That's not necessary," she insisted.

"No trouble."

"It is to me."

"I just want to make sure you get safely to your car."

"I didn't drive," she blurted out when his grip on her arm grew tighter.

Brilliant, Cassie. So much for a quick getaway. She could have kicked herself for throwing him the advantage. She would have if she were sure her dress would stay firmly in place.

But Jake's reaction was suddenly different from what she'd expected. His dark eyebrows drew into a tight knot on his forehead. He glanced away and dragged his fingers over a head of course dark hair, letting his hand rest on the nape of his neck. She damned herself for wanting to lose her fingers in his hair. Three years since she had a decent relationship and her body picked now, of all times, to come back to life.

"Please tell me you weren't planning on walking home in this neighborhood," he said tightly.

She straightened her spine. "Of course not. What do you take me for?"

He tossed her the most irresistible wry grin. He didn't have to say a word for her to know what he was thinking.

"I'm not what you think."

Another grin. This one was more irresistible than the last. Her knees suddenly turned to rubber, making it difficult to stand. She cinched her purse strap higher on her shoulder and folded her arms across her chest.

Jake cocked his head to one side. "And you're so sure you

know what I'm thinking?"

"You think I'm something I'm not. And I can assure you, I am definitely *not.*"

He had a full-blown smile now. One with straight white teeth and a dimple on his left cheek she was sure wreaked havoc with more women than her.

"You're not all that hard to figure out, CJ."

Indignation swelled inside her. Despite her obvious attire, she didn't like his assumption. She hadn't had sex in three years, and she definitely wasn't going to have it tonight with him.

"If you'll excuse me, I'll go catch a cab and be on my way home. Alone."

Jake shook his head and sputtered. "CJ, you couldn't be further from the Land of Oz. Cabs don't come to this neighborhood, honey. *They* know better."

Cassie groaned inwardly. That would explain the cab driver's behavior earlier when he dropped her off. Admittedly, she didn't frequent this part of town and was more thankful that the cab driver knew how to get here than curious about his reaction. As neighborhoods go, the street didn't look ominous, but looks were deceiving.

A crescendo of laughter had Jake glancing over his shoulder to look at the man on the other side of the room. He was the owner of the bar, Cassie recalled Jake saying.

With his movement, Jake's jacket gaped open, and she had the first glimpse of what this man hid behind his black leather armor. A Beretta was tucked firmly inside a holster against his chest. It was hidden well, but easy to find for someone trained in what to look for. Cassie knew the gleam of the metal when she saw it. She knew the weight of it in her hand and the smell of gunpowder when it ignited.

Dark memories had her heart hammering wildly in her chest. But the boisterous conversation on the other side of the bar shifted her back to her reality. Cassie glanced in that direction, but she couldn't see a thing past the wide expanse of Jake's shoulders.

As Jake leaned his arm on the bar, Cassie's breath lodged

in her throat. Her pulse hammered. And she wished to God she hadn't been curious enough to look.

* * *

Jake saw terror flash across CJ's face. Great, she was finally beginning to understand how stupid it was for her to be here. But just as he was about to lead her to the door, her arms abruptly came up to his chest. She gripped his leather jacket, leaning into him as if she were about to climb into his lap.

Confusion mixed with heightened awareness of this enigmatic woman suddenly so close to him.

"Gun!" she screamed. With an unbelievable force, Cassie yanked him forward to the floor until his body was stretched over the length of hers. The air in the bar exploded into a spray of bullets and flying glass shards. Chairs and tables tumbled over as people screamed and scrambled for cover.

The room and everything that was happening exploded right in front of him and registered at lightning speed. Primal instinct took over. Screams, bullets, breaking glass and the sound of his own heart pumping were deafening. Jake wrapped his arm around CJ's waist, shielding her body with his own as he slowly dragged her around the corner of the bar to relative safety on the other side. She buried her head in his chest as he encased her body, protecting her from the flying glass from the shattered mirror behind the bar and the bottles of booze bursting with every hit from bullets.

It seemed to take forever for the explosion of gunfire to stop. In reality it was probably less than thirty seconds. But as soon as it started, it was over. It took another thirty seconds for Jake to get his bearings once the massacre had ended.

From outside, the cold wind whistled through the blown out windows and brought with it the sound of tires peeling out as a car sped off down the narrow side street. Before Jake even lifted his head, he knew the car was gone. Whoever did this would go unpunished unless he could find a witness.

His chest tightened where CJ's face pressed against his shirt. He didn't have to see her face to know she was crying. Her fingers clutched his shoulders in a death grip and her body shuddered helplessly beneath him.

It would make it easier on this case to have a witness, but Lord help him, he didn't want it to be this fragile woman in his arms.

CHAPTER TWO

Cassie looked at the clock on the wall as she sat downtown at Detective Jake Santos's desk in a cold metal chair in the middle of an open room filled with desks and paperwork. It was two AM. And she was alone.

In the far corner of the room, officers absorbed details of the shoot-out at Rory's. Jake, or rather, Detective Jake Santos, had disappeared. That left her nothing to do but relive the horror of the evening, or busy her mind formulating yet another wild scheme of murder. She had the most delightful daydream of her fingers curled around Maureen's throat. Since she wasn't a violent person by nature, there was no harm in letting her daydream run rampant. Maureen deserved it. Cassie had just witnessed enough violence firsthand to last her ten lifetimes and it was all Maureen's fault.

Jake appeared in front of her holding a Styrofoam cup, startling her.

"You okay? Still awake?"

"I don't think I'm going to sleep for the rest of my life. But other than that, I'm okay," Cassie said weakly. She wasn't okay. She wasn't okay the first time, all those years ago on that hot Miami night when she'd witnessed her first murder. Why should it be any different now?

But she would be, as soon as she got some sleep and some distance from this horrendous evening. As soon as she submerged herself deeply into work again.

Jake took her hands in his and then curled her fingers around the cup. "Drink it. But I warn you, it's deadly."

She looked into the cup and grimaced. "You pass this off as coffee? I thought you were supposed to prevent murders."

"We do what we can, but some things are beyond our

control. Your fingers are like ice cubes. This will help."

Jake shrugged out of his leather jacket and draped it around Cassie's shoulders. Immediately the heat from the jacket, left over from being encased around Jake's warm body, engulfed her. It smelled of rawhide and man. Wrapped in it, Cassie felt small and fragile. *Protected.* She welcomed the heat and the presence of the man who'd supplied it.

Once again, the horrible scene in the bar flashed before her eyes before she could stop it. She remembered it in all-too-vivid detail—the exploding glass, the cries of fear and pain...having Jake's arms wrapped around her like a shield.

He dragged a chair next to her and spoke in a low voice. "I have to ask you some questions."

"I figured as much." Cassie forced a smile.

"What were you doing at Rory's tonight?"

"Research."

He lifted his gaze from his notepad and darted a quizzical look at her. His shoulders sagged and he let out a slow breath, tossing the pad of paper to the cluttered metal desk.

"I'm telling you the truth," she insisted.

"Truth? Okay, let's start with the truth. At the bar, you told me your name was CJ. When we first got to the station, you said your name was Cassie Lang. Your driver's license says Juanita C. Alvarez. So I'm asking you again—"

"The C is for Cassandra," she said, cutting him off. "It's my middle name. Juanita is my birth name, but people don't usually call me that. Just Cassie. CJ was for CJ Carmen, the main character in all my books."

"Your books? What kind of books?"

"Crime novels."

"You were using the name of a character in a book?"

She sighed. "Yes and no. When I created my character, CJ Carmen, I just reversed the first two initials of my own name."

"And Cassie Lang?"

"My pen name. That's what my readers know me as. I'm a crime novelist. Since I'm used to doing public events, it's become habit to introduce myself by my pen name."

Jake blew out a quick breath, looking more haggard than sure of himself as he had at the bar. "Then what were you doing at Rory's dressed like…?" He flipped his hand so his palm was facing up, gesturing to her scanty clothes.

She sputtered and rolled her dark eyes. "I just told you, research."

"Researching who? Ritchie Trumbella?"

"Who's Ritchie Trumbella?"

"The guy lying in the morgue with about fifty bullet holes in him."

Cassie's mind was flooded with the gruesome scene in the bar again. Would it ever go away? "That's right. That poor man."

Jake raised an eyebrow. "That poor man is the reason three other civilians and a federal agent were killed tonight. Not to mention the countless number of other unsolved murders he's contributed to over the years. Most of those victims are most likely chilling at the bottom of a quarry somewhere."

"There was a federal agent at Rory's tonight?"

"He came in with Ritchie. Seems I wasn't the only one working a case against the crime boss."

"I told you the truth. I never laid eyes on that man until tonight. I don't know anything about this Ritchie Trumbella."

"You were awfully interested in him when he walked through the door. I saw you…watching him."

"I was watching a lot of people. You even. It's just research. Actually, character sketches. He is…was quite an interesting character, don't you think?"

Jake blinked hard and shook his head.

"The way you behaved in the bar…you have some experience."

"I'm not a prostitute," she said quickly.

"No kidding. That much I figured out in about five seconds. But you knew all about the gun you saw. And the car. You described it all in perfect detail."

"It's what I do for a living. Well, not actually what I do, but what I know. I've studied all about crime. I research different bits of criminal activity, and then I replay different situations in my mind to use in my books. When the gunfire broke out tonight, I acted on pure instinct. I don't know what happened or where it came from. I'm not usually like that."

Jake's expression changed, becoming darker and more intense. "You pulled me to the floor before the gunfire broke out."

"When you moved, I had a clear view out the window. I saw the car slow down just outside. That man, Ritchie, had his back turned. Everyone was talking, laughing, not paying any attention to what was happening outside."

"And then?"

"It just felt strange to me. Like when you know something is going to happen but you have no way of really knowing for sure. I saw the car window being rolled down and the gleam of what I thought looked like a gun coming out of the window. Like I said, it was pure instinct. Call it an overactive imagination if you want. I've been accused of that all my life. For once, I didn't stop to think before acting."

"Well, I have to say I'm glad." Jake's eyes bore into her. "You saved my life tonight."

Gratitude. It looked uncomfortable on his face. Jake Santos was probably used to being on the receiving end of thanks for getting someone out of a tight jam.

"You're welcome."

He smacked his hands on his denim-clad thigh, giving her a razor sharp look as he stood. "But you had no business being at that bar tonight."

"Hey, it's a free country. At least, it was the last time I voted. Rory's is a public place."

"Rory's is the pit of the universe. If you'd done enough research, you would have known enough not to go there at all, especially the way you're dressed."

"What's with the Neanderthal attitude all of the sudden? Who saved your life? Or did you already forget?"

"I'm a trained police officer. I'm trained for situations like this."

"And I was—"

"I know, doing research."

Irritation rose up in Cassie. She was tired; her toes were cramped from being in foot-deforming heels all night. The last thing she needed was a lecture from some Lone Ranger cop. All she wanted now was to get back to her safe apartment in the nice section of town, peel off her dress and slip into her favorite flannels. She'd be doing just that if it didn't mean she'd have to give Jake his jacket back.

"The night could have easily ended different. Your body could be sitting in a freezer downtown with the rest of them."

Jake's eyes more than his words struck Cassie hard this time. There was something that resembled fear there, as if her getting seriously injured or killed in that gunfire somehow shook him.

Warmth spread from the center of her chest outward just thinking about it. Men like Jake didn't see the best of the world. They were as rough around the edges as a man could be.

Cassie had always played it safe in her life. It was probably why she'd never married. Most likely why she hadn't allowed any of the dates she'd had in the last three years to go beyond a mere sweet kiss goodnight at the door. It was definitely why she didn't write romance novels. How could she write about something she'd never been any good at?

Thoughts of what she could experience with a man like Jake Santos made her heart race and caused little rivulets of sweat to trickle down the valley of her chest beneath her dress. She pictured him as a lover, holding her in those strong arms, turning her inside out with passion only a man like Jake could unearth.

"I'm fine. Really," she said softly.

He nodded, his blue eyes locking with hers. When was the last time a man's gaze held such intensity for her? She couldn't remember.

"Are you up to looking at a few photos?"

She nodded and Jake tossed a few mug shots to the metal desk.

Her eyes grazed the small pictures and immediately zeroed in on one. Her heart pumped furiously. There he was staring up at her from a two-by-two snap shot. Pointing to the picture, Cassie said, "This is him. The gunman."

"Are you sure?"

"Yes, it's him." She'd never forget that face.

"What about the driver of the car?" Jake asked. "Do you remember what he looked like?"

Cassie thought about it a moment, and then shook her head. "It all happened too fast. My mind fixated on the gun and the face of the shooter…" She pointed to the picture Jake had just shown her. "Do you have him in custody yet?"

"No, but we're working on it. Between your description of the car and you IDing the gunman from a picture in our files, we shouldn't have any trouble nailing him."

"Who is he?"

"His name is Angel Fagnelio. I was supposed to meet him at Rory's tonight, but he was a no-show. Now I know why. He'd been dealing with Ritchie, was going to cut me in on it. But the talk on the street is that Ritchie double-crossed him. We haven't figured out the whole story yet. We were lucky this time. You're very observant."

"That's my job," she said, feeling warmth fill her cheeks with his compliment.

"Anyway, now that you've given a positive ID we can put out an APB on Fagnelio and bring him in."

"What if he finds out I identified him? What if he sends someone after me?"

"Your name isn't being released. As long as you stay put for a few days until we bring him in and get the rest of the information we need for the DA to bring him to trial, you won't have anything to worry about. We might even get lucky and gather enough information so you won't have to testify."

"When can I go home?"

"Now, if you'd like. I'll drive you."

Cassie shook her head. "That won't be necessary."

She glanced at the big numbered clock on the far wall. It

21

said three-thirty. *Perfect dream time.* "May I use your phone? The other officer at the scene took my purse with my cell phone in it."

A quick ride to her apartment would have been wonderful. But Jake Santos was probably as eager to get back to his own life as she was to get home to hers.

"Dial 9 for an outside line. I'll get your bag." Jake pulled the phone on his desk closer to her before lumbering away toward the coffee machine. He hadn't finished his coffee, so Cassie assumed it was to give her a modicum of privacy.

As she punched in Maureen's telephone number from memory, a little devilish grin pulled at her tired cheeks. She waited three rings before someone picked up.

"Hello?"

"Are you awake?" Cassie asked evenly, trying to keep what little dignity she had left by not out and out blasting Maureen in front of the entire precinct. "It's me."

"Me, who?"

Cassie ground her teeth. "Cassie Lang, a.k.a. Cassie Alvarez, a.k.a. woman of the night? You know, the one sent out into bedlam—"

"Cassie. Okay, okay."

There was mumbling in the background. Cassie recognized a man's voice and guessed that Maureen's boyfriend had spent the night. Interrupting a romantic interlude gave Cassie none of the satisfaction she'd craved earlier.

"Why are you calling at this unbelievable hour?"

"I'm at the police station."

"Oh. My. God!" Maureen's voice was now crystal clear and she was fully awake. *Let the guilt begin.* "You got yourself arrested? You were only supposed to take notes."

"Arrested? Are you insane? How about shot at and dragged across a glass-laden barroom in a dress that couldn't warm a cantaloupe."

Maureen's high-pitched gasp distorted the connection. "Shot? Are you hurt? Are you okay?"

"I'm fine." Cassie blew out a frustrated breath. She was

too tired to lay on a guilt trip, no matter how much Maureen deserved it. Her energy was completely depleted and Maureen's sudden concern poured enough water on her flames to cool her down. "I'm just tired, and I want to go home."

She looked up just as Jake was approaching. He'd offered to drive her home. If she didn't take it, she'd have to wait for a cab. He had to go home, too.

"Are you okay, I mean, really?" Maureen said, cutting into her thoughts. "Adam and I will pick you up and bring you over here tonight. You probably don't want to be alone."

"I'm fine. It'll be dawn by the time you get here. I just didn't want you to hear about the shooting from someone else or read about it in the morning papers."

It was a lie. Jake assured Cassie her name wouldn't be used in the papers. Even if Maureen remembered Rory's was one of the bars she'd suggested Cassie go to, she wasn't likely to put two and two together. But Cassie was no good at delivering guilt trips. She could murder all she wanted in her dreams and on paper, but in reality, she was a softy.

"I'll see you in a few days," Cassie said before she hung up the phone. For a split second, she wished she hadn't refused Maureen's offer to stay at her apartment tonight. She really didn't like the idea of being alone.

As if he'd timed it that way, Jake sat down on the edge of his desk just as she placed the phone in the cradle. He handed Cassie her purse.

"All set?"

Cassie peered up at Jake, into slate blue eyes that seemed to burn with fire and ice at the same time. "Is that offer for a ride still good?"

* * *

The streets appeared colder and particularly lonely as his sports car ate up the pavement toward Cassie's apartment. Every once in a while, he'd glance at her as they passed under a glowing streetlamp.

She'd pulled her dark hair down from the upswept style

she'd been wearing all night. Chocolate curls framed her face and covered her shoulders, blending into one with the color of his leather jacket. It made her look even more vulnerable than she had appeared earlier.

What they'd gone through tonight was enough to send most people over the edge. Or at least in search of a bottle of Jack Daniel's to help them forget. Instead, Jake's mind wandered to elicit thoughts of a woman who was sweet enough to rival sugar cane. He wasn't about to give in to his sweet tooth no matter how much of a shock to his system tonight had been.

"What you said at the bar, about not being married, is that true?" she asked.

As they passed under another streetlamp, the light illuminated her face and then left it dim. The image of her lips remained in his mind until the next streetlamp grew near.

"Yes, it's true."

She nodded and looked out the window away from him. "Oh."

A moment passed in silence.

"Why do you ask?"

"I thought maybe it was a line you used when you were undercover."

She didn't elaborate further. Had she been thinking about him all this time? Wondering? Jake didn't know if he liked the implications of why. He knew he'd been doing a whole lot of thinking and wondering about Cassie Alvarez and how all those names rolled into one woman.

He drew in a deep breath of air, feeling a slight tremble in his hand as it gripped the steering wheel. He didn't want to know anything more about Cassie Alvarez, or any of her aliases, than he had to know. All his years on the force filled him with the gut instinct that he should just drop her on the curb, make sure she got into her apartment building and then drive away without looking back. After this case was wrapped up, he'd do exactly that.

"What about you?" he asked, going against his reasoning. "Ever been married?"

"Almost, once."

He squashed the sudden protective feeling that swept through him. The birthdate on her driver's license showed she was twenty-nine years old, a good six years younger than him. No matter how innocent Cassie appeared to be, she probably had relationships in her past just as he had. He just wished the image of her with another man didn't feel like a kick in the gut.

"Did you grow up here?"

A grin tugged at his lips as he stole a quick glance at her. "Still researching?"

She slouched a little in her seat and smiled sheepishly. "Some habits are hard to break. Call it small talk this time."

"New Jersey. West Orange to be exact. Most of my family still lives there."

"I grew up in Stamford. But I went to school in the city."

"Really?"

She chuckled. "Why does that surprise you?"

"It doesn't."

They rode in silence for a few blocks, past more streetlamps and lonely locked storefronts.

"Okay, maybe I'm a little surprised. I'm having trouble figuring out why an obviously intelligent and accomplished woman like you thought she could just walk into a place like Rory's alone and walk out unscathed," he finally admitted. "I mean, did you even think about how dangerous a place like that is?"

"I certainly didn't expect to be in a war zone. I guess being on deadline makes you do…stupid things."

He pushed his foot on the brake to stop for a red light. He thought he heard a soft sigh and wondered if he'd imagined it or if it was real.

"I guess maybe I've just become immune," she said.

'Someone like me who sees this stuff every week, I don't think I'd ever be immune to what happened tonight. So I find it hard to believe someone—"

"Like me?" she said, eyeing him with such intensity he hadn't noticed the light had turned green. "Forgive me, but

25

beyond knowing my name and professional alias, you know very little about me."

"I'm all ears."

"We have one block to go before you reach my apartment building and not enough time to give it justice."

A sudden sadness enveloped her, but she quickly brushed it aside.

Jake drove the last block in silence, fighting his strong desire to know something more about Cassie. He needed to stay detached.

He double-parked in front of her building and left the car running.

"Thank you for the ride," she said, slipping out of his leather jacket. "I'd say I had a nice time, but given the events of the evening, and the fact that we weren't on a date, I don't think it's appropriate."

"How about nice to have met you?"

She paused for a second with her hand on the door handle. A slow smile played on her full lips, but she didn't answer. She just pushed the door open and climbed out.

"I'll call you," he said as she stepped out onto the sidewalk.

Cassie swung around to look at him, the question written across her tired features.

"If I need more information for my report," he clarified.

This time she didn't smile as she nodded. Jake waited as she took the steps up to the front door, unlocked it and stepped inside. He made sure the door had locked behind her before pulling away from the curb.

It had been an endless night in a string of long nights. As he drove his car onto the boulevard, the streets were vacant. Jake usually welcomed heading home after a long shift. Especially after a night as eventful as tonight.

But this time, something pulled at him, making him want to turn back toward Cassie's, toward something he didn't want to face. It had been years since he'd felt that kind of pull. The department shrink had warned him he was treading on thin ice thinking he could handle the stresses of his job without it affecting him. But Jake wasn't giving in. Not this time.

He said he'd call her if he had any questions. Part of him searched his mind for a reason to make that call. But the only thing Jake came up with was that he wanted to see Cassie again.

CHAPTER THREE

That couldn't possibly be the door, Cassie groaned silently as she lifted her heavy head from the pillow. Her head was still hammering and her sense of time had shifted somewhat. But she could swear she'd just crawled into bed moments ago.

If this is Maureen...

Whoever felt the need to assault her door at—she focused on her brass wind up alarm clock on the nightstand—9:30 AM, was at it again. She dropped her feet to the carpet with all the heaviness fatigue had left her with, wondering how she could have managed to sleep a total of three hours and not feel like she'd slept at all.

When Jake had dropped her off at her apartment last night and she'd bolted her apartment door shut, Cassie had showered to scrub off all the makeup and stink from Rory's. After that, she sat in her living room with every light in her apartment on, just staring, afraid of what nightmares would assault her in her sleep. She finally forced herself to go to bed at 6:30 AM, reasoning that if she woke from a bad dream, at least she'd wake in the daylight.

The pounding on the door continued. Taking the time to throw a short floral cotton bathrobe over her nightshirt, Cassie glanced through the mini-blinds to the street three floors below. The night had been replaced with a glorious sunny morning. Jake's empty sports car sat double-parked outside the entrance where he'd dropped her off last night, as if he'd never left.

The ferocious pounding on the door matched the kind of power she imagined Jake could deliver if provoked. The kind Cassie had felt last night as his arms wrapped around her and he shielded her body, pulling her behind the bar to safety when the gunfire broke out.

"I'll be right there," she said, and cleared the sleep from her throat. She drew in a deep breath, pushing her tangled hair away from her face before yanking the door open. She was met by Jake's handsome and somewhat *scowling* expression, mid-knock. He slowly lowered his fisted hand.

"You didn't even ask who it was," Jake barked.

"Good morning to you, too."

"It could have been anyone here to do God only knows what."

Crossing her arms across her chest, Cassie replied, "I knew it was you."

"How?"

"I'm psychic."

He didn't look convinced, nor did he appear in the mood for any of her attempt at teasing, and at this hour of the morning, Cassie didn't care.

"How did you get into the building without being announced?" she asked.

"Perfect timing. I was coming in as someone was leaving through the front door. I think a crime watch meeting with your neighbors is way overdue." Jake stared at her. "Aren't you going to invite me in?" he asked.

"Give me a minute, I'm thinking."

He spun past her into the living room as if he hadn't heard her and tossed the morning paper to her cherry coffee table, already cluttered with reference books she'd dragged home from the library a few days before.

"Well, think while you read this. Got any coffee?"

"Ah, I'll make some in a minute. Make yourself at home."

She pushed the door closed and padded barefoot to retrieve the newspaper.

Jake's heavy sigh had her turning to him. He looked exhausted, as if he'd had even less sleep than she'd had. The dark shadow lining his jaw showed he hadn't bothered to shave yet. Normally, Cassie liked men with a clean-shaven face, but something about the way Jake looked, rugged, almost outdoorsy, made her stir inside. It started small and began to build. She shifted in place to shake off the tingling feeling.

Jake cleared his throat. "You read. Just tell me where."

"Where?"

"Coffee. Preferably extra-strength, if you have it. I'll make it."

Uneasiness skittered through her, settling in her stomach. It wasn't the same stirring she felt just seconds ago. Cassie refused to believe it to be a premonition, so she passed it off as fatigue.

Jake's presence in her home was too intimate. He'd been an enigmatic stranger at Rory's, and a highly professional police officer at the police station last night. He was much the same now, except in her apartment, surrounded by her personal things, Cassie felt almost...*naked* in a way she hadn't felt for some time.

"Colombian coffee on the refrigerator door. Filters in the cabinet above the coffee maker on the counter," she said.

As Jake treaded to the kitchen, Cassie plopped down on her slipcovered sofa and draped the afghan over her legs. This man had been privileged to see more of her than any man had in three years, and she hadn't even known him a full twenty-four hours.

It wasn't only modesty. Scratches from the flying glass and bruises from hitting the floor were now surfacing on her skin. Cassie hadn't felt them when she'd showered last night or before she went to bed, but now that the adrenaline rush had worn off, they were nagging at her.

She reached for the newspaper. "What am I reading?"

"Front page," Jake called out from the kitchen.

Cassie slapped the newspaper on her lap, fingering the edge of the paper as she examined the headline. "The President vetoed—" she started to say before Jake came back into the room and cut in.

"Bottom of the page, big bold print."

Her eyes grazed the page of the *Providence Journal Bulletin* until they settled on the article Jake was referring to. Her whole body collapsed as the newsprint screamed at her. ***Crime*** *novelist Cassie Lang involved in deadly shoot-out.*

Cassie's heart stopped beating and her hands shook so violently, the newspaper slipped from her fingers and fell to the floor. When she finally found her voice, it was barely audible to her own ears as she spoke.

"You said you weren't going to reveal my name."

Jake was at the doorway, leaning his shoulder against the doorjamb.

"I didn't."

"Then how? Who?"

He came into the room slowly and eased himself down on the sofa beside her, draping his arm across the back in what seemed like a comforting gesture. The whole thing felt like watching a movie in slow motion. Those bottomless blue eyes she'd locked onto last night held assurance meant only for her benefit. She only wished it brought the comfort she craved.

"That's what I'd like to know," he said.

"Just tell me one thing. Did you find Angel Fagnelio?"

"No."

To his credit, Jake didn't try to sugarcoat the truth. Cassie didn't know why that made her feel better but it did. But only momentarily.

"He's in hiding," she muttered.

"We're looking. I need to know if you recognized anyone at that bar last night. Anyone at all."

"No. Why would I? I'd never been there before."

"Who knew you were there?"

"Just Maureen Phillips."

Goosebumps invaded her skin like wildfire running across a dry field, and she hugged herself to keep from shivering. Jake inched closer and hesitated, as if he didn't like what he was about to say.

"Not Maureen," she insisted, taking the burden from him.

He scrubbed his hand over his jaw before replying. "Who is she?"

"My editor."

"Anyone else who might have known? Someone Maureen

might have told?"

"It just happened last night? Who could she have told between the time I spoke to her at the station and the newspaper went to press?"

Cassie squeezed her eyes for a moment, wishing she could will away the newsprint on the page like writing on a chalkboard. Wishing she could be invisible again. But suddenly she felt so exposed.

"Ah, her boyfriend, Adam Coel, was there when I called. I'm sure she probably mentioned it to him. But—"

"Do you know him well?"

"A little. We've spent a few weekends in the Catskills together over the eight or nine months since she's been seeing him. But he'd have no reason to call the papers about this? And it was so late."

"Why did you go to Rory's? I mean, what made you decide on Rory's as opposed to some other bar in the area to do your research. That part of town is filled with places like Rory's but not nearly so notorious for criminal activity."

"Maureen suggested a few places."

"Your editor suggested you become a hooker for the evening?"

Cassie tossed him a wry expression. "I was not a hooker. I was pretending. Big difference. Besides, Maureen had no idea I'd gone to Rory's specifically. We did a Google search while we were on the phone. I made a list, closed my eyes and picked one."

Cassie forced air into her lungs, much like a gulp. Her head was swimming. As a novelist, she'd learned enough about crime to know that this morning's headline was akin to having a target on her back. Last night, she was just another nobody who happened to be in the wrong place at the wrong time. Sure, she was a well-known author, but still invisible to anyone who didn't read her books. It was doubtful anyone at Rory's was part of her readership.

But today, she was a material witness who could finger a killer who now had the means to identify her. *And he was still out there…*

She peered up at Jake, hoping to find some assurance. In the end, the lines etched on his tired face and the tightness around the edges of his mouth didn't give her any.

"Then how did Maureen know you were there last night?"

"She's the person I called from the station."

He nodded. "You have to admit the publicity—"

"No!" The sharp tone of Cassie's voice startled even her.

Jake stiffened as if bracing himself for yet another unpleasant battle. "How can you be so sure it wasn't Maureen?"

"I just am. I may have wanted to kill her last night, figuratively of course, but we're friends. She'd never put me in harm's way."

Jake lips spread to a cynical grin.

"Look, I know going to Rory's wasn't the smartest thing I've ever done, but I've known Maureen for six years. If she really thought I'd be in danger, she never would have made the suggestion. In fact, if I hadn't been so late getting there in the first place I'd have gotten all the information I needed and been long gone before the shooting. We both thought it would simply be an hour or so of people watching. Maybe talking a little to some of the other girls who might show up. Seeing how they interact with people who came into the bar. That's something I do all the time for my books."

His dark eyebrows stretched high on his forehead. "You said that last night. You just watch people when they're not looking?"

"Yes, that's how you really get to know them. It's not like voyeurism or anything sick like that. I don't peek at people through their windows or do anything illegal. I just watch people acting naturally, take in their mannerisms and try to make characters out of them. Once you meet people, they put on a fake face to impress you."

"So you were interviewing me as a prospective—"

"I was doing research. I had no intention of going to bed with you."

As soon as the words were out of her mouth, she was sure

33

her sensual thoughts of Jake had betrayed her. He gave her a slow, sexy grin, rewarding her with his dimple. She'd been caught.

"Maybe not last night," he answered in a low voice.

She closed her eyes and tried to squash the longing that suddenly engulfed her. Fear replaced it.

"What happens now?"

Jake nodded once, straightening his posture. Whatever had just passed between them was gone, and the man standing in her living room was suddenly serious and professional again. "You're going to be fine. For starters, I'm bringing you down to the station to work out the details of what to do until things settle down."

She snapped her gaze at him and huffed. "Don't patronize me. A crime boss has just been murdered and the one person who can finger his murderer is me. I may have been a little naive last night, but my mind is pretty clear right now, and I know what trouble I'm in."

"You'll be safe."

A wry laugh escaped her that sounded almost hysterical to her ears. "You saw how easy it was for you to waltz right into a *secure* building. Are you going to have someone stand guard outside my door twenty-four hours a day?"

"If we have to, yes."

"And what will that accomplish? These people don't ring doorbells. They don't pick and choose who to hurt. And they don't care who gets killed in the process. A spray of bullets, a bomb and broken brake line to make it look like an accident? Hell, they don't even care of it looks like an accident."

"You're going to be fine."

Cassie looked at Jake in disbelief. He was totally serious. "What about you? You were there, too. Aren't you afraid someone in Ritchie's family will come after you because of your connection with Angel Fagnelio? And Fagnelio knew you were there. He didn't care."

He hesitated. "That's a problem."

"You think?"

34

"I thought I'd gained Angel's confidence these last few months. Perhaps I was wrong. Or perhaps his desire to get back at Ritchie was worth wasting me too. I don't know. This group isn't exactly the warm and fuzzy type. Since Fagnelio made the hit on Rory's, none of the other informants are talking. They're all pretty nervous. I'm pretty sure Ritchie Trumbella was the target and everyone else was just in the way. But that's just a guess."

"And now I'm in the way." She dropped her face into her hands, not wanting to think about how differently last night could have played out. Within seconds, she felt Jake's wide hand stroking her back. Heat enveloped her where his touch made contact and slowly spread outward.

"There's a lot riding on this. But the most important part of all of it is that someone leaked your name to the press. That shouldn't have happened. But since it did, you need protection. You say it wasn't Maureen—"

"It wasn't. I'll admit Maureen has had some wild ideas in her time. She had me dress up as a clown and deliver singing telegrams once so I could think about ways to get into highly secure buildings. But all that stuff was harmless. She would never put me in danger just to sell some books."

"How famous is Cassie Lang?"

She shrugged. "I have some fans. I don't get recognized at the market or anything. People aren't running after me to get my picture, if that's what you're asking."

"Maybe one of them saw you and called the press."

"You flatter me. I've had a good sales record, but I don't think someone would turn their head twice if they recognized me."

"You're wrong there, Cassie."

She forced air into her lungs. She tried to convince herself it was to calm her down after learning the disturbing news she was a target. Certainly not because of the way Jake Santos held her gaze as if he were balancing a fragile piece of crystal.

The coffee maker cut into the sudden silence with a loud burping noise as the pot filled. Normally Cassie couldn't function without at least two or three cups in her. The fear she had racing through her veins now rivaled anything caffeine could give her.

Jake eased off the sofa. "Why don't you go pack an overnight bag while I pour us some coffee?"

"A suitcase?"

"We'll probably be moving you to another location."

"That won't be enough," she said, not moving or looking up at him as he strode toward the kitchen.

Jake turned back, resting his hand on the doorjamb as he looked at her. He was powerful, magnetic. She was infinitely glad he was here, yet at the same time she feared everything about him.

"No, it won't," he said, the deep timbre of his voice echoing the severity of the situation. "But it'll have to be enough for now. Anything else you need you can get on the way."

"Like a computer? My work? How about my life?"

"We're talking about your life, Cassie. Now go pack. The sooner we get you to a safer place, the better."

He wasn't demanding, but Jake made his point clear. She should put her trust in him and go. Why did that fill her with a fear she hadn't felt in a long time? Why did she think that by giving up her trust to a man like Jake Santos to take care of her, to keep her safe, she'd risk endangering her heart?

* * *

District Attorney Martha Landers gave a new definition to dog spitting mad. She had always been a powerhouse, Jake recalled, but after reading the file on Ritchie Trumbella and Angel Fagnelio, she was ready to have someone's head readied for the guillotine.

Jake was first in line. As they walked down the hall toward the interrogation room where his partner, Kevin Gordon, was talking to Cassie, Martha let him have it.

"Did it ever occur to you to check to see if there was another ongoing investigation? You were tripping all over the FBI's case and didn't even know it!"

"Courtesy would have gone a long way if the FBI had informed the local PD about their own investigation. This is our turf," Captain Russo said. "We've cooperated with the FBI before. We play nice if they do."

"The FBI doesn't give a shit about playing nice," Martha said in disgust. "And they don't have to. I spent an hour on the phone with the head of the Bureau in Quantico this morning convincing him I love my job and want to keep it. They have jurisdiction on this, our turf or not. They'll be here to collect their witness within the hour."

"*Their* witness. That doesn't give us much time," Russo said.

Martha folded her arms across her chest, stretching the shoulder seams of her blue power suit. She had been working in the DA's office longer than Jake had been on the force. Except for the slight tint of stubborn gray at her temples that hair color couldn't tame, and the deepening crow's feet creasing her eyes, she hadn't changed much. "I suggest you tread lightly. If the FBI suspects you're even looking at Ms. Alvarez wrong... Where is she?"

"Here. She's with Kevin." Jake opened the interrogation room door. Cassie sat at the table. Across from her was his partner, Detective Kevin Gordon. Kevin was his usual charming self, laughing and leaning his chair on two legs. He pushed back errant strands of hair that had fallen from the tight ponytail he wore while working to keep his shoulder-length dark blond hair at bay.

Martha smiled politely at Cassie. "Ms. Alvarez."

"Hello," Cassie said.

"Detective Gordon, can I steal you away for a minute?"

Moments later, they were standing in the hallway. Martha appeared uncomfortable as she spoke. "My hands are tied on this one. Not that the outcome would be any different for Ms. Alvarez, but I wish you'd kept me in the loop regarding your investigation of Ritchie Trumbella. It would have saved me a little embarrassment with the Bureau. My complexion doesn't look so good with egg on it."

"We didn't have anything to give you until last night," Kevin said. "It goes both ways, you know. But whatever they were investigating had to be more than just local or they wouldn't have invested this much time."

"Bond fraud."

Captain Russo whistled.

"Jeez, no wonder the feds are pissed," Jake said.

"They lost an agent last night in the shooting. He'd spent over two years deep undercover cozying up to Trumbella. They've been closed-mouthed about much of it, but I do know the investigation was focusing on a connection with a company called The Aztec Corporation out of Colombia."

"Never heard of them. South America?" Kevin asked.

"There is a unit out of Chicago that has been working on this for some time. They traced a connection to the Aztec Corporation to Massachusetts. But that connection somehow ended here in Providence. Anyway, they're a long way from home if they're working up here."

"With Ritchie Trumbella," Russo said.

Martha shrugged. "That's the way it looked. And that's all I know. With their inside agent gone, they're back to square one. They want to salvage whatever they can by leaning on Angel Fagnelio. They want him to roll."

"Me, too. If we can find him," Jake said.

"Which means they want to keep their witness safe," Martha said with a sigh. "I feel sorry for the girl. Cassie Lang. I've read her books. She's good. I'm not sure how they're going to be able to keep her hidden until they bring Angel Fagnelio to trial. That is, if they find him."

* * *

A few minutes later, Jake opened the door to the interrogation room. His breath caught in his throat when he saw Cassie sitting in the cold metal chair, looking lifelessly at the empty chair across from her until he, Kevin and the captain walked into the room.

"Sorry to keep you waiting, Ms. Alvarez," Captain Russo

said. "Agent Tate will be here shortly to give you an update on what's going to happen next."

"Tate? As in Charlotte Tate?" Jake asked. "I thought she was in Virginia."

"She transferred to the Chicago office a year ago," Russo said. "She's in charge of the investigation. She's calling the shots."

Jake cursed under his breath.

Cassie's stomach dropped. "What's wrong?"

"Nothing," Jake said.

Cassie gave Jake a hard look. "Don't give me that."

Both Kevin and Captain Russo exchanged a look. "Working with the feds can be…difficult at times," Kevin said.

"But it's nothing you need to worry about. It's just logistics." Russo reassured.

Jake noticed the bags under Russo's eyes were more pronounced these days. Since he'd lost his eldest son to a drug overdose nearly a year ago, he'd let himself go, gaining a thick middle that made the buttons of his white shirt pucker, courtesy of too much take-out and maybe a few too many beers when the day grew long. The hours he kept at the station were taking their toll on him as well, and had less to do with his commitment to the force than his being unable to go home and face what he'd lost.

"I'll try to do some damage control," Russo said. "Special Agent Tate wants Ms. Lang, ah, Alvarez turned over to FBI custody within the hour."

After Russo left, an eerie silence filled the room until Cassie sat up straight in her chair.

"Everyone talks about me like I'm a piece of property they can just hand off from one person to another. I don't like this."

"It's in your best interest to be in protective custody right now," Jake said delicately.

"But it's up to me, right? I don't have to go with them."

Kevin stood up from the table, his chair grinding against the floor as it pushed back with his movement.

"You'd be foolish not to. In a perfect world, Fagnelio will

39

be apprehended, cop a plea and then give up a wealth of information about the bond fraud ring. But this is Providence. Things don't work out that easily."

"What are you saying? When can I go home?"

"Probably not for a long time." At Kevin's frank comment, Cassie gasped.

"What do you mean?"

"It means that if you go out on your own, while Fagnelio is still at large, not only will you have his people tailing you, you'll have the FBI breathing down your neck. You won't be able to walk to the coffee shop on the corner without having someone's eyes on your back. The FBI has one star witness— you—and they're not going to want to lose you under any circumstances." Kevin's voice was uncharacteristically harsh. "You're better off cooperating or it could be worse than if you went with them."

Jake had trusted Kevin with his life from day one. Kevin was a good cop and there was no one Jake felt more comfortable working in the field with than his partner. But right now, Kevin was being a colossal ass.

"Back off," Jake warned.

Kevin took in the hard look Jake gave him, then glanced at Cassie. His expression relaxed.

"I apologize, Ms. Alvarez. You'll be fine as long as long as you're at a safe house until this thing goes to trial," Kevin said.

Cassie abruptly stood up. "Until trial? I don't want to go to a safe house. I want to go home. I thought this was only going to be for a few days until Angel Fagnelio was put in jail."

Jake felt the weight of fatigue dragging him down. The last thing he wanted to do was face Charlotte Tate again. Lord knew he had good reason. But if the plan was to take Cassie into protective custody, then he had to agree it was best.

"I'm afraid you don't have a choice."

Her shoulders sagged. "What do you mean?"

"You're a material witness. Whether you want to go or not…it's not up to you."

Tears welled in her eyes. "But I'm not the criminal."

40

"That's why you have to be protected."

"Yes, but...isn't a witness banned from contact with anyone when they're at a safe house?"

"Yes," Kevin said. "It's in your best interest."

"My best interest. You mean, to keep me from my family...my friends? No. Don't treat me like I'm the one who..." Awareness illuminated her eyes like the bright lights of an interrogation lamp. Slowly, she unknotted her arms and brought them down stiffly to her side. "Wait. You think I'm the one who leaked my own name to the press, don't you?"

"No," Jake said quickly. But the look on Kevin's face said it all.

No one had uttered the accusation yet, but Jake was sure it was on the minds of every cop in the precinct. No one knew who'd leaked Cassie's name to the press and only one name kept coming up as a possibility.

Cassie's book sales were sure to skyrocket from the publicity now that her name was attached to the gruesome crime. She was adamant that Maureen couldn't possibly be the one who talked to the press. Jake had his doubts about Maureen, but he'd swear on his last breath it wasn't Cassie.

Something deep in his gut told him Cassie was telling the truth. He could put his faith on instinct. But Kevin was another story. The dark shadows crossing his partner's features echoed the thoughts of every single other officer in the department. And Cassie knew it.

"You don't believe him," she was saying to Kevin. "You think I did this?"

"It doesn't matter now how it happened or what I think," Kevin said, callously brushing her hurt feelings aside. "The point is the damage is done. Someone wanted this to be front-page news. Now it is. And now Angel Fagnelio has a nice picture of the FBI's star witness."

"We need to concentrate on finding Angel Fagnelio and making our case against him."

Cassie flashed her wide sable eyes at Jake. She seemed to shrink in fear right before his eyes. "You mean you don't even know where he is?"

"He's gone into hiding."

She stood up straight and drew in a deep breath as if the room had sucked out all the oxygen. "I don't care what the FBI wants. I want to go with you."

Jake shouldn't have been so taken aback, but he was. "You heard Captain Russo. It's in the hands of the FBI."

Kevin shook his head. "The FBI is equipped to protect you in ways we're not. You'll be safe with them."

"I'll be alone."

Jake shook his head, but kept his voice firm. It would do no good to give Cassie false hope when he knew that in a matter of minutes, Charlotte Tate would be wiping the floor with his face because of his involvement with Fagnelio.

"I'm in the middle of a case."

"A case I'm a part of now. All the more reason why you should be sticking with me."

Did she know what she was asking of him? "You have that much faith in me?"

"Yes."

Kevin's wry chuckle had Jake turning his attention away from Cassie. "Before you two go working something cozy out together, let me see what Tate has up her sleeve, okay? She's due here any minute and if my memory serves me right, she just hates anyone else running her show."

Jake waited until Kevin closed the door behind him before speaking again. In the dead silence of the room, the walls began to close in on them. Cassie nearly jumped out of her chair when the heater kicked on in the room, humming as a hot gust of wind blew out of the blower. Thrust with it was the scent of lemon and ammonia, as if the room had been recently cleaned with industrial cleaning liquid.

Cassie hugged herself as if she were cold despite the sudden blast of heat filling the room. "You don't seem like you have a whole lot of faith in this Agent Tate."

"I have my reasons, but they have nothing to do with you or this case. She has an excellent reputation with the Bureau.

She'll see to it you're comfortable wherever they take you."

"And that's it?"

Jake took in her accusing expression. "What?"

"You just pass me off now?"

"That's not the way this works. You should know... Haven't you researched the FBI for one of your books? A federal agent was killed last night during an ongoing federal investigation. They're in charge."

"I can refuse protective custody."

Jake shook his head, not even wanting to think of the possibility of Cassie out there on her own with Fagnelio still loose. "You'd be foolish not to cooperate. They'll be reasonable, but if you're not, they can make your life hell. And they will. I've seen them do it."

"Someone leaked my name to the press last night. The only people who knew I was involved were officers working here in this building and the FBI. I didn't do it. And you're the only one I believe didn't do it. That leaves everyone else outside that door or who was involved with this case."

"Cassie—"

"This is my life, Jake. Mine. I want to decide. You're the only one I trust."

Jake gave her a half grin. "That's funny."

"What is?"

"Last night you accused me of knowing nothing about you except your aliases. And yet you know nothing about me."

Her small chin protruded slightly, her sable eyes were infinitely deep and round with resolute trust. *In him.*

"I know you protected me last night. That's good enough for me."

Jake nodded, his head swimming. It wasn't uncommon for victims of crime to look up to the officers who protect and serve the community. But Cassie Alvarez was forgetting one important detail about last night. One he didn't think he'd ever forget. She was the one who saved his life, not the other way around.

"I appreciate your faith in me, but I'm not what you need

right now."

Cassie shook her head, her dark chocolate curls moving to and fro over her shoulders. "You couldn't be more wrong, Detective Santos."

He watched her gracefully step closer to him, stopping by the side of the table. There was just enough distance to keep him from touching her if he reached out.

Cassie's lips tipped up to one side. "You're exactly what I need."

CHAPTER FOUR

Jake rubbed the tight spot in the center of his chest where his air constricted. Bertie was right. He had a soft spot for lost women.

Of course, his sister wasn't one of them, as she so frequently reminded her younger brother. *Nosiree.* In fact, every single Santos woman had a strong mind of her own and knew how to use it. And Jake had plenty of experience dealing with strong-willed women, having grown up surrounded by five older sisters.

Cassie looked up at him, her eyes holding a determined fire and a vulnerable innocence that closed around him like a vise. He had a feeling, despite the delicate position she'd been thrust into, she wasn't going to back down without a fight. He'd seen that determined fire before, knew when the battle was lost and when to back down to it.

"I can do what I can to make sure you're treated right—"

"Oh, really? And how do you plan to do that?"

"The FBI is equipped to handle this type of situation and are ready to do—"

"Well, I'm not," she interjected again. "And I don't like being treated like a piece of steak tossed out and torn apart by a junk yard dog."

Jake wanted to agree with her. He wanted to say that he had no confidence Charley Tate would care one way or the other if the FBI treated Cassie right. She wanted her witness to finger Angel Fagnelio and force him to unload a lot of intimate details of Ritchie Trumbella's operation.

Cassie was the ticket to that. Agent Tate was interested in one thing, and one thing only, and that was furthering her career. Cassie was the ticket to that as well. And it didn't matter

45

whose toes she stepped on to keep her pretty patent leather boots clean.

But it wasn't right for him to inject his personal feelings about Agent Charlotte Tate on Cassie. Not with so much at stake. Cassie was the one who had to live with the consequences of what happened last night and what decisions were made on her behalf now.

He was just about to say that when the faraway look in her eyes gave him pause.

"What is it?"

"Concurrent jurisdiction," Cassie said quietly.

Jake quirked an eyebrow. He'd forgotten momentarily that Cassie wasn't just an ordinary citizen. As a crime novelist, she had done her homework. He hadn't read any of her books. He hadn't even heard of her until last night, but he had no doubt she knew what she was talking about. Hell, even a powerhouse like Martha Landers had read her books.

"What about it?"

"Having a deadly shooting in a local bar—to which I was witness—along with having an FBI agent killed sounds like it would fall within the guidelines of concurrent jurisdiction, wouldn't it?"

"It could."

"That makes me your witness as well as the FBI's." Her face suddenly brightened, as if she'd found the secret piece of a puzzle no one could solve but her.

"Technically, yes," he said.

Being involved in a barroom shooting would tilt anyone's world on its axis. But Cassie wasn't sitting back and playing the wounded victim. She was taking the bull by the horns and wrestling it to the ground.

Lost woman, my foot, Jake thought with admiration. *Bertie would love her.*

Cassie leaned forward and placed her palms on the table. An air of triumph filled her otherwise clouded expression. For the first time that morning, she looked confident, as if she'd been struggling for air and finally filled her lungs.

"Then that settles it."

Jake gave a wry chuckle. "It doesn't work that way. It may look nice and neat on a piece of paper, Cassie, but reality works a little different than your crime novels."

"How so?"

"Well, there's the little matter of the FBI wanting you in *their* custody."

She straightened up and crossed her arms over her chest. "Neither the FBI or the District Attorney has a hostile witness. They don't need to arrest me and lock me up to get me to testify because I'll agree to do that in both cases. The only question now is my protection until Angel Fagnelio is put behind bars."

"Which the FBI seems to want full control over."

"So do I," she said determinedly. "And I'm choosing what I know and what I trust."

"Bond fraud and the murder of an FBI agent are a mite bit heavier than a local bar shooting."

Abruptly, Cassie dropped into the metal chair and pulled one leg up to her chest, hugging it with her arms. Her expression suddenly collapsed. "I just remembered something."

"About the case?"

"No, something from one of the first books I wrote."

Baffled, Jake stared at her blankly. "What are you talking about?"

"One of the main characters in the book was a low ranking member of the mob who turned state's evidence after his wife was killed. He wanted to change his identity, live off Uncle Sam's dime while planning his own operation on some tropical island. *Grieve* for his wife in high style."

Jake shook his head. "We're talking about your safety. Real life, Cassie. Not some make-believe character in a book."

Haunted eyes, fringed with thick black lashes, lifted to meet his gaze. He didn't need to have her soft body trembling against his, like it had last night, to feel her fear. It was all there in her eyes, like a line of mirrors reflecting a thousand images back at him.

Cassie forced in a deep breath of air, opening up the

stored information held neatly in her mind after years of research. She'd sworn after her cousin's murder she wouldn't allow herself to feel this helpless again. All the research, all the books she'd written about crime with CJ emerging victoriously, suddenly fell flat on dry ground. She was no stronger than she was eight years ago, she realized. She was still the same powerless witness in a violent crime she had no control over.

In her years researching crime, Cassie had prided herself on her meticulous attention to detail. She wanted all her books to reflect the true nature of the crimes they depicted. How could she have forgotten this one important detail?

"I'm talking about my choices, Jake. The FBI arrested the character in my book and locked him up in jail for his own protection when he didn't get what he wanted. I'm their material witness. This Agent Tate could do the same to me whether or not I cooperate. Sure, there is concurrent jurisdiction, but the FBI could leave me with no choice at all until they're done with me. And that could take years. I hate that. I'll never get my life back."

Jake moved behind her where she sat defeated in the cold metal chair. Placing his strong hands on her shoulders, he gently kneaded her tightly knotted muscles, bringing forth conflicting sensations. Part of her welcomed his warmth and strength.

What was it about this man that made her whole body come alive with a single look, or a brush of his hand? With his fingers burning the flesh beneath her shirt, she couldn't keep her mind from wandering into dangerous territory.

She was drawn to him in a way that she'd never felt before. He was her safety net. Her safe harbor. It was only right that she'd cling to feelings of security now, wasn't it?

This wasn't like her. Cassie prided herself on keeping a level head where men were concerned. It was true a part of her didn't want to go through the same heartache she had three years ago, the last time she'd been involved in a serious relationship with a man. But things had changed since then. She couldn't blame Dennis for becoming bitter. How could she expect him to spend the rest of his life with a woman who didn't feel anything when he touched her?

Jake was impossibly close. She could feel the heat of his body against her back as he moved his fingers into the tender flesh of her shoulders. His hands were strong and warm, reassuring. In less than twenty-four hours she'd let her guard down with Jake Santos. Why couldn't she have done that with her fiancé?

Cassie couldn't let it happen. It became painfully obvious three years ago that she was no good at romantic relationships. That's why she'd purposely chosen not to write about them. She knew crime. She could deal with guns and broken bones, not broken hearts.

Cassie had written her main character, CJ Carmen, as an able-bodied heroine who knew just what to do in every situation she encountered. She didn't cower in a barroom brawl or hide from her enemy. She stood up and gave as good as she got. She wouldn't want a man like Jake Santos to shield her from bullets. She'd turn the tables and protect him and everyone else around her.

And when it was over, she'd have no trouble taking a man like Jake Santos to her bed and sharing the pleasures that only a man and woman could share. She wouldn't have to pretend to feel anything, as Cassie had done with Dennis. CJ was comfortable with the primitive dance of giving and taking on all planes. She could meet Jake Santos, and all the desire and passion he could unearth in her, head on and give back just as much.

But Cassie wasn't CJ.

Jake's deep voice pulled her from her reverie. "You seem a little more relaxed now."

Cassie straightened her back, trying to pretend Jake's touch had no effect on her, that she hadn't been thinking of what it would be like to have his rough hands roam the length of her body. Now wasn't the time to be thinking of meaningless, mind-altering sex. She had to figure out how she could stay alive while taking back control of her life.

"I'm fine."

Jake stepped away from the chair, leaving her cold in his absence. Voices out in the hall drew their attention to the door. Kevin opened it.

"Are you two ready for this?" he asked.

"No, but then I wasn't ready to be witness to a barroom shooting last night, either. So I guess it doesn't matter."

Jake placed a hand on her shoulder. "Whatever happens, it's going to be okay, Cassie. Just remember that."

As she rose from her chair, Cassie wondered just whose benefit those words were for. She didn't feel it. In the short time she'd known Jake, he'd been up front with her. She could trust him. And that was the most vital thing she could cling to right now.

The noise in the hall grew louder as they approached the interrogation room door. Jake turned back to her, his eyes settling on her for a brief moment as he hesitated.

"You're shivering. Are you cold?"

Cassie stood then, mindlessly wiping her sweaty palms on her denim-covered thighs, feeling shakier by the moment with the prospect of being caught in a tug of war, with her being a frayed rope. Regardless, she had to put one foot in front of the other and keep doing it until she felt her unraveling world twist back into place.

She slipped her hands into her front pockets to hide their obvious trembling. "I'm fine. Really."

The look of compassion on Jake's face was almost heartbreaking. She was just a material witness in a case he was involved with. He was doing his job. Cassie wasn't a part of his life for any other reason. Playing the nice, agreeable witness would most likely make Jake's job, and everyone else's, a lot easier.

His lips stretched into a smile, revealing the lone dimple that marked his cheek, and her heart beat at a dizzying rate.

Trust. Yes, she could trust Jake Santos.

"Come on," he said. "Let's go meet the woman of the hour."

* * *

"I want her out of the city. In fact, I don't want her anywhere near the state of Rhode Island."

Captain Russo had succeeded in pulling some strings all right. But what he'd managed to pull, Special Agent Charlotte Tate managed to snag right back.

"She wants to remain at home."

"That's out of the question," Charley said, pacing the floor. "We can protect her better in Virginia."

"She wants to be home," Jake said.

"Near you?" Charley said sarcastically. "I don't even want to know what that's all about. But I warn you, Jake. If you've done anything to compromise this investigation—"

"Easy, Charlotte." Agent Radcowski had remained quiet for most of the discussion. "I'm sure the detective is as eager to see Fagnelio's head roll as we are. After all, he could have been killed last night, too."

"I'm just relaying what Cassie has said to me," Jake said. "You have my report. It's complete. I haven't slept since last night and I'm not in the mood for—"

Charley swung around mid-pace to face him. "I don't really care what you're in the mood for."

Radcowski cleared his throat. "We're all a little jumpy this morning. Agent Novak was a friend of mine as well. His loss at the Bureau will be felt for a long time. But let's stay focused. Keeping Ms. Alvarez in Providence is out of the question. I've been to the safe house in Virginia. It's very pleasant and she'll be comfortable there."

"Try convincing her of that." Jake stood. "Are we done here?"

"Just one more thing," Radcowski said, glancing at Jake's report. "You said you didn't see anyone. Does that mean Fagnelio never mention anything about Agent Novak?"

"He knew him as Junior Canfield," Jake said. "That's all in my notes."

Radcowski nodded. "And you didn't suspect there was a problem when Mr. Fagnelio didn't show for the meeting?"

"I did. I was about to leave with Ms. Alvarez when the shooting happened."

Charley grabbed the report and quickly scanned it. "That was nearly a half hour after the time you were supposed to meet Angel."

"A little less, actually."

"Did you recognize Ms. Alvarez as Cassie Lang, the author?" Charley asked.

Jake shook his head. "I didn't know who she was at the time."

Charley lifted an eyebrow. "Her statement says she was doing research, dressed up like a hooker. You were soliciting?"

Captain Russo rolled his eyes. "He was on the job. She looked out of place and he tried to get her out of there."

Charley looked directly at Jake. "I'd like Jake to answer this."

"I could tell she wasn't a hooker within five seconds of meeting her. As soon as you see her, you'll know why."

Charley gave him a hard look. "Okay, where is she?"

* * *

Watching Cassie with Charley now, Jake had to admire the power of Cassie's will going up against the Federal Bureau of Investigation as if she were talking to the PTA. The people in this room could protect her life, but they could also make it a living hell if they were so inclined. And Cassie seemed unaffected by that.

It was clear right from the onset of their meeting that Charlotte Tate wasn't in any mood to negotiate, but Cassie insisted on having her say. Even something like Charley's impenetrable personality Cassie seemed to win over with a mix of police know-how and undeniable charm.

Maybe it was because they were both women and women spoke the same language. They understood it. Or so his eldest sister, Caroline, kept telling him. In fact, she'd called it a handicap that all men were afflicted with; the inability to speak the language of the female race.

Regardless, Cassie seemed to melt the glacial stare Charley had given Jake and agreed to a conference before any final decisions were made on Cassie's behalf. Since Charley Tate hated to be forced from the power seat, this was a major coup for Cassie, one that perhaps Cassie only won because of her status as a crime novelist.

The conference room was filled with a mix of police officers and FBI agents alike. As Cassie stood at the head of the room and addressed them all, Charley kept herself at the sidelines, merely listening. And Jake watched her.

Not a thick black strand of hair in her perfect hairstyle was out of place. She'd cut her hair since the last time he'd seen her. Instead of waves of raven hair flowing down her back, it was now shoulder length. She no longer wore bangs that emphasized her youth. Instead, she combed her hair back, making her eyes appear larger, more direct.

Jake could see how Tyler, his former partner, had been attracted to her. Charley was a looker, no doubt about it.

"I understand how serious this case is and how much you want to capitalize on Angel Fagnelio's involvement with Ritchie Trumbella by having me as a witness," Cassie stated, tapping the eraser end of a pencil against the table. "But it is vitally important to me that I not be used as a pawn in the legal system."

The room erupted in a wave of rumbles.

"You don't need to worry. I intend to cooperate with both the police and the FBI," she continued above the noise. "And I'll go to a safe house that you feel will give me complete protection only until Angel Fagnelio is securely behind bars."

"We appreciate your cooperation," Charley said, starting forward. "And we'll do—"

Cassie held up a hand. "Hold on, I'm not finished. I've done enough research to know that protective custody isn't always the sweet piece of cake it seems like in the movies. You all may be doing your job, and I'll even agree that this is necessary. But at the end of the day, you'll get to go home to your own lives. I'm the one who has to live this way twenty-four hours of every day."

"As I started to say, we'll certainly try to make you as comfortable as possible. I understand how hard this must be for you, Cassie. The safe house is designed—"

Cassie cut Charley off yet again before she could finish, rising up stronger than a tornado raging through the flatlands of Texas. Jake had to laugh when the agents directly in front of her seemed to shrink in their seats. How could one woman be sass, steam and innocence all rolled up into one?

He stole a quick glance at Charley and saw how her lips had thinned and her face had become tight with frustration.

Cassie's fists were clenched by her sides. He wasn't sure if it was from nerves or if she were ready to take a slug at anyone who didn't agree to her demands.

Sweet Lord, you've just met your match, Charley.

"I'm not asking for the world here. As I stated, I intend to cooperate. But there are some things I need if I'm going to be away for a while."

When no one made a move to interrupt, Cassie continued.

"The first thing is quite simple." Her delicate chin jutted out just enough to show her fire, enough for Jake to notice the deep color of her eyes and how they sparked as she spoke. "When I go to this safe house, I don't want to be hovered over like a two-year-old. The events of the last twenty-four hours were traumatic enough without having an agent assigned to count and report on how many times I go to the john to take a pee."

A rumble of laughter rolled through the room.

"It won't be like that," Charley cut in harshly.

Cassie wasn't intimidated. "I'm not a fool, Agent Tate. I know how this system works. I want my computer, some references books and to be left completely alone. It's the only way I can write."

"You're going to need to be under constant supervision. Round the clock," Charley said, coming up alongside Cassie.

"I understand that," she said. "Detective Jake Santos can guard me there."

The room came to life with whispers that spread around the closed room and echoed off the stark white walls. Jake was sure he'd heard a few snickers in there as well.

"I'm afraid that's not possible, Ms. Alvarez." Charley finally took her place at the front of the room with Cassie. "The agents I've assigned to the safe house are fully trained to act as your bodyguards."

"None of them are agents I've met or trust. I won't be able to relax unless I feel I'm safe, and that means I need someone I can trust completely."

"That's out of the question," Jake said. Cassie looked at him, her jaw set, and he knew he was in for a fight.

Agent Radcowski spoke up. "Agent Bellows will be driving you to Virginia. Agent Tate and I will follow in a day or two. There will be details to sort out but I can assure you, you will have your privacy there. You won't even know an agent is there."

"It's Jake Santos or I'm not going," Cassie said resolutely.

Charley parked herself in front of Jake and said in a low voice that oozed anger, "You and I need to have a serious discussion."

* * *

Richie Trumbella's autopsy report lay closed in a manila folder on Captain Russo's desk. Coffee rings marked the blotter underneath and were accompanied by happy- and sad-face doodles. An ashtray filled with stale cigarette butts, emitting the scent of spent tobacco, lay next to a jar of butterscotch candy. Jake sat on the corner of the desk, staring at the Captain's artwork. He waited for Charley to close the door behind her before looking up.

"What have you done to my witness!" Charley charged. "I agreed to let Ms. Alvarez speak to the agents on this case as a formality because I understand how difficult this must be for her. It's also given me the opportunity to judge my witness from a distance and get a little insight into her state of mind before she's transferred to the safe house in Virginia. We don't need any more publicity focused on our witness. The press is already all over it. She needs to leave here quietly. The last thing I need is for her to have a hissy fit because she wants you to babysit her."

Jake stood up. "The last thing I want is to babysit anyone. I'm just as interested in finding Fagnelio and getting him behind bars are you are."

"You can't very well do both, now can you." Charley sighed and crossed her arms across her chest. "I don't even want to know how you did it, but somehow between last night and this morning you managed to turn our star witness—our *only* witness—into a lovesick admirer of yours."

Jake cursed low. "You've got it wrong."

She laughed wryly and began pacing in front of him. "I've got eyes, Santos."

"Cassie has a mind of her own."

"You mean to tell me you didn't have anything to do with this little escapade?"

"I don't work under the same deceptive umbrella you've held up to move yourself ahead, Charley."

She stopped pacing and glared at him. "You're never going to let that go, are you?"

"Tyler has to live with it. Why not you?"

She pointed her finger towards the closed door. "Do you have any idea how hard it was to gain the respect of every agent out in that room? How long we've all been working on this case? I'm not going to let you waltz in and—"

"I've been working three months on this," he boomed over her.

"I hate to interrupt," Captain Russo interjected, leaning back in his chair. "If we're going to make sure that everyone in the building can hear, why not just go up on the roof and have at it. Otherwise, I suggest you keep it down."

They settled into a strained silence before both Charley and Jake dropped into the chairs opposite Captain Russo's desk. After a few controlled breaths, Charley turned to Jake.

"I've worked a long time to put that incident behind me,

Santos. Despite what you think, I never meant to hurt either you or Tyler. A decision had to be made at the last minute and I made it."

"And you hung us out to die in the process."

"I was doing my job. So were you."

With that, Jake stood and planted his fists deep in his pockets in an effort to control his fury. It amazed him how after five years he still felt an overwhelming anger from her deception. "You lied to Tyler just to get a damned promotion. You lied to us and it almost killed Tyler. He was a good cop."

"I know that!"

Charley closed her eyes and was quiet for a moment. Jake didn't want to think what he'd seen in her eyes was sadness and regret. He didn't want to think about Charley having feelings at all. All he could think of was seeing his partner lying in a pool of blood and Jake not being able to do a damn thing. Not being able to radio for help because he'd been sprayed with bullets himself. He'd been lucky the Kevlar vest he'd been wearing spared his flesh the bullets. But with two broken ribs and a punctured lung he was unable to get enough breath to do anything to help his partner. If it hadn't been for Kevin…

"I know Ty was a good cop," Charley finally said, her voice low and thready. "I wish it hadn't been so, but Tyler made his own decision to leave the force. Despite what you think, I had nothing to do with that."

She cleared her throat and blinked away the last trace of emotion he'd seen misting her eyes a few short moments ago. The glacial stare she seemed to reserve just for him was back.

"But we're not talking about the past or Tyler Jacobsen here. I want to apprehend Angel Fagnelio and squeeze as much information from him as I can about the Trumbella family. Cassie Alvarez is the key to that, and for some strange reason she wants you to be her bodyguard. I want to make sure my witness is cooperative and protected from Angel Fagnelio, as well as herself."

Jake folded his arms across his chest. "What the hell does that mean?"

"It means I still don't know who called that tip in to the papers. Cassie has something to gain from this, and it could potentially compromise this case if she's hell-bent on furthering her career with the publicity."

"Oh, come on, Charley. You saw how scared she is. She didn't do it."

"Can you be that sure?"

All he had was his gut feeling. "Yes."

"Now whose judgment is a little cloudy?" She turned to Russo. "He's off this case."

"What?"

"Wait a minute," Russo said. "We have a shooting to investigate. Junior Canfield or rather, Agent Novak, wasn't the only person killed at Rory's last night."

"This is my case, Charley. You can't just yank me off it," Jake said.

"In case you didn't hear right, Ms. Alvarez has requested that you be there with her at the safe house." Turning to Captain Russo, she added, "Don't worry. The FBI is prepared to share information as necessary with your office as long as it doesn't interfere with our own investigation. And since Jake is a witness to what happened, even if he didn't see the shooter, it's in our best interest that he remain alive."

"What's that supposed to mean?" Russo asked.

"It means, Fagnelio called a meeting with Jake and then sprayed the place with bullets. I don't know why, but I aim to find out if he was a target, and if so, why. I don't have to remind you that this federal investigation takes precedent over your case."

"I'm not going," Jake said, turning to Russo.

Charley started to protest, but Russo held up his hand to stop her.

"Yes, you are. If I have to drag your ass to the car and tie you inside, you're going."

"What? What about Fagnelio? What about this damned case I've been working on for three fucking months!"

"Kevin will take over it and work with the FBI. Jake, there

isn't a doubt in my mind that Angel Fagnelio knew you were undercover. That dirt-bag lied straight to your face and set you up to die. Wait until we have him in custody. Once Fagnelio goes before a grand jury, you won't have anything to worry about and neither will Ms. Alvarez. Trumbella's organization is responsible for too many deaths already. I don't want to add you to the list."

Jake started to protest.

"Enough!" Russo charged, slamming his fist on the coffee-stained blotter on his desk. "The decision has been made."

Charley picked up a butterscotch candy from the nearly empty glass jar on the desk and twirled it between her fingers. "I'll call the office in Virginia to tell them to expect you along with Ms. Alvarez. Pack your bags. You're leaving within the hour."

She took one step toward Jake.

"But I warn you. If anything goes wrong, if you cross me just one time because of our past association, I'll drag your ass right out of there and you can kiss your career good-bye."

And that was Cyclone Charley, Jake thought cynically as he watched her strut out of the office, leaving the door ajar.

CHAPTER FIVE

The empty road stretched out endlessly ahead of them like a string of railroad ties on a track with no train. The four-door federal-issue sedan quietly hummed down the Blue Ridge Parkway toward the brim of the Smoky Mountains. Their driver, a federal agent whose name Cassie had already forgotten in the long line of names she'd heard this morning, was concentrating on the road that was taking them far away from her home in Providence.

They'd be safe out of the city. But even Cassie knew that mobsters didn't recognize city or state limits, much less view them as an obstacle.

As soon as Angel Fagnelio was caught and brought before the grand jury, Cassie would be called back to testify. She had to face him, just like she had all those years ago when she'd faced her cousin's murderer in a humid Miami courtroom that stormy day.

Cassie's heavy sigh wrapped around her as she stared out the window, watching the last remains of the sunlight dip below the tree line. Rhododendrons lined the roadway, bare of any flowers that might have made this journey brighter.

Why in God's name did she live in a world of concrete and pavement when she could look out her window and see the peaceful countryside of Virginia? In the city, she didn't have beautiful sunsets over the mountains or rolling green hills that stretched on forever. There was just her small apartment in the safe part of the town. There was Angel Fagnelio, and hundreds just like him, crawling the streets, waiting to hurt innocent people who were just going about their daily lives.

Cassie's whole definition of safe had changed drastically in the last twenty-four hours. She had believed she was safe in the city. She thought she'd gotten over the black feeling of fear that consumed her eight years ago. But it was still there, imbedded deep inside like an angry cancer just waiting to grow.

Rolling her head back to the headrest in the back seat, she turned toward Jake and watched his profile. He'd been sleeping for the first leg of the journey out of Rhode Island and through Connecticut. Now he sat tall and stiff in the seat, his long body barely fitting into the space. His strong jaw was squared as if he were rolling something back and forth in his mind, or trying to force it out. His dark blue eyes were intense with thought.

Cassie wanted to believe Jake was just concentrating on what was ahead. But as time wore on, she got the distinct impression he was forcing himself not to look at her.

Was he angry with her for insisting he come? It wasn't that she'd blame him. In one fell swoop, she'd turned not only her life around, but Jake's as well.

She had the whole Federal Bureau of Investigation ready and willing to put out the red carpet for her if it meant she'd cooperate as their material witness. Once she was in the room giving her demands to them, she knew they would have granted her anything to get Angel Fagnelio convicted for his crimes.

Charlotte Tate was another story, and even Cassie had to admit she was surprised when the special agent came into the conference room and agreed to Cassie's request.

While they were at her apartment, Jake had promised it was going to be all right. And she believed him. Maybe now that they were alone together, he'd changed his mind?

"You look tired. I'm surprised you're not still sleeping," she finally said, wishing she could close the gap between them and ease the tension plaguing him. She wanted to place her hand in his, touch his cheek, now shadowed with dark stubble. Anything to bring the connection back she felt earlier when they were alone at the police station.

Jake answered quietly. "I'll sleep more when we get where we're going."

Cassie glanced at the driver to make sure he wasn't paying attention, then back to Jake. "You're angry with me."

"What makes you think that?"

"You've been cool all afternoon."

He hesitated a fraction of a second. "Have I?"

She nodded. "You haven't said much, but when you do, you look...well, angry."

His sigh echoed defeat. "I guess I am. Seeing Charley brought back a lot of memories I'd just as soon forget."

He turned to look at her then, and she saw his smoky eyes were filled with warmth. He wasn't completely plagued with the tightness she'd seen all day. Some of it had subsided.

"I'm sorry if you mistook my...coolness for being angry with you. I'm not. Kevin always says I was born with an intense stare. He got used to it."

"Then I guess I'll have to get used to it, too."

Jake went back to watching the road with his intense look. She went back to watching the strong lines of his profile.

He glanced at her then, and she knew her fears were true. His eyes were haunted.

She leaned forward in her seat to talk to the driver. "I'm sorry. I forgot your name."

The driver glanced in the rear view mirror. "Agent Hogan."

"That's right. Can you at least tell me how much longer it's going to take for us to get to this safe house?"

Cassie had long since brushed aside her annoyance that the exact location of the safe house couldn't, or *wouldn't* be disclosed to them. She'd been given strict orders to call Maureen and her parents to tell them she was going out of town and wasn't sure when she'd be back. But she was safe and she would get in touch with them. She was also given strict orders not to use her cell phone or email.

As much as she hated the idea of being locked up for Lord only knew how long, she was looking forward to getting there and having a nice hot bubble bath before crawling beneath the sheets.

"A few hours still. If you're tired, why don't you nod off for a bit. It'll make the drive go quicker."

Cassie leaned back in the seat. "I can't sleep," she muttered.

"You're too wound up," Jake said.

She cocked her head to one side and tossed him a wry grin. "No kidding, Sherlock. You're just as bad. I've seen more relaxed stiffs in the city morgue."

"Do you have to do that?"

His question, as much as the stark look on his face, startled her, filling her with a sense of foreboding. She felt herself shrink down in the seat.

"I was just teasing."

"I meant, go to the morgue. Do you have to do that in your research?"

Eight-year-old memories Cassie wished she could will away stormed her mind at an alarming speed.

"Just once," she said quietly. "It wasn't for research."

When she paused, choking on her own reaction to the memory, she saw that he was waiting.

"My cousin was murdered eight years ago. Even though she witnessed it, my grandmother couldn't believe he was really gone, so my aunt and I took her to the morgue. It was horrible."

"I'm sorry."

"Me, too," Cassie said shakily as the memory of her grandmother falling to the floor and weeping uncontrollably flooded her mind.

"I thought because you write about it…"

She tilted an eyebrow. "What? That I get off on blood and gore?"

He lifted his shoulder in an idle shrug.

"Guess again. I hope I never have to see someone I love like that again. Not in this lifetime. Seeing Emilio that way…was quite enough."

Jake heaved a sigh, and she heard him mutter an oath under his breath.

"Were you close to him?"

Cassie shook her head, swallowed a bit of emotion that bubbled up her throat. "That's what makes it more horrible to me. Before he died, I remember seeing him exactly three times in my life."

Jake's eyes widened as he glanced at her.

"I was visiting my family in Miami when it happened. My cousin and I were the same age, but I never got a chance to get to know Emilio when I was growing up because we lived so far apart. I'd gone down for a visit during spring break at college and spent a few days with my grandmother. Emilio and I really hit it off. I was hoping to finally get the chance to get to know him more during that visit."

A blanket of sadness covered her as she turned away, twisting her attention away from the memories to the relative safety of the scenery. Dark roads, barren hills, trees that had yet to produce buds that would pop out in spring. And they would. It was only with absolute death that spring didn't come.

The sun was now long gone. The headlights shone bright on the dry road ahead of them. They drove in silence for a few minutes. Every once in a while Cassie's mind would wander to that day on her grandmother's porch.

The sight of an animal's illuminated eyes at the side of the road brought her back to the present. She was in a car with Jake Santos and an agent she'd met three seconds before climbing into the car. She wasn't eighteen anymore, but she *was* once again on the run.

"How'd it happen?" Jake ask.

"Emilio?"

He nodded.

"Well, like I said, it was spring break. My father was livid I'd gone to Miami."

"He was angry you went to visit your family?"

"Yes, well, no, not really for visiting my family. It was because I went to Miami without telling him. I didn't tell anyone. I just showed up on my grandmother's doorstep one day. She was so thrilled."

Cassie laughed just thinking about how her grandmother had called all her neighbors from the front porch to tell them her little Juanita had come home.

64

"My father didn't want me to travel to Miami. He'd said if I wanted family around, he would have paid for them to come visit us in Stamford. He just didn't understand."

"I'm afraid I don't, either."

She laughed quietly, without the bitterness she'd felt her whole life about her father's reasons for not wanting to return to Miami.

"My dad didn't have an easy childhood. Things were rough for his family when they first came over from Cuba. That's something I was spared because I grew up in a nice middle class Connecticut neighborhood, well away from the prejudice he'd encountered in his life. He worked hard, not only building his business up in Stamford, but building his self-esteem."

"Something to be proud of."

"Yes, and I am. Unfortunately, it built a wide gap between me and my only other family here. It wasn't just the cultural differences either. He tried hard to blend into the mainstream, leaving his culture behind. He wanted to be American in all ways that counted. I doubt I'll ever know everything that caused him to leave Miami. He doesn't speak much of that time. But I got a good glimpse of it the day Emilio died."

"You mean, you were there...when it happened?"

Cassie swallowed hard. She'd always wondered if things would have been different if she hadn't gone to Miami. Maybe Emilio would still be alive.

"I remember it was this gloriously perfect sunny day, and Emilio and I had just come home from the beach. I loved the beach and the warm water.

"Anyway, we were just sitting on the porch with my grandmother, dumping the sand from my beach bag."

She paused for a minute, running her hand over her cheek as if to wipe away the image. But it remained.

"A man started yelling in Spanish. He'd apparently followed us up from the beach. I didn't understand any of it because I don't speak it fluently. My parents only spoke English, even in the house. The next thing I knew my grandmother was screaming and the man had grabbed me by the hair. He'd pulled a gun, was waving it around like a flag and laughing. Emilio was shouting in Spanish. I had no idea what he was saying. Then I was thrown aside and Emilio was lying on the ground bleeding."

Cassie swallowed down the acrid taste of bile. The sound of the gunshot, the smell of gunpowder still seemed to choke the air around her with startling clarity, even after all these years.

"The man who shot him didn't even run. He wasn't scared at all. He just stood there laughing as Emilio bled on the dirt, like taking my cousin's life was nothing. Then he looked at me and my grandmother—I'll never forget his face—he said we were next."

Jake swore then. It didn't shock her, like the plethora of expletives she'd heard that day during the shooting. Or the look in the eyes of her cousin's killer.

"So this is nothing but a reoccurring nightmare," Jake said almost to himself.

Sighing, she said, "That's putting it mildly. I testified then. My grandmother didn't. Even though she witnessed the murder, she refused to believe it happened. She was too frightened. I don't blame her. It was pretty horrible.

"My father was furious at me, both for going to Miami and for doing what I thought was right."

Jake reached across the seat and covered his hand over hers. She ignored the immediate zing of energy that shot through her and gladly accepted the comfort he offered.

"Fear makes people do funny things, Cassie. I see it all the time. Your father must be feeling it all over again now."

"I couldn't tell my parents," she said quietly, gazing out at the darkness. Although by now, they probably knew.

Cassie hadn't told anyone, except for Maureen. She knew her parents would worry, so she'd asked Maureen to tell them she was going away for a few days. It would be surprisingly easy for Cassie to keep her whereabouts from her parents, at least in the short term. Cassie lived such a solitary life while she was working on a book. She'd hardly leave the house except to go to the library and pick up some food at the grocery store. Even then, Chinese take-out and pizza were her best friends. There was no one at home to fret about her or wonder when she came home. She didn't even have a cat to worry about feeding.

There were times when a deadline loomed and she would drop out of sight for months, communicating with her mother only via email or a quick phone call. She could do both at the safe house and reassure her parents that she was fine without having to deal with her father directly.

Jake squeezed her hand gently. "At a time like this you could use your parents' support."

"How much support can I get from them if they're in Stamford and I'm tucked away in a safe house? Besides, my father would only blame me again."

"They're going to find out, Cassie. It was in the papers."

"I'm sure they read about it. But I asked Maureen to call them. They're going to worry. At least this time I wasn't to blame."

Jake frowned. "It wasn't your fault then, either."

She smiled weakly. "Thanks. I did blame myself for a while though. I figured if I hadn't gone... Dad said it was better to forget it ever happened. Forget we'd lost Emilio like we had. After it was all over, he insisted my grandmother and my aunt come live with us. He didn't want any of us to talk about the shooting ever again. And no one did. We never forgot Emilio, but it was as if he'd died some other way. He was just gone. I know my father blamed me, even if he didn't put it into words."

The vacant sound of the tires crushing the pavement beneath them mocked her, surrounding her like the tide of blinding fog now rolling over the hills.

With a shake of his head, Jake said, "I don't understand how you do it. How can you write about crime and not relive that horror every single day?"

"It's because of that incident that I write about crime. My character, CJ Carmen, is a strong woman. I wrote her that way so she wouldn't feel all the fear that I've felt since that happened.

"A month after that creep was convicted for killing Emilio—over a wink, mind you. Emilio's mortal sin was winking at this guy's girlfriend on the beach. Anyway, I started writing *Fire in the Night*, my first crime novel. All that anger and fear just came pouring out of me. It was very cathartic. I learned a lot, too. Most of all, I learned my father was wrong. About some things anyway. There are things about our culture that may not be wonderful. But it's not all bad. There's good there. People find themselves in situations they have no control over. Like this. But it doesn't make it all bad."

Jake pulled his hand from Cassie's, cursing himself inwardly for lingering there and for feelings just holding her hand stirred inside him.

"You can hardly keep your eyes open."

"I told you, I'm fine."

"Don't give me that."

She dragged her seatbelt off and grabbed her overnight bag from the floor. She pulled out a little pillow that had flowers embroidered on it.

"What's this?"

She shrugged shyly. "Whenever I travel I always bring this along. It makes sleeping in a strange bed less weird."

Cassie reached over and undid his seatbelt, then tucked the pillow into her lap.

"What are you doing?"

"I'm making you a comfortable bed. At least, as comfortable as I can make you in this car. You can't sleep sitting up. This way you can stretch out a little. Come here, lay your head down on the pillow."

He did as he was told. The heat of her body against his shoulder seeped into him with the contact. The sweet scent of perfume drifted to him. No, it wasn't perfume, it was soap. The warm scent of lavender was what had been filling his head all afternoon in these cramped quarters, driving him insane.

"We're going to be traveling on the Blue Ridge Parkway for a while, right?" Cassie asked the driver.

"Yes, ma'am. You have about an hour."

Cassie looked down at Jake. "An hour is good. I'll wake you up when we get there. Oh, wait, I have a blanket, too."

Reaching forward, she wrestled with her overnight bag. Her breast brushed against his cheek.

Good Lord! "Let me get up," he said.

"No, I have it." Gripping the edge of the blanket, which was half out of the bag, Cassie began pulling and then bouncing the bag up and down until it made a racket on the floor.

Abruptly, she stopped pulling at the blanket and was silent. He glanced up at her as she leaned over the seat, her shoulders moving up and down slightly, and her hair swinging to and fro with the movement. The soft noise bubbling up from her throat sounded like...soft sobs.

A smoldering fire burned the center of his chest and slowly spread outward, making it hard for him to breathe. Was she...crying?

"Cassie?"

She tilted her head then, just enough for her hair to swing away from her cheeks, and he saw the soft features of her face. She wasn't crying at all. She was laughing. Tears streamed down her cheeks, but she was definitely laughing.

"What's wrong?" he asked, completely dumbfounded and on the brink of hysteria himself.

"The blanket is stuck," she said, still laughing. He held on to the bag and she gave a quick yank. The light blanket pulled free.

Throwing the blanket over him, she said, "This is so absurd."

"What is?"

"This. Everything. You and me on the run like Bonnie and Clyde. Well, not quite like Bonnie and Clyde. We're on the run from bad guys instead of being the bad guys."

Her laughter faded and her face grew serious as she sighed. "I need to keep my head clear. I know how all this works. I've researched it. Written about it. But when I get frustrated about all that is happening, I forget. I just hate this sense of my world being out of control."

"Me, too."

She heaved another heavy sigh, her breast stretching the

fabric of her shirt just a little to draw his gaze in that direction.

"Starting now, I'm back on track. I promise." She put her hand up as if she were taking an oath. "Now that you're comfy, get some sleep."

"Are you always this bossy?" he asked, not able to keep the smile from stretching across his tired face. He was amazed at how good it felt to smile. He wasn't sure he had at all that day. If he had, he most surely was with Cassie when he did it.

"I do my best, detective," she said, giving him the most irresistible grin.

He closed his eyes, but Jake found no release in sleep. Visions of the dead, shattered glass and screams invaded his mind, startling him awake just as he drifted off. He didn't know if it was memories of the sweet smell of Cassie that made sleep impossible.

CHAPTER SIX

The mountain road leading to the safe house was ominously dark. Enough drizzle clung to the windshield to need the wipers, but not enough to keep the wipers from sticking to the windshield for lack of moisture. Instead, they made a crying sound that seemed to warn them of danger. Of what kind, Jake wasn't exactly sure.

Now that they were almost at the safe house, Jake was thankful he'd had a little sleep behind him. He was equally thankful for his full belly due to Cassie's insistence a bunch of teenagers weren't going to recognize her and call the local papers if they went through the drive-through window of a fast food restaurant.

He was glad for Cassie's impulsiveness.

Agent Hogan pulled onto a dirt road just off the driveway leading to the safe house.

"We're almost there," he said, looking at the two of them from the rear view mirror. "I need to stretch these legs."

An ancient mobile home set back from the road, almost hidden by a stand of trees at the bottom of the hill, came into view. At first glance, the unkempt trailer appeared to be deserted. But Jake knew that was just a diversion for the locals. From this vantage point, about a quarter mile from the safe house, the only road leading to and from the safe house could be monitored by state-of-the-art surveillance equipment located inside the trailer.

"Is this it?" Cassie said, her face contorting into a grimace.

Agent Hogan chuckled wryly. "This is the guard's station. Very inconspicuous. You're going to be staying up on the top of the mountain."

"You mean, people actually live in this place?"

71

She was studying the tattered shell of the mobile home just as she had been scoping the crowded bar. Jake knew in an instant, Cassie was storing the information away for later use in one of her crime books.

"I assure you, as bad as it looks on the outside, it's state of the art inside," Agent Hogan said. "And very comfortable for anyone who has to spend any amount of time in there."

She chuckled nervously. "I'm glad it won't be me."

Hogan jammed the car into park. He left the engine running and opened the door. "You'll be staying up on the hill. It's much bigger. Just sit tight for a minute. I need to check in with the guard on duty."

"Not to worry," she murmured as he closed the door.

Agent Hogan met another man halfway to the door. The man looked at the car and then walked over to them. Jake rolled down the window and introduced himself.

"Agent Bellows," the man said, shaking Jake's hand. "I thought you'd never get here."

Hogan arched his back and grimaced. "We hit traffic through the city."

Agent Bellows got in the car and shifted it into gear. He turned to Jake and Cassie. "I'm going to bring you two up to the house. I've already done a check and it's well stocked for you. You should be comfortable."

"What about Agent Hogan?" Cassie asked. "He didn't eat anything while he was driving."

"It was a long drive. I thought I'd let him use the bathroom and grab a bite down here while I take you two up."

"I appreciate that," Cassie said.

They drove up the narrow road toward the house. When they arrived, they got out of the car.

Bellows handed Jake the keys to the house. "Give me a call when you're secure."

Jake just stared at him. "You aren't going in with us?"

Bellows shook his head. "The lady is the one who said she didn't want agents hovering over her, and Agent Tate wants to keep her happy. Besides, we already did a sweep of the house less than fifteen minutes ago, and we've been watching ever since. You got a fully stocked kitchen that should last you a week. The guards down the hill will be checking in with you and doing a check of the grounds at least twice a day. Agents Tate and Radcowski will be here tomorrow to do a more formal briefing once they're finished in Providence. I want to do a quick walk around the perimeter. I'll wait to make sure you're both inside before I head back down."

When Bellows disappeared into the darkness behind the house, Jake said, "You okay?" One glance at her, and Jake realized she was anything but. Her hands were bunched up in front of her if she were clenching her fists and her dark brown eyes suddenly looked like a cat caught by a pack of wild dogs.

"Hey?"

"Yeah. I'm fine."

"Agent Bellows said they'd be checking in with us periodically so make sure you have a robe on if you're walking through the house. You don't want any strange men catching you in your pajamas."

"Except you."

She peered up at him, about to say something, but didn't. She had the strangest look on her face that made him want to reach out and touch her. Her dark lashes dipped, hiding the fatigue in her eyes. He didn't have to see her face in the light to know she was blushing. The image of her cheeks turning crimson last night at the bar was still imprinted in his brain, causing havoc with his peace of mind in cataclysmic proportion.

"You were the one who insisted on having me here," he said in a low voice.

"I didn't mean it that way. I just meant that there was going to be at least one man seeing me in my..." She drew in a shallow breath and shook her head slightly. "Never mind. I don't know what I meant."

She started laughing, and Jake couldn't help but feel lightheaded by the sound of her voice.

"You've had the privilege of catching me first thing in the morning in my pj's, but this is going to be a first for me. Seeing

73

you, I mean."

He cocked his head to one side, silently questioning whether he should confess. "I don't want to disappoint you, but I'm not the pajama type."

Her reaction was exactly as he'd anticipated. She sucked in a deep breath and held it. When she finally let it out, she tugged on her bottom lip with her teeth and averted her gaze. But not before he saw the flames of desire burst to life in her dark eyes.

He'd been thinking the same. The thought of sleeping with Cassie's naked body pressed against his was torture. What made it more tortuous was the fact it would never be reality.

"Well, are we going to go inside where it's warm, or are we going to continue to stand outside in the rain?" she asked.

Jake lifted his face to the black sky and felt cold moisture misting his face. Yes, it was still drizzling lightly. Not enough to cool him down though, which is probably why he hadn't bothered to notice.

Cassie followed behind him to the back of the sedan. After popping the trunk, he pulled out her laptop computer and a suitcase, handing them to her.

"I'll get the rest and meet you in front of the house. Drop the bags on the porch and wait for me."

Jake dug into the trunk for his overnight bag and the bigger suitcase Cassie had packed. When she didn't move, he turned to her.

"If it's all the same, I'll wait for you," she said.

"There's nothing to be afraid of, Cassie. They told us, this place was checked less than half an hour ago. My walk through will just be more out of curiosity than anything. Once I check the rooms over and get all the bags inside, I'll lock up tight and call in to Agent Bellows at the station."

She nodded nervously. "Okay, but I'm going to be your shadow. So don't get jumpy."

Nerves were getting the best of her, he decided. It had been a long twenty-four hours and he guessed that neither one of them would fully relax until they were settled. Better to get that done sooner rather than later.

"Are you getting bossy with me again?" he said, hoping she'd take his teasing good-naturedly and finally begin to calm down.

He dropped the bags on the porch and unlocked the door. The way she clung to his back as he opened the door, as if he was the last hold on earth to her peace of mind, gave him his answer. *She was terrified.*

The soft glow of light from the kitchen in the back of the house shined beams across the deep-pile living room rug. Jake reached up and skimmed his hand against the smooth-papered wall to find the light switch. When he did, he flicked it on and bright light filled the open room.

This safe house was called a cottage, but one look and it was obvious it was anything but. The living room was square and wide with a cream sofa and settee propped in the center of the room. Against the inside wall stood a full oak-paneled entertainment unit. A cushioned window seat in a floral design sat between a row of bookcases resting against the far wall. The living room was open to the kitchen area, filled with brightly shined stainless steel appliances and a white and gray marble countertop that gleamed under the track lighting above.

The FBI had taken pains to make the safe house comfortable. Jake knew that equal pains had been taken to hide the state-of-the-art equipment meant for keeping both "clients" and agents comfortable and secure for a dangerously long time.

He squashed down the feeling of being impressed and went about searching the rest of the house. Cassie held tight to his heels at every turn. He could feel the heat of her behind him as he moved, heard each little burst of breath as she remembered to breathe. And she was literally on his heels when she plowed into his leather jacket and stepped on the back of his boot.

He'd felt it, but he knew she felt the connection between his hard boot-heel and the toe of her canvas sneakers more.

"Ouch," she muttered softly as they moved on through the kitchen.

"You don't have to follow that close."

She did it again.

Jake spun around. "Cassie, the lights are on and no one, *but us*, is here," he said delicately. "I know you're nervous, but I assure you, here, more than anywhere else, you'll be safe."

She opened her mouth to speak but quickly clamped it shut.

The sound of the car engine firing up drew Jake's attention to the window. He quickly walked over to the window and peered outside. Red taillights bounced down the driveway toward the road.

"Agent Bellows has finished his perimeter check. See? All clear."

Chewing on her bottom lip, Cassie pointed down the hallway. "Shouldn't you have checked the coat closet?"

Jake heaved an exasperated sigh, knowing his unrest was fueled by fatigue more than frustration.

He peered down at the delicate features of her face. As it had last night, the small beauty mark to the side of her full lips teased him. He'd wondered last night if she'd purposely put it there for show. Now, seeing her cleanly scrubbed face and creamy complexion, he knew for sure that it was something nature had blessed her with, a true mark of beauty.

He needed some distance from this woman, and the only way he'd get that was when they were both locked in their own bedrooms for the night. Deciding the quickest way to achieve that would be to appease her, he gripped the doorknob of the coat closet at the entry of the hallway and yanked it open.

"See? No Bogey Monster in there," he said, trying to keep the grin that tugged at the corners of his mouth from showing.

Cassie knotted her arms across her puffed-out chest and glared at him.

"In one of my books—the one I was telling you about at the station—there was a gunman waiting for the agent in the coat closet."

"How'd he get in?"

"He strangled the guard."

Jake glanced at Cassie over his shoulder. "Do you really

think it was such good therapy for you to write crime novels?"

Straightening her spine, she sputtered, "Of course."

"I think you were right last night. You have an overactive imagination."

Jake checked the remaining rooms while Cassie stayed rooted behind in the hallway, fuming. He might have imagined it, but he thought he'd actually seen steam rise from her head.

"Are you done making fun of me yet?" she called out as he checked the last room.

Jake peered at her face and that nagging emotion welled inside. His heartbeat hammered in his ear just seeing her vulnerability, making it hard for him to breathe.

"I'm sorry. I didn't mean to hurt your feelings. I'm just tired."

She hesitated for a moment, looking at the floor, the door and then at his face. "Did you check the closets in the bedroom?"

He had to keep himself from laughing. Bogey Monsters aside, Cassie was right about one thing. Everything about this whole situation was absurd. Here he was, Mr. Keep-Yourself-Detached, looking at an incredibly beautiful, sensual woman, and he was supposed to keep her safe?

What the hell was he thinking? And Lord have mercy, that was just the problem. He was thinking way too much about how much he wanted to take Cassie to bed when he should be staying focused on the job he was sent here to do.

In all the years he'd been on the force, all the women he'd ever known who'd come and gone from his life, he never had trouble keeping himself detached and focused on his work. A mere twenty-four lousy hours with this tiresome woman, and he was forgetting all he'd worked so hard to achieve. He couldn't keep his mind focused on anything except the way her bottom lip jutted out just slightly when she pouted. Or the way her laughter bubbled up inside her.

How Cassie could even laugh at all, given the situation they faced, was beyond him. But she did. And every time her lips spread into a slow smile, Jake's mind went into a complete nuclear meltdown. All he wanted was to crush her soft, tiny body against his and kiss her until he couldn't breathe, until the rest of his body found the release that would make all the craziness he felt inside make sense.

He needed to stop this madness right now. As attracted as he was to Cassie, there was absolutely no way he was taking this woman to bed.

"I think maybe we should go to bed, ah, get some sleep."

* * *

Cassie stared at Jake's face, trying hard not to read into the multitude of expressions stretching and changing his features. She was being ridiculous. She knew that. As much as she tried to convince herself what Jake said was true, she couldn't keep the hairs on the back of her neck from dancing on end.

Maybe Jake was right. Maybe she had been writing about crime too long and it had tainted her, making her unable to deal with reality. She wasn't living the story in one of her books.

But then most people didn't live with the reality of getting showered with bullets as they had last night at Rory's. That was not something out of one of her books. That had been real.

She rolled her head on her shoulders, easing out some of the tension plaguing her. Last night and the long drive had taken its toll. She needed a hot bath and some distance from this incredible pull she felt toward Jake, so she could regroup.

"Okay. Where?" she conceded.

"The center room here," he said, reaching dangerously close to her in order to open the door behind her. "It has a private bath with no windows. You'll feel safe there."

Stepping inside, he reached for the light switch. Cassie was completely unprepared for such a beautifully decorated room. Sure, the rest of the house was gorgeous, but this room looked as if it had been decorated just for her. A queen-sized bed rested against the interior wall. The mound of floral throw pillows piled high against the wooden headboard looked like a huge welcome bouquet. The soft violet of the carpet brought out the delicate stripes in the wallpaper. In the corner by the bathroom door sat an empty secretary's desk, just waiting for her and her laptop to set up home.

Cassie had always dreamed of writing in a secluded place, free from noisy traffic jams and telemarketing calls. But never once in her wildest fantasies had she dreamed it would be like this. She had all the peace and quiet she needed now.

She drew in a short breath, amending her thought. How could she have any peace when Angel Fagnelio was still out there? Until that was resolved, she didn't know if she'd ever find peace.

"I'll take the room right across the hall. Just knock if you need anything."

When she turned to the sound of Jake's voice, she saw that he was by the doorway, stepping back into the hallway.

"Are you going to bed now, too?"

He stopped and looked back at her over his broad shoulder. "Just as soon as I check in with Bellows and tell him we're all locked up for the evening."

"I'll just get my bag then."

She eased past him, filling her head with the scent of his lingering aftershave and the faint smell of the coffee they'd drunk on the drive up. He was still rooted in the same spot when she returned with her suitcase and her laptop.

"I guess this is where we say goodnight," she said, finding it hard to meet his gaze. She knew if she did, she'd see the same heat she'd seen last night when she'd gotten out of his car all dressed in that wild outfit Maureen convinced her to wear to Rory's. It would be her undoing because then he'd see the erotic fantasies that had been swirling around her head during the drive.

If she closed herself in her room and locked the door, she'd feel safe from Angel Fagnelio and his ugliness. She'd also be safe from the emotional whirlwind she was caught in every time Jake flashed his drop-dead-sexy smile.

"Goodnight," he whispered.

For a minute, one nanosecond, she thought he was actually going to bend his head and kiss her. His gaze dropped to her lips and lingered there. As powerful as her fear had been all day, the desire to have Jake dip his head and cover her lips with his was wildly intoxicating. She wanted to feel the power of being wrapped tightly in his arms again, feel the heat of his strong body crushing her without the fear of bullets and flying glass and death. She wanted his passion and strength. That would keep her safe.

But Jake didn't kiss her. He stood ramrod still, his penetrating eyes echoing what she felt as his gaze washed over her.

"Goodnight," she said. "Could you do me a favor?"

"Sure."

"When you're finished with your phone calls, could you just come by my room and knock on my door before you go to bed?" She dipped her gazed and chuckled softly. "I know it sounds silly—"

"No. It doesn't. I'll be done in a few minutes."

"Thank you, Jake," she said softly.

Cassie closed the door to the bedroom and was alone for the first time that day. Something deep inside, call it gut instinct or woman's intuition, just didn't feel right. And no matter how tired, she wasn't going to sleep until she allayed her feelings.

Turning from the closed door, she hugged her middle. Not from a sudden cold chill now that the heat of being near Jake was gone. What she felt was spine-tingling jolt nagging her insides.

But she was being ridiculous. *Wasn't she?*

Bogey Monster.

Jake had teased her to try to ease her irrational fear, but they were still there, nagging at her. Cassie's sensible mind knew there was no such thing as the Bogey Monster. There was only Angel Fagnelio and whoever it was that leaked her name to the press, making her as wide open a target as a duck at a carnival shooting gallery.

She'd silently watched him sleeping in the the car during the ride. She'd even allowed herself to brush her fingers across his forehead to push a thick lock of hair out of his eyes, giving in to the wild temptation she'd felt all day.

Jake wasn't a man she'd run away with on a romantic weekend. He wasn't going to be her lover for the weekend or even for one night. He had a job to do. To protect her, keep her alive. That was the only reason either one of them was there.

Cassie dropped her laptop case on the desktop with a big clunk, not caring she could have ruined it. The suitcase was heavier. She used two hands to lift it to the bed, then zip it open. She grabbed her nightgown and turned toward the bathroom door. But her eyes settled on the big oak closet door instead. There was a hook for her bathrobe and suddenly her mind raced to her suitcase and the fact that in her haste to pack she'd forgotten her bathrobe completely. What else had she forgotten? How much of her life had she left behind?

She walked over to the enormous bed and plopped down at the foot of it, staring at the closet door. Bringing her hand to her cheek, she chuckled.

Bogey Monster.

"In *Hidden Evil*," she muttered to herself, thinking about her third book. "There were no bad guys in the closet waiting to shoot CJ."

She paused breathlessly. *But there was a man with a gun under her bed.*

Like radar, her gaze swept over the big beautiful bed with pillows piled ridiculously high in the center. *No, this big beautiful bed can't hurt me.*

Jake's muted voice filtered in through the closed bedroom door. He was still talking to someone on the phone.

"You're being ludicrous, Cassie," she muttered to herself, clutching her face with both hands now and laughing. "This isn't *Hidden Evil*. This is life. Reality. This isn't a make pretend book you've dreamed up. And you're not CJ Carmen."

Still, Cassie's mind kept racing to dark thoughts and before she knew it she was dropping to her knees at the foot of the bed.

"Okay, if there's anyone under here, be prepared for battle," she said, chuckling almost hysterically. "And if there isn't, then I guess I better prepare myself for some serious psychoanalysis, because I'm losing my mind."

Of course, there wasn't going to be anyone hiding under her bed. The house had been checked. But she knew that the only way she'd be able to put her head down on one of these gloriously pretty pillows and sleep tonight was if she checked for herself.

Her hand trembled as she reached for the white dust ruffle. Pulling the eyelet fabric up, she had to squint her eyes to focus. The small desk lamp was on, but it was dimly lit in the corner of the room, making it hard to see under the bed. Blinking, she fought to focus her eyes. Then again. They burned as she focused them so she rubbed them with two fingers.

Cassie didn't really believe in the Bogey Monster. Her sensibility told her she certainly wouldn't find one under her bed. Nor would she find a masked man wielding a gun or a knife or any other weapon. Her creative mind was just working overtime, as it always did, and this time it was getting the better of her. She was just being silly.

Still, Cassie had to look for herself.

Through the dark shadows, something came into view.

You're being ridiculous.

But Cassie knew she really wasn't. She rubbed her eyes again. Even as her mind registered relief that there was no masked intruder hiding under her bed, waiting to kill her, what she did register most definitely would.

CHAPTER SEVEN

Jake scrubbed his hand across his rough face with one hand. He hadn't bothered to shave that morning and now, with an extra day's beard growth, his jaw itched like hell. But he'd be damned if he was going to take the time to rid himself of his whiskers before he climbed into bed. He'd just finished calling the guard's station and decided to check in with his partner before turning in.

"She insisted I look in the closet, Kev," Jake said, shaking his head as he eased himself deep into the wing chair by the telephone. "She's nuts. But do you know what's more nuts?"

Kevin laughed. "You did it, right?"

"Yeah. I'm surprised she didn't insist I look under her bed."

"Man, you got it bad," his partner said, a hint of knowing in his voice.

"It's not like that," Jake lied. It was exactly like that, but he wasn't about to admit it to Kevin. "I got roped into this."

"You looked like hell when I saw you and that was this morning. You must look a whole lot worse now. Maybe you frightened the poor woman."

"Fuck you, asshole."

"Just keeping things real."

He leaned over to turn the fancy lamp sitting on the end table off, but before he did, something caught Jake's attention and he missed the next thing Kevin had asked.

"What's that?"

"You're mumbling again. Sure sign of dementia."

Jake normally would have laughed but he was distracted by what had caught his eye.

Kevin continued. "You sure you're okay with all this?"

"Ah, yeah."

It was hidden well in the seam of the lampshade. Jake pulled at the threads that had been stitched until the device fell into his palm. It was the size of a flat pea. He probably wouldn't have noticed it at all except that the lampshade was slightly askew, most probably tilted when Cassie bumped into him earlier. The naked light bulb made it glaringly obvious at this particular angle.

Terrific. Charley had appeased Cassie by telling her she wouldn't be watched like an insect under a microscope. She'd kept her word. But only because the agents on duty fully intended to bug the house. Jake was sure all the rooms were filled with these tiny devices. He'd have to figure out a way to warn Cassie about it without making her feel self-conscious.

"It's been a hell of a day, Kevin. Did you manage to get any info on those names?"

"A bit more than I bargained for. Maureen Phillips, Cassie's editor, came up clean. Not even so much as a parking violation with the DMV. But the other name—"

"Adam Coel?"

"Yeah, him. Seems he's had a little bad luck streak at the local casino. In hock up to his eyeballs and in desperate need of some major cash."

Jake let out a quick sigh. "So he's a possibility."

"Maybe, but I doubt it," Kevin said, still sounding unconvinced. "Legitimate newspapers don't pay for big stories. And it doesn't seem likely someone requiring the kind of cash Coel needs would give it up for free. Seems more likely he'd have gone to the tabloids and sold his story to the highest bidder."

"Keep checking for me, will ya?"

"Sure. But there's more."

When Kevin hesitated, Jake braced himself.

"I dug up some information on Angel Fagnelio that I thought you might find a little interesting."

"Such as?"

"Debra Cantelli was Angel's sister."

The floor felt like it fell out from beneath Jake. "That can't be."

"I didn't think so either, so I double checked."

So had he, Jake thought dismally. At the beginning of his investigation he'd done a full sweep of Angel Fagnelio's file. But if this was true, it was obvious he hadn't done his homework right.

"It's true, Jake. Both had different fathers, different last names. She lived with her father most of the time. Probably why we were never able to make a connection. Debra was older by ten years and only went to live with their mother after she was of age. She practically raised Angel when his mom hit the bottle too hard, which was pretty much all the time."

He wiped his hand over his face and tried to clear his mind, tried to make some sense out of the last few months and how it connected to his past.

"Angel knew all along I was undercover," Jake said grimly.

"That would be my guess. Puts a new spin on who he was actually targeting last night at Rory's."

And how close Jake had come to being sent away in a body bag. If it hadn't been for Cassie's quick action, he was sure that's the way it would have gone down.

"All things considered, I'd say you could use a good night's sleep, Jake," Kevin said.

"Yeah, right."

He didn't want to rest, Jake thought. He wanted Angel Fagnelio.

"Do you have him yet?"

"Not yet, but you'll be the first to know when we do. You're gonna call in periodically? Let me know how you're doing? Gloat about the good food and fill me in on any change in the sleeping arrangements?"

That hint of amusement was back in Kevin's voice. It grated on Jake's tired nerves more than fingernails against a chalkboard.

"There's not going to be any change," he shot back.

"Same ol' Jake. I'll bet you were an altar boy."

85

Jake ignored the disappointment in Kevin's voice. "Three years."

Kevin laughed. "Oh, man. I can't believe you get a cushy gig out in the middle of the mountains while I get to work my ass off here. You know, Russo's been riding my case since this morning. He's still at his desk."

"Doesn't that guy ever go home?"

"No." There was a small silence between them. They'd both been there when the call came in about the death of Paul Russo, Captain Russo's only son. The old man had never been the same since and would probably work himself into the grave before he'd face an empty house.

"Don't work yourself too hard. At least not on the job," Kevin finally said, his rich laughter floating through the telephone line before the connection was cut.

Jake stared at the tiny bug in his hand until the dial tone blared in his ear. Only then did he place the phone back in the cradle.

A few long strides down the hall, and Jake was in front of Cassie's bedroom door. He lifted his hand to the doorknob, catching himself before walking in. She might be getting dressed. Curling his fingers into a ball, he rapped his knuckles lightly against the door three times instead.

No answer.

He knocked again.

Silence.

Staring at the white paneled door, he hesitated before turning the knob. He'd only left Cassie a moment ago. She couldn't possibly be asleep yet. But then again, as tired as she was...

The lamp on the dresser was still glowing when he crept into her room. A quick glance to the bathroom showed the door was open and the light was off.

"Cassie?"

She sprang upright from the floor at the foot of the bed. Sheer black fright clouded her delicate features, and it took but a second to figure out what she was doing.

"Geez, it wasn't good enough to check the closets?"

She shook her head vehemently, waving her hands back and forth. It took no more than two seconds to realize her fright wasn't about her overactive imagination.

"What's that I smell?" he asked.

Slowly she shook her head as if she were paralyzed and fighting to move. Her breathing was shallow and quick.

"I think it's gas," she said quickly. "It's coming from the heating unit under the bed. I thought maybe I was imagining it and hyperventilating, but if you smell it too then—"

He took another whiff and then dropped to the floor, checking under the bed to inspect it himself. As soon as his face got close to the bed ruffle, the smell was stronger.

"What the... We need to move quickly."

"What?"

"Get out of the house!"

In two quick movements, he was pulling Cassie up from the floor and dragged her across the room to the door. Cassie stumbled once as he dragged her around the bed, knocking into the dresser. The lamp pitched and Jake quickly grabbed it before it fell to the floor.

"Wait. I need my laptop," Cassie cried.

"We'll get it later."

Jake dragged Cassie through the house. The air was definitely cleaner in the living room, but it was filling up quickly.

When Jake reached the living room door, he turned the doorknob, but it wouldn't budge.

Cassie gasped. "It's locked?"

Jake didn't need to confirm it. There was no time. He raced to the kitchen door and found that it wouldn't budge either.

"We're locked in?" Cassie said on a sob.

"Breaking the bolt on the door might cause a spark."

There was no time to speak, or breathe. He had to think and then act. They had to move *faster*.

Ten seconds went by.

Think, think, think. Surveillance cameras were littered along

the driveway and the front of the house. There was no telling
how many other cameras were positioned at the other corners
of the safe house. It wouldn't take whoever did this long to
figure out he and Cassie had escaped.

If they escaped.

"Jake the smell is getting stronger!"

"Pull up your shirt and cover your face." She did as she
was told. "That's right. Don't breathe too heavy or you'll take in
too much.

They needed to act fast. Jake looked into Cassie's terrified eyes
and gave her a silent plea to stay quiet. The two of them
sprinted through the kitchen to an office at the far end of the
hall in the back of the house.

"Don't turn on the light. Don't touch any of the light
switches. Even the smallest spark could blow the house up."

Jake felt his way along the top of the window and
unlocked it slowly. The window opened with a rush of much
needed fresh air. He pushed the screen out with one quick
movement.

"Climb out and I'll ease you down to the ground. Then I'll
jump out," he said.

Jake filled his lungs with fresh air as he lowered Cassie to
the ground.

"Hurry, Jake!" Cassie said.

Jake jumped to the ground and took Cassie by the hand.
Just as he suspected, the light on this end of the house was dim.
They could use that to their advantage.

"Quickly, into the woods."

"Aren't we going back down to the guard's station?"

The heater in the basement kicked to life. Jake could hear
the whine of the motor turn on and then shut off...and then
turn on again.

"Run!"

Jake dragged Cassie behind him like his shadow. She kept
up with every step without question, without the slightest drag.
If he was wrong, they'd make it to the woods, turn around and
wait for Agent Bellows and his crew to come up the driveway

and check on the problem. But if he was right, they had mere seconds left until the whole safe house turned into a Fourth of July fireworks display gone bad.

Time dragged on at a turtle's stroll as they ran. The wood line was in sight. They needed to get as far away from the house as they possibly could, needed to clear the boulders lining the property, needed shelter. They raced over the boulders clinging to a prayer.

And then it happened in slow motion. White hot fire burst forward, bowling them over like a tidal wave crashing to shore, sending them tumbling down the slight pitch leading into the woods.

The heat was intense, singing his skin with its fury. His lungs felt as if they would explode.

When they stopped rolling, Jake forced himself to look back toward the path they'd just escaped from. It was gone. The whole house erupted into the sky like a mushroom explosion in a military testing field. Bright spitting fire burned angrily from what was left of the safe house, licking flames high into the sky as fiery wood and ash rained down all around them.

He hadn't landed near Cassie after the initial explosion. Frantically, he searched the brightly lit area for some sign of her. He was sure they'd both cleared the line of boulders before impact.

"Cassie?" he called out. He couldn't hear anything. Not the fire, not the sounds of the night or even his own voice.

And then he saw her. Cassie was scrambling on her hands and knees. Somehow, within seconds, Jake managed to grab hold of her, pulling her to the base of a spruce tree with low-growing branches at the entrance to the woods. Flames sprayed like hellfire, hitting the intrepid spruce, which acted as their shield.

Jake held Cassie tight beneath his body, their chests locked together as he protected her from falling debris the hammered tree limbs couldn't hold back. They had to move before their meager shelter burst into a fireball.

He glanced down at Cassie's face, saw the shadows of

destruction and smelled the scent of burning pine needles and sizzling sap. His heart stopped beating when he pushed her hair from her face. Her long dark lashes fluttered open as she peered up at him.

"Seems to me we've done this before, Detective," she said, her voice shaky.

Her face was streaked with ash, and she managed a weak smile. Jake couldn't fathom how she did it, but she did.

Rolling to his side, he said disbelieving, "We were almost just incinerated, and you can joke about it?"

"I have to," she said on a choked sob.

It was then Jake saw the tears well in Cassie's eyes and knew she was in shock.

"If I don't, it'll take control of me, and I have to be in control. As horrible as this is, if I can't get up and say, 'Hey, I'm alive. Isn't that great?' I'll cry. And I don't want to cry anymore. I can't cry anymore, Jake."

The full impact of what had just happened hadn't really hit yet. He was numb and would probably be like that for a while. But it would hit them both. And when it did, he wanted Cassie to be as far away from this *safe* house as he could possibly get her.

"Jake, that was no accident."

"I know. It's not going to take the Gestapo more than a few minutes to race up this hill, Cassie. Pretty soon, this whole area will be swarming with Feds. We need to get out of here."

"Jake, who did this? Who keeps doing this to me?" She kept gulping for air, and her bottom lip was trembling. Despite what Cassie had just said, she was going to cry, and she had every right to do it.

Later.

"Listen to me, Cassie. Are you hurt?" His voice was firm and commanding. He had to get through to her.

She shook her head stiffly. In a few hours, they'd both be feeling the effects of rolling down this hill and being blown back against the trees. He'd find some way to deal with it then.

But not now. Right now, they had to move.

"Who is doing this to me, Jake?"

"I don't know. We'll figure that out later. Can you walk?"

She nodded quickly.

"Good. If you can walk, then you have to run. You have to run right now. Do you hear me, Cassie?"

"What about the car?"

"We'll never get out of here with that car. Hopefully, no one will know for at least an hour or so that we weren't inside the house when it blew."

Jake quickly tugged Cassie to her feet and pulled her through the woods as fast as he could, scraping past low branches and brush. They had to move fast. In the confusion that was sure to come, they just might be able to escape.

* * *

Cassie couldn't feel her feet anymore. They were frozen. The Smoky Mountain night air bit into her skin like a mosquito on a hot night. She could no longer feel the branches that were tearing into her skin as they ran. Somewhere deep in her mind she knew it had nothing to do with the outside temperature. It was just raw fear of knowing she was being hunted like an animal.

Jake held her hand and pulled her along. It was too easy to lose each other in the thick of the forest and the dark of the night, he'd said. In the beginning, she was right up with him, running alongside, forgetting that she couldn't feel her feet or the squeeze of his hand as he held hers. After an hour or two— she wasn't sure how long the minutes or hours dragged along— she was now lagging behind.

"Shouldn't we try…to make it…to the road?" she asked, her words coming in short bursts.

Jake finally stopped moving and glanced back at her. It had stopped drizzling. The clouds had parted and a half moon had hung itself high above them at some point during the last hour. There was enough light poking through the bare tree limbs for Cassie to see Jake's face, see the hard lines of worry as well as the primal instinct of survival.

"We're safer hidden in the woods."

"We don't know where we're going."

He glanced up at the moon, then turned his head toward the darkness ahead. "Listen for a second."

She did as he asked. She'd finally regained her hearing, but all she could hear was her heart hammering against her chest and the crack of a twig beneath her sneakers. There were more distant noises. And owl maybe? She couldn't tell.

"There's the highway. I can't guess how far, but it sounds like it is coming—." Jake abruptly stopped as he turned back to look at her. Cursing under his breath, he pulled off his jacket. "You're freezing. Why didn't you tell me?"

"I'm fine. I didn't feel cold when we were running."

"I should have noticed."

He helped her into his leather coat and began rubbing up and down her arms. The movement stimulated her circulation.

Her eyes fell to his empty holster.

"Jake, your gun is missing."

He stopped rubbing her arms and snapped his attention to his holster, his hand folding over the empty pouch. He cursed again.

"The leather snap is completely broken off. It must have happened when we rolled down that hill after the explosion."

"What are you going to do?"

"We can't go back for it now. Dammit!"

She pulled the leather jacket tighter and felt a chill shoot through her whole body.

"We have to keep moving," he said. "We should reach the highway soon. We have a better chance of catching a ride without being detected, especially this time of the night. Tell me the truth. How are you holding up?"

Her legs ached and a scrape along her neck was starting to sting and throb. Cassie was thankful she really couldn't feel her feet. Now that she had a little taste of warmth again, all she could think about was dropping to the ground and falling asleep. *Not a good sign.*

"I'm good to go," she said.

"That's my girl," he said with a hint of a smile.

Less than an hour later, Cassie was standing by the side of the road watching a tractor trailer slow down to a stop.

She ran behind Jake as they made their way to passenger side door. Jake climbed up the rig and spoke to the driver through the window.

"We're headed north. Are you going that way?" Jake asked. Cassie couldn't hear the driver's response, but when Jake opened the rig's door and reached down for Cassie's hand, she thought she'd faint with joy.

Moments later she placed her head down on a pillow in the back cab of the gigantic eighteen-wheel truck.

"You're an answer to a prayer," Jake had said to the driver when they'd climbed in.

"I'm no answer to anything," Bernie had said. "I could use the company."

Cassie let Jake do the talking. She took a moment while they talked to look at the driver.

His name was Bernie and he was a small man with thin straight brown hair that was getting even thinner at the center of his head. His beady eyes reminded Cassie of a mouse, but his smile seemed sincere.

Cassie had quietly questioned Jake about the wisdom of taking a ride while they were walking the road earlier. But Jake insisted any risk in taking a ride was far less than being found wandering on the road by the very people responsible for that gas leak. Now that her head was on a soft pillow, she was infinitely glad that Bernie had found them.

"The cab has a hell of a heater," Bernie said. "But just in case you're still shivering, there's a nice wool blanket on the mattress there, too. Snuggle up and stay warm, why don't ya. Can't think of why y'all decided to leave home without a warm jacket."

Bernie was talking to Jake now, but looking at Cassie through the mirror on the dash. She was wearing Jake's black leather jacket and she knew it looked ridiculously huge on her. She let the scent of Jake, and the comfort it brought her, wrap around her like the jacket as she stared back at the eyes peering at her in the mirror.

"How far up north are you going?" Jake asked.

"I'm headed to Toronto."

A spark of an idea that felt like hope zipped through Cassie's mind. "We're going in that direction. Our place is in the Catskills," she blurted out.

Jake's snapped his gaze back to her. She sat upright in the bed and nodded her head. She could tell by the way his eyebrows slightly furrowed at the center of his forehead that he knew she was up to something, but wasn't sure.

"That's right," Jake said, playing along with her. After all, they had nothing else but a ride going a few hundred miles away from people who just tried to kill them.

Cassie couldn't see the driver's face to be sure if he bought the story.

"Well, it's a good thing I rolled on by," he said brightly. "I can take you all the way. That is, if you don't mind a detour or two for drop off and pick up along the way."

"No, that would be great," Cassie said. *Perfect in fact.*

"Don't mind if I mention, you two look like road kill. I just had myself a few ZZ's at the truck stop a few miles back. I'm good for another twenty or so hours. Looks like you both could use some shut-eye though. I'll wake you when we stop for breakfast. I know a good truck stop that has the best steak, eggs and hash right off the interstate."

"I appreciate that. Breakfast is on me," Jake said.

Bernie haled a laugh that seemed out of character for a man of his stature. "Well, I hope your wallet is padded, because I have a hearty appetite."

"You and me both."

Jake climbed into the back of the cab and crawled on the mattress, pulling the blanket over both of them before settling in close to Cassie. Immediately she was engulfed by his heat.

It was more than just body heat. Jake was strong and warm and she craved the comfort and protection he provided. He didn't put his arms around her and it surprised Cassie just how much she wished he would.

It was probably for the best, she reasoned silently. Part of her feared the way she'd crumble in Jake's arms if she allowed herself. She couldn't do it. She had to stay in control.

But there was also this small fragment of her that wanted to say "to hell with control." Why couldn't she allow a man to be strong for her?

Disappointment settled in the pit of her stomach, making her slightly nauseous. It was exactly the reason all her past relationships had failed. Her only serious relationship had ended three years ago because she refused to let herself lose control, even in bed.

She'd rationalized that maybe she was just one of those women who didn't enjoy sex. But she knew that wasn't the reason. In giving herself to a man fully, even sexually, she'd have to give up part of the control she'd fought so hard to gain since her cousin's murder.

Rolling over to her side, she inched closer to Jake and gazed up into his eyes. His face was just a whisper away from hers. With each streetlight the truck rolled past, his face illuminated and then vanished as if it were never there. Cassie fought the overwhelming urge to reach up, place her hands on his cheeks just to keep him there. Just so she knew she was not alone in her horror.

"Do you think we can trust him?" she whispered, barely audibly.

Jake leaned forward, his mouth a mere fraction of an inch from her ear.

"I don't know. But we have to trust someone. We're in no condition to go any further until we get some sleep. How are you holding up? Are you okay?"

"I'm…afraid," she admitted, cursing herself when her bottom lip began to tremble. She clamped her teeth down hard to keep it still as the image of the explosion invaded her mind.

"I know. But we have to sleep now."

"What if he does something? What if he calls the police?"

Jake chuckled softly. "What's he going to do? He's lonely. He just wants some company. Besides, I sleep light."

"You don't have your gun, Jake."

She'd seen the empty holster as they emerged from the trees, heard Jake's quiet curse as he tore it off his body and tossed it to the ground.

"We're not going to need it." He kissed her head softly, breathing deeply with his lips against her skin.

With Jake's body simmeringly warm next to her, Cassie finally drifted to sleep. She dreamed of sunshine and laughter, and of her childhood in Connecticut. She dreamed of Jake's sexy smile and his body of armor that made her feel so safe in a world forcing her out of control.

The brakes of the truck groaned, pulling her from the safety of her dreams. She fought to stay there until Bernie's call pulled her completely from dreamland.

"Wake up you two. It's time for breakfast. And I, for one, am starving!"

* * *

They jumped from the truck and headed to a small diner off interstate 81. Traffic roared by them, seemingly unaware of the scent of bacon grease and cinnamon buns drawing Cassie and Jake toward the door.

They filled themselves while listening to Bernie ramble on about where he'd been and where he was going. As Jake had suspected, the poor guy was no threat, he was merely lonely. The craziness of talking small talk with this stranger in the wake of what they'd gone through to get there seemed surreal, but also a welcome break in the tension.

The driver grabbed the sports section of the newspaper and excused himself to the bathroom, telling them he'd meet them at his rig.

Jake waited until the waitress refilled their coffee and walked away.

"What's in the Catskills?" he asked, keeping his voice low.

"I was wondering if you'd caught on to that last night. Maureen has a small cabin just outside the Catskills."

"Maureen, huh?" he said with half a groan. Cassie didn't

seem to notice. If she did, she didn't comment.

She held her coffee mug in both hands and took a sip before continuing. "I've been there a few times. She hardly ever goes except in the summer because she hates driving, especially in the snow, so it'll be empty. It's not that far from the interstate."

"How secluded is it?"

"About a half mile into the woods. You can't see it from the road because it's well hidden by pine trees. Even if Maureen were questioned, I don't think she'd think to tell anyone about it. No one will look for us there."

Jake turned the notion over in his head for a minute. They needed to hide, at least until he could talk to Kevin and find out what the hell had happened last night.

"It could work. We could hide there until I figure out what is really going on. Do you remember how to get there?"

"It's not that hard. I think I could find it." She stared at him as he rubbed his hands together. "You're going to need your jacket though."

Cassie still had his leather jacket on. She'd offered it to him when they got out of the rig, but he'd refused. If they had a half-mile walk up into the mountains, he'd probably need something more than the cotton shirt he'd worn last night. He'd been freezing when they emerged from the woods and Bernie stopped the rig. It was going to be a lot colder hiking all the way to the cabin in the Catskills.

"No, you keep it."

"I can't stand seeing you cold. It's not fair for me to take your jacket. Even a half mile walk up the road is long without a warm jacket."

"I saw some hooded tourist sweatshirts for sale in the display case on our way into the diner."

"You shouldn't use your credit card. They'll be—"

"Able to trace it. Yeah, I know. I have enough cash. Maybe we'll get lucky and they'll have some gloves and warm socks, too."

"I saw the morning paper on the way in. I'm not on the

97

front page this time."

"That's a good thing."

"I figured there might be something about the explosion."

"Not likely. The FBI will want to keep that under wraps. Bad PR, you know?"

"Jake, that wasn't an ordinary gas leak."

They hadn't talked about it last night. They were both too much in shock and primal instinct was to keep moving and survive. But in the light of day…

"No, it wasn't. I don't believe in coincidence and there was too much gas being pumped through that heating unit in your bedroom."

Cassie was quiet a moment. A faraway look made her look so lost.

Jake drained the rest of his coffee and placed the cup on the table before grabbing the check.

"I'm nervous enough about being out in public like this with so many people who could recognize you."

"Looking like I do, *feeling* like a do, I sure hope not."

As if on cue, Jake saw Bernie stroll out the front door of the diner, newspaper tucked under his arm.

He pushed out of his seat. "Our ride to the Catskills is leaving soon. Let's roll."

CHAPTER EIGHT

The sun had long since dipped low on the horizon when Cassie and Jake finally reached the hidden cabin in the woods. It was snowing lightly now. Luck staying by their sides, Bernie proved to be in more than just good spirits. He was making good time and offered to drive them up to the bottom of the road leading to Maureen's cabin. It saved them one hell of a walk in the cold.

They reached the small shack-like cabin with frozen feet and chapped lips. But thankful they only had a half-mile walk instead of having to walk the entire way from the highway exit.

"Are you sure this is it?" Jake asked.

Cassie sighed. "Please stop asking me that. Yes, I'm sure."

"It's the size of a tin can."

"It looks smaller than it really is. On the plus side, it won't take long to heat up. At this point, anything with heat will be heaven."

Jake gripped the doorknob and pulled it back and forth, each yank became more urgent. "The door's locked," he said, grunting as he slammed his flat palm against the wood.

Cassie knew his outburst was fueled by fatigue. She felt it herself. The minimal sleep and being bowled over by the explosion had her bones screaming for relief and had her barking right back at him.

"I wouldn't have brought us here if I didn't know how to get inside. Maureen keeps the key hidden in this stump," she said, brushing away the snow-covered lump by the porch stairs. "It's one of those plastic planters that has a hidden...here it is."

With the frozen key in her hand, she quickly ran to the door and unlocked it. Relief poured into every inch of her. They were finally going to be able to relax and let their guard down for the first time in days.

She pushed through the rough planked door with anticipation. The inky blackness that greeted her inside was only marginally inviting. Void of the warmth she craved, the cabin felt similar to an ice chest, but still less abrasive than being exposed to the wind.

At the sound of the light switch clicking on and off, Cassie swung around.

"Does Maureen forget to pay her light bill?" Jake asked.

"The cabin is solar powered. Although, apparently nothing is kept turned on. There is a wood stove in the corner. Do you know how to work one?"

"Yeah, I can fire it up if I get some light."

"We always had power when we came before. But it was always during the day and we had the benefit of daylight. Maureen might have turned everything on when we got here. I just don't remember."

"Do you have any idea how the system works?"

"Not really. She said it was fairly easy to figure out though. I think enough of the system is kept running to keep the batteries charged. There is a supply closet with a stack of batteries and a panel in the back."

Jake took a step and plowed into Cassie. Unprepared for the blow, she lost her balance and fell into one of the chairs. She recalled the new striped slipcovers Maureen put on the old furniture last summer when they were here last. Cassie couldn't see the bright colors in the dark, but she did feel the cold, soft fabric as she fell against the chair.

"Are you okay?" he asked. As Jake found her in the darkness, his hands gripped her leg and brushed against the swell of her bottom, sending a shiver through her.

Her pulse quickened and blood pounded through her veins, warming her fast. Her only warmth for last two days had been Jake. Even now, with the two of them frozen and tired, just having him stand behind her made heat coil inside her and spread to her extremities.

A little disoriented, Cassie fumbled for a firm grip on the

arm of the chair and pushed herself upright.

"I'm fine. I just fell into the chair."

"Stay with me," he said, as if he'd been affected by the mere accidental brushing of his hand against her derriere.

"I'm right here," she said, her voice an earthy whisper.

She heard his heavy breathing, felt his fingers tighten around her.

"Um, the kitchen is open to the living room. Stay behind me. There are some candles in one of the cabinets."

Jake had his wide palms on her hips, his fingers digging into the denim material, as she cautiously moved through the dark with her hands stretched out ahead of her. When she bumped into the counter, she quickly ran her hands along the cabinet drawers, blindly searching each one until her fingers grazed the waxy surface of a long, skinny candle and a box of wooden matches.

She waited until she lit a match to grip two candles firmly between the fingers of her other hand.

Jake was impossibly close as she twisted around to face him. Cassie craned her neck to look up at him, nothing but the glow of the match illuminating his features. His face was surreal in the flickering flame.

"Light the candle," he said softly, his lips barely moving.

Even with the minimal light the flame emitted, she could see a cloud of mist from his breath. With her body sandwiched between the cold counter and Jake's warm body, she tried to steady herself, but her head spun.

Pain pierced her fingers. She dropped the match and they were plunged into darkness again.

Jake's arm instantly snaked behind her. With the rolling of the wooden sticks and the unmistakable strike of the match, a small flame glowed, dimly lighting the room once again.

"You burned yourself." He quickly lit the two candles she still held in her hand and blew out the match.

He took her sore fingers to his lips and kissed them tenderly, so much more so than she would have expected a man as rugged as Jake could be. She knew the hard-edged intense

101

side of him and pictured him as much in bed, rough, wild, completely on fire and burning her with the same intensity.

But here he was with the pad of his thumb gently caressing her blistered finger, handling her like a fragile piece of glass that would shatter with the slightest pressure.

"It's just a small burn," she murmured.

"No burns are small."

In response to his gentleness, she curled her fingers around his, wanting much more than to simply have his hand caress her fingers. She wanted him to touch her intimately. His eyes were extraordinarily dark despite the minimal light. He gazed down into her eyes, silently whispering words she felt in her heart but didn't hear with her ears.

Cassie willed herself not to give in to the impulse of reaching up to push her fingers through his thick, coarse hair.

Jake dropped Cassie's hand, quickly forcing his gaze away from her tempting lips to the counter behind her. "We can use these mugs as candlestick holders for now," he said, occupying himself by placing the lighted candles in the mugs he'd just retrieved from the hooks under the cabinet. Anything to keep himself from feeling the emotional war raging inside.

He'd been ready to kiss Cassie. All he had to do was bend his head and press his lips against the sweetness of her soft mouth, feel the fire she had burning inside her.

He'd almost done just that last night in the back of the truck. He'd kissed her forehead. To give her comfort, he reasoned. But he'd fought mightily to let it end there. He'd wanted more from that kiss. He wanted to hold her in his arms as she slept beside him. The feeling was as overwhelming now as it had been last night.

As tired as he was, he'd slept straight as a board with his hands glued firmly beside him, hoping he wouldn't subconsciously reach for her in the middle of the night. After a few hours of sleep, he'd pulled himself from the mattress and climbed to the front of the cab with Bernie, deciding chitchat with the truck driver would surely cure his libido.

It worked.

But being this close to Cassie now, and in such confined quarters, was bringing the memories of carnal dreams he'd had last night rushing back.

Clearing the sudden lump that lodged in his throat, he asked, "Where is the power panel?"

"In the pantry."

He couldn't help but laugh. "This shack is about as small as a pantry and it *has* a pantry? What about bedrooms?"

"Just one very tiny one. Maureen has this enormous bed in there that leaves next to no room for anything else. But the bed is big enough for both of us."

Jake's heart slammed against his ribcage. "No, you take it."

He ignored the wounded expression on Cassie's face. She was tired. So was he. But the small pout of her full lips made his heart break just the same.

She straightened her spine and jutted out her chin. "I'm not going to attack you in the night."

Maybe she wouldn't, but Jake couldn't be certain he could say the same. A little sleep and a walk into hypothermia land hadn't changed that fact that he still wanted her desperately.

"You're being ridiculous. We slept in the same bed last night, and it didn't matter to you."

"We didn't have a choice last night. Tonight we do."

Glancing around the dimly lit room, he saw the large sofa in the middle of the floor in front of an ancient potbelly stove.

"That should do me fine for the night. That way I can keep the fire going."

She looked past him toward the sofa and then peered up at him again. "I can't let you sleep on that thing. *I've* slept on that sofa, and I know how uncomfortable it is. You need your sleep just as much as I do."

He didn't say anything. How could he tell her that he didn't trust himself not to reach out for her in the middle of the night? That the only thing he was thinking of had nothing to do with sleep.

"Let's work at getting some lights and some heat in the cabin. We can argue about the sleeping arrangements later."

103

It didn't take much to figure out how the solar electrical system in the cabin worked. While Cassie turned on the power, Jake gathered some stacked logs from a small woodpile out back and filled the woodstove. Within a short time, the cabin filled with welcoming heat.

"These should fit you and be comfortable to sleep in while your clothes dry," Cassie said as she walked in from the bedroom. In her hands, she carried a pair of dark gray sweatpants and a matching sweatshirt.

She'd changed out of her wet clothes, too, Jake noticed. Her hair was damp, combed free of tangles and pulled back in a tight ponytail at the base of her head. She wore a pair of green spandex stretch pants that accentuated the curves of her slender hips and the smooth lines of her thighs and a short Kelly green and blue flannel shirt. She'd taken off her soaked sneakers and socks and now had a pair of fluffy bear slippers on her feet that look incredibly ridiculous and adorable on her at the same time.

Jake glanced down at the pile of clothes she still held in her hands. "Maureen keeps men's clothes here?"

"I think they belong to Adam. Or maybe they belonged to her ex-husband. She got the cabin in the divorce, along with the Jeep she keeps parked out back."

"There's a Jeep?"

"Yeah, Maureen's afraid of driving in the snow without four-wheel drive. She hates driving in the city even more, so she keeps the Jeep here. It doesn't get much use. We had to jump start it last summer to get it going."

"I thought you said she doesn't come up here in the winter?"

"She doesn't. At least not since her divorce was final. But she keeps a vehicle here just the same. It costs a lot less than keeping it in the city."

"That's good news for us. It'll save us having to walk to town to get some supplies."

Cassie fiddled with her hands. "How long do you think we'll need to be here?"

Jake ran his hand over his scruffy face. "I have no idea."

"They must know by now that we escaped the explosion," she said, rolling her shoulder.

"I'm guessing they knew within the hour. Surveillance cameras would have shown us running into the woods."

"Why didn't they come after us?"

Jake had wondered that himself. "The only thing I can think of is that Agent Bellows didn't want to bring on more suspicion than what the explosion was bound to do."

"You think he did this?"

"It's the only logical thing I can think of. He checked the perimeter of the house when we went inside. And when we went to open the doors, they wouldn't budge. My guess is he knew that the explosion would break free whatever he used to jam the doors. If not, he needed to cover his tracks before the fire department got there."

"But why? Why would the FBI bring me there only to try to kill me. Why would I be a threat to them?"

"Not the FBI. But you being able to finger Angel Fagnelio in that shooting has probably rattled someone's cage. Angel had to have been working with someone from the FBI and I'm guessing it wasn't Novak."

He got a good look at Cassie now. He'd tried his best to pull his thoughts away from her, but now he allowed himself to really look at her for the first time. She wasn't scared anymore. Her face was freshly scrubbed as if she'd washed away the worry creases along with the dirt and grime from the explosion. Maybe it was the fatigue or because she was in familiar surroundings that she seemed more at ease.

He took in the sight of her. Cassie's hair was wet and her face cleanly scrubbed.

"When did you take a shower?"

"While you were fiddling with the stove. You didn't hear the water running?"

Jake shook his head. "I guess I was too busy trying to get the fire going."

"It was...lukewarm," she said with a smile. "But even that was okay because the water pressure is pretty strong. I needed something to pull some of these aches out of me. I think I'm going to sleep for a hundred years now." She looked at him thoughtfully. "You should take one, too. You might have better luck with the hot water, now that the system has been on a while."

"Am I that offensive?" he said with amusement.

Cassie quirked a smile, cocking her head to one side. "Only mildly offensive. But the hot water will ease the tightness in your muscles. Don't you feel like a truck rolled over you?"

"That's basically what happened when we rolled down that hill. It was worse last night," he said, rubbing his two-day-old beard again. It was beginning to itch. "I could use a good soak and a shave though."

She tossed him the clothes, which he caught in both hands like a football. "I think I saw some fresh razors in the cabinet. Why don't you do that now while I see what I can scrounge up for dinner out of the canned goods in the pantry. I'm starving."

Twenty minutes later Jake emerged from the tiny bathroom to the smell of food. Cassie had outdone herself by cooking up a pot of canned beef stew and biscuits from a box mix. In truth, it didn't matter what Cassie had prepared. It was hot. It was food. And Jake would have eaten anything she put in front of him.

He hoped that as soon as the dishes were cleared and washed, Cassie would just go to bed. It would be easier that way. Looking at Cassie in the soft lighting of the cabin only seemed to magnify another hunger inside him that wouldn't easily be sated.

The sofa didn't look inviting at all, but at this point, Jake didn't care. He dropped down to the middle cushion and leaned back. Closing his eyes, he squeezed the tension spot in the center of his forehead with the pad of his thumb and index finger.

"You've got to learn to relax, Jake. Every time I look at you you're all bunched up into tight knots."

With a rush of cool breeze, Cassie moved behind him. Placing her delicate fingers on his shoulders, she gently kneaded

106

his tightly knotted muscles the hot shower hadn't eased.

"That feels good," he murmured, keeping his eyes closed. Too good. Warning bells pealed loudly in his head, but he ignored them. She wasn't going to bed. And he needed her to go to bed. *Alone.*

A soft chuckle escaped Cassie's lips. "I know. It felt good when you were doing it to me the other day."

Jake remembered the feel of her body easing beneath his fingers as he'd touched her. Was that really just two days ago? It didn't quite seem possible. Time was passing so rapidly and yet it felt as if he and Cassie had been running from a phantom for so long.

"You know all about me," Cassie said, her voice like smooth velvet to his ears, like a breath of a whisper.

He liked the sound of her voice, the way it was strong and sure sometimes, like the other day when she was determined to get her way with the FBI.

And now, when it was low and sexy as hell.

His thoughts betrayed him, making him wonder what she'd sound like when she was making love to a man. Did she talk at all? Whisper sweet words against her lover's ear? Or just moan as desire took hold of her? He had a hard time pushing away the image of her calling out his name as she reached climax.

His body reacted to his thoughts and he felt himself grow hard. Shifting his place on the sofa, Jake shook his head to rid himself of the image invading his mind. But it remained.

He stole a quick glance at her, knowing he shouldn't. Knowing he'd see the unspoken words he heard in her voice.

"No, I don't," he whispered. "I don't know anything about you, Cassie."

She smiled sweetly as her fingers kept working magic, gently kneading the knots in his shoulders. It was like a slice of heaven.

"You know I write crime novels. In fact, you had a field day teasing me about it the other night. You know about my life, my family. You've seen my apartment, my editor's hideaway.

107

You've even seen me in my pajamas. I'd say you know more about me than most of the men I've been involved with over the years."

"Have there been many?"

"Not enough to be even remotely scandalous," she said with a light chuckle. "But we aren't going to talk about me anymore. I want to know about you, Jake Santos."

He closed his eyes again and tried to concentrate on what Cassie was doing to him, to let the tension gripping him ease. In the end, it was futile. Instead of relaxing, her gentle ministration wound him tighter and tighter into knots. Hell, having her in the same damned room as him was enough to give him a full blown heart attack!

"I've been on the police force for nearly—"

"Oh, no you don't. I don't want a resume."

She stopped kneading his shoulders and moved in front of him, kneeling down on the floor at an intimately close range.

"I want to know what's in here," she said, gently pointing her finger to the center of his chest. "Starting when you were a child and going all the way up to what you had for lunch the day we met at Rory's."

His lips tugged into a wry grin. "This could take a long time."

Tilting her head to one side, she gave him an irresistibly sweet smile, but it never reached her eyes. "I don't think we're lacking for time. Not here anyway."

Jake straightened himself on the sofa, moving over to the end. Reaching over, he tapped his hand on the seat at the opposite side. Cassie obliged by sitting where he'd indicated. The wide gap between them made it easier for Jake to think.

"I already told you I grew up in West Orange. I'm the youngest of six kids and the only boy."

She held up her hands in a time out signal to halt him. "Whoa! Five sisters? Five? And you're the baby?"

He couldn't help but laugh, thinking about his childhood. He was always trying to get away with something or another until one of his sisters bagged him. They'd called it the sister patrol. He didn't have a prayer.

"I'd hardly call me a baby. But yeah, I have five of the toughest, sweetest sisters a guy could ever have."

"They must love you."

"They tortured me ruthlessly when I was growing up."

Cassie giggled. "I'll bet they didn't. I'll bet they spoiled you rotten, and you loved every minute of it."

Jake smiled warmly. It was exactly that way. But even now, he had a tough time admitting it. He'd been outnumbered too long.

"You try having five older sisters and wait your turn in line for the bathroom. The only bathroom in the house, mind you. They bossed me around and never let me get away with anything."

"Oh, you poor thing. Someone save the man," she teased. But she sobered quickly. "They must hate you being a cop."

"They sure as hell weren't happy about it when I went through the Academy. I think my youngest sister, Beth, still hasn't quite accepted it. If it was up to her, I'd be designated to desk duty until the day I retire and get my gold watch."

"Only Beth?"

He shrugged. "They worry. But I can't see me changing things any time soon. I love what I do."

"Did you always want to protect people?" she asked when the conversation lulled.

His cheeks flamed just a bit. "Nah. When I was little I wanted to be a cowboy."

She laughed at the serious look he cast her until he too was laughing.

"How in the world did you get from cowboy to cop?"

"Well, there was the issue I had with horses."

"Which is?"

"I'm terrified of them."

Her already large eyes widened with surprise. "Really?"

Jake shrugged and then abruptly stopped laughing. He didn't much like thinking about the dark side of life. His profession alone was enough to give him a healthy dose of it without drudging up old memories.

"When my sister Jenna was in college, some guy tried to mug her."

"Oh, God, that's awful."

"Yeah. Being Jenna, she wasn't about to let the prick get away with her paycheck so she fought real hard to hold on to her purse. My parents didn't have a lot of money and with six kids, there wasn't much to dole out when college came rolling around. My sisters sometimes worked two and three jobs to get through school. Law school tuition was steep, and although Jenna knew Mom and Dad would have helped her out, she wanted to do it herself.

"All five of my sisters are pretty tenacious when they put their minds to it. But especially Jenna. She's a little rough around the edges sometimes and it puts people off before they get to know her. Most of my friends were scared as hell of her when I was growing up."

Jake chuckled with the memory and then sighed. Cassie wasn't laughing. She was watching him intently, hanging on his next word.

"Her hard edge makes her a damned good lawyer. But deep down, Jenna's as soft and sweet as they come and that mugging did something to her. Until that point I don't think she ever thought there was a situation she couldn't handle by herself."

"Everyone needs someone, sometimes."

He nodded. "At first she seemed okay with the mugging. My parents were a wreck and insisted she go to the hospital to get checked out. Being Jenna, she just went off about being fine and couldn't figure out what everyone fussing about. She didn't want to talk about what had happened and didn't want anyone else to, either."

Jake blew out a slow breath, puffing his cheeks. "If you'd seen the bruises on her face…." He clamped his eyes shut as if that would wash the image away like turning off the TV. But he could still see the quiet fear in his sister's eyes.

"He didn't…sexually assault her, did he?"

Jake shook his head quickly. "That's what I thought at first. Maybe something happened and she couldn't handle telling anyone. She was knocked around but she insisted he'd only tried to steal her purse, and because she fought back, he'd beat her up."

Jake got up and walked to the wood stove, opened the door. He stoked the fire and loaded another two logs into the stove, trying not to relive that day like it was yesterday.

"I'd gotten up during the night to...you know, just to check on her, and as I walked to her bedroom door I heard her crying."

"That must have torn you apart."

"You have no idea. I'd seen Jenna cry before, but always when she was watching some chick flick on TV or something like that. I wanted so bad to go into her room, give her a big hug, talk with her...something. Just to tell her it was over and she was okay. I was so afraid the guy raped her and she was suffering with it all alone. But I wanted to kill the bastard for putting his hands on her."

"Did you go to her?"

He shook his head. "She would have hated for me to see her that way, and knowing Jenna, she would have pulled herself together just for my benefit. I figured she needed a good cry and I'd only keep her from it if I went to her. So I sank down to the floor in the hallway and sat there, just to make sure she was okay. Just because, I don't know, I needed to."

He scratched the back of his neck, feeling the tension gripping him from the memory. "She cried most of the night. The next morning at breakfast she acted as if nothing had ever happened. That's when I knew, strong as my sisters are, they need to be protected. The guy never did get her money, but I'm sure he got one hell of a beating back from Jenna for his effort. That's the only solace I got from it."

Cassie sighed. "Did she ever talk about it again?"

"Not voluntarily. A few months later I asked her about it, and she tensed up like it had just happened. She insisted her body wasn't raped, but the man who'd mugged her had raped

111

her sense of well being, and that was almost as bad. That was something she was never going to forget."

"So you do this for your sisters?"

Jake glanced at Cassie's beautiful brown eyes and shrugged. "Everyone has a sister or mother or someone who's afraid to walk across a parking lot to their car. Now I have nieces and nephews to add to the mix. I don't like thinking about what they might face as they get older. Someone has to make it safe for them, so why not me?"

Sadness clouded Cassie's face. "I envy you your big family. I'm an only child. I would have loved having a sister or brother."

"My sisters are like mother hens, every single one of them. I made up for not having a brother by having five brothers-in-law that take care of my sisters well. And I have more nieces and nephews than I can keep track of half the time."

Cassie tucked her knees up to her chest and looked at him as if he was telling her a fairy tale, hanging on his every word.

"You look much more relaxed now that you're talking about your family."

Rolling his shoulders, he said, "I'm always relaxed."

Cassie shook her head. "No, you're not. At first, I thought you were so tense because of the shooting at Rory's. Then I thought you were angry because I insisted on you coming with me into protective custody."

Jake's gut coiled. Had he really given her the impression he didn't want to protect her? It wasn't his desire to be the one to keep her safe that had plagued him for days. It was doubting his ability to do it effectively. Because in these few short days Cassie had gotten under his skin. He had feelings for her he didn't want to explore. Couldn't if he was going to be able to protect her. The more time they spent together, the harder it would be to keep from doing just that.

"I'm sorry I've been such a bear."

A flash of humor brightened her expression. "Don't worry. I'm getting used to it. Besides, it's understandable under these circumstances. Who'd ever thought a few days ago we'd be here like this now? When I was slipping into that disgustingly small dress to go to Rory's I thought I'd be chained to my computer by now, writing about the life of a prostitute climbing her way out of a world she didn't want to be in."

"With CJ Carmen's help, of course," he said.

She dipped her head as color crept into her cheeks. "You laugh, but I bet you'd like CJ."

"She must have a lot of spunk, like you."

Cassie's face was suddenly serious. "I wish," she said softly. "I'm nothing like CJ."

"You do a pretty good job yourself, Cassie."

"You really think so?"

Lord, Jake couldn't help himself. He reached out and touched her face, brushing his thumb across the beauty mark that teased him so often, knowing he'd be in trouble before he did it. Her skin was as soft as a rose petal, just like he remembered, tormenting him in a way that made his groin tighten. His breath lodged in his throat.

Jake wanted to kiss her. Knew he shouldn't. But dammit, he was going to. He'd done things far crazier than indulging in a simple kiss.

"Jake?"

Her breathing was shallow and she spoke on a whisper that sounded much like a plea. It wasn't just him. Cassie wanted him to kiss her and that was all the convincing he needed to do it.

CHAPTER NINE

Jake's hand had a will of its own, reaching up to touch Cassie's silky hair and digging his fingers into the dark waves until his hand settled on the back of her neck. He didn't need to coax Cassie forward to reach her lips. The distance he'd been seeking when he had invited her to sit with him on the sofa now made it easy for him to scoop her up into his arms and pull her into his lap.

She didn't protest. Instead, Cassie willingly wrapped her arms around his shoulders, gazing into his eyes with a white-hot desire that surged him on. Her full lips parted with the escape of a soft gasp. His gaze settled there, knowing what pleasures he'd find in taking the next step.

With her small body curled into his lap as if they were form-fitted for each other, the way a man and woman should be, he bent his head and covered her soft mouth with his. She was exquisitely perfect, sweet and tantalizing. His hand slid to the small of her back, stroking her, pressing her hard against him so he could feel more of her.

A soft moan bubbled up from her throat. He kissed her there and made a trail of tiny kisses along her neck eliciting the desired response. She smelled of baby powder and clean soap. A heady fragrance mixed in with the smoky scent of the fire.

Cassie clung to him, squirming in his lap and driving him mad. Framing his face with her hands, she pulled him back and kissed him hard, deepening their kiss, thrusting her tongue deep into his mouth with an explosion of passion. Her fingers dug into his neck with every thrust, every moan of pleasure.

Cassie was not the fragile woman he'd originally thought. She knew what she wanted and was bursting like a powerful inferno.

They parted much too soon for Jake's liking, breathlessly clinging to each other and trembling. As he gazed at her, he was reminded how utterly long it had been since he'd taken any form of pleasure with a woman. Cassie's lips were moist and swollen from their crushing kiss, her hair a wild mass that hung forward, framing her face. Her long black lashes fluttered open to reveal a well of desire he wanted to drown himself in.

Good God, he wanted to make love to her. He wanted to drink her in until there was nothing left. It was all he could think about. It would be easy to just pick her up and carry her into the bedroom until...

The awareness that he couldn't do that very thing slammed into him. *He couldn't...*

Jake sat straight up stiffly and eased Cassie off his lap. It didn't matter if she noticed the visible signs of his arousal. He needed the space. He needed even more to get the hell away from her.

If he dared to look at her, he'd forget all the reasons why he couldn't make love to her and he'd come undone. *Damn, how he wanted her.*

"I shouldn't have done that."

Cassie was still breathing deeply when she spoke. The heartbreaking confusion clouding her delicate features was unmistakable.

"Done what? Kiss me or pull away? If it's the last one we can rectify that easy enough."

She reached for him again, wrapping her arms around his shoulders. He had to close his eyes, shut down his mind, to keep from pulling Cassie back into his arms.

Jake drew in as much air as his lungs could hold and held her back before attempting to speak.

"Kissing you is not a good idea."

Her expression collapsed. "A few seconds and you've already had a change of heart?"

He didn't say anything. How could he tell her the truth? After the shooting five years ago, he'd thought sleeping with a woman was his salvation. Not consciously, of course. That had come out later after many sessions with the department shrink and a lot of soul searching on his part. He couldn't even recall the faces and names of some of the women he'd been with during that period of time. He'd been reckless, testing his boundaries just to feel alive. He'd survived where other officers had not.

It nearly destroyed his peace of mind and quite literally could have destroyed his life. But he'd gotten over looking at woman as sexual objects and distanced himself from any romantic attachments so he could focus on getting himself back to the thing he needed. His job. Jake wasn't about to destroy himself again just because the woman he was charged to protect was sexy as hell.

"Was it the kissing or the idea that wasn't good?" Cassie asked, her lower lip jutting out. But she valiantly fought to keep from showing her pain.

"I don't think I have to comment on how *that* kiss was. You were right there with me. It was..."

Mind blowing? The most incredibly intense experience he'd ever had with a woman, and it was just a kiss? If just kissing Cassie was enough to cause a complete meltdown inside him, he could only imagine how perfect making love to her would be.

Jake didn't have to imagine it. He knew. Making love to Cassie would be incredible. And that startled him to the core because despite his past, despite the aggressive need he'd felt after the shooting, being with Cassie would be making love, not just sex.

But he couldn't say that to her. If he did, he'd be reaching for her again, scooping her up into his arms. He'd be carrying her to that tiny bedroom and placing her down on that enormous bed. He'd be making love to her all night, and then some, until his body finally quit.

He wanted that as much as he wanted his next breath. But he couldn't tell her that.

"You don't have to worry about hurting my feelings," she said softly, abruptly pushing up from the sofa.

Although they were right in front of the woodstove, the

sudden distance from Cassie left him cold. He already ached to have her in his arms again.

She chuckled without any humor. "I never got high marks in the kissing department."

Jake almost choked on his words. "Says who?" How could anyone think kissing Cassie was anything but a cosmic explosion?

She shook her head and wrapped her arms around herself. Dipping her head, she avoided his probing eyes.

"It doesn't matter."

"Cassie, if any man ever told you something like that then he was nothing more than an idiot."

Her dark eyes lifted to meet his straight on. The uncertainty in her expression made his chest squeeze so tight he couldn't breathe.

"Do you mean that?"

"My pulling away from you has nothing to do with not wanting you. In fact, that's all I've been able to think about."

"Me, too," she admitted, her lips stretching into a coy smile.

"But that's the problem. I can't protect you if..."

"We make love? That's what you were going to say, right? You want to make love with me just as much as I want it."

Good Lord, he was in trouble. It didn't take much to know how Cassie felt, but hearing her say the words aloud was torture.

"Yes, Cassie. I want to make love to you," he said, his voice just above a whisper. The need inside him kicked so strong and violently, he couldn't breathe. "But that's not going to happen."

He pulled himself up from the sofa and stood, standing on the opposite side of the throw rug on the floor. It was much too far away from where he wanted to be, but at the same time it was a safe enough distance to keep him from reaching out and touching Cassie. To give in to all that he wanted.

"Trust me. It's better this way," he said, realizing as he said the words that he was trying to convince himself more than her that it was true.

117

"I don't happen to agree with you," she said, lifting her chin just a bit as if to keep him from seeing the hurt from his rejection by showing her strength. "But I won't beg."

"Cassie—"

"It's okay, Jake," she said, cutting him off. "Really. I appreciate your honesty. I think it helps to keep a line drawn between us, if that's what you need. And you're right in one way. There's too much going on right now, and we're liable to get confused about how we really feel about each other."

He nodded, the disappointment striking him like a kick in the stomach. Even worse because he'd been the one to deliver the pain.

Damn he'd been a colossal jerk leading Cassie on with that kiss, and then rejecting her when all he wanted to do was make her smile as she had done so many times before. She wasn't smiling now. She was trying to be strong. But Jake knew she was hurting.

And so was he. His body still ached for her.

Cassie wordlessly turned and walked toward the bedroom door.

"Goodnight," he called out.

Cassie stopped at the doorway, placing her hand on the doorjamb. But she didn't turn around.

She was waiting for him to come with her into the bedroom. To finish what they'd started. To give in to what they both confessed to wanting.

In his heart, Jake knew that. But the professional side of him, the one who'd vowed never to use a woman to take away the pain again, the one that kept screaming for him to detach from his feelings for Cassie, held him back.

After a few agonizingly long seconds, when it was clear he hadn't moved and had no intention of following her, Cassie stepped into the room and quietly closed the door.

Jake pried his clenched fists apart, feeling pain in his joints from holding them so tight.

He'd survived gun fights on gang-plagued streets. He'd stared down the barrel of a gun thinking it would be the very last thing he would see before he left this earth. But not following Cassie into that bedroom had to be the hardest thing he'd ever done in his entire life.

* * *

Angel had broken into his own home in the middle of the night like a damned cat burglar, stalking through the alleyways and staying hunched in the shadows until he saw the cars change. He'd been watching them, just as they had been watching his house. *His home.* Damn them.

Fucking police had never been able to catch him before. What the fuck made them think they could now?

Climbing through the open window, Angel immediately felt the warm air from the radiator rise up to meet him. At least his mom had paid the electric bill before hitting the bottle. After two days of hiding in the cold, he welcomed the warmth. He didn't have time to take comfort though. He wouldn't be here long.

He paused when he saw the nearly empty bottle of vodka on the kitchen table and cursed quietly. Could there be any more torture?

The blaring of the telephone was only marginally louder than the noise of the television in the next room. But even that would be enough to at least rouse his mother from the drunken stupor for which she'd buried herself. It wasn't enough that they'd buried Debbie. Santos had to kill them all.

With renewed rage, Angel wrenched the phone from its cradle before the third ring and waited for the caller to identify himself before giving his own identity away. The familiar voice had him taking a sigh in relief.

He glanced down the hallway toward his mother's bedroom on his way to the kitchen. The door was shut and the television was on. He could hear the laughter from a sit-com rerun that his mother always enjoyed. Thinking about the empty bottle he'd found, he figured she wasn't enjoying much of anything tonight.

"I told you never to call me here. This line could be

tapped," he growled.

"If you're stupid enough to go back home where someone can tail you, you deserve to be caught. I'd know if there was a tap on your damned phone. What the hell are you doing there? You were supposed to meet me."

"I needed cash. My picture is all over the news. I can't show my face anywhere for fear someone will turn on me. And no one wants to know me right now. You said you had things covered. Is it done?" he asked, his voice just below normal level. Although the only other person in the house was his mother and she wasn't likely to hear. Not in her current state.

The voice on the other end was low and muffled. "You always did ask too many damned questions."

"I don't see your face plastered on the damned television screen." He slammed his fist on the counter and then quickly stepped into the hallway to see that his mother's door was still closed.

His poor, sainted mother. She'd gone through enough heartache. It was all Santos' fault. All of it. Why didn't he just die in that bar with that bitch? It would have been sweet. It wouldn't have brought back Debbie, but at least there wouldn't be a witness, nothing to connect that shooting to him.

He couldn't hear any movement in the bedroom. His mother was probably passed out. It didn't take much these days.

"Just tell me if they're dead."

"Not yet. They escaped the explosion," the voice on the line said.

"Dammit. You said you'd take care of it."

"And I will. We've got a lead. Seems a Good Samaritan, a truck driver on his way to upstate New York, called the hotline. Was going to sell what he knew to the tabloids but then got a stab of conscience and decided to do the right thing. Don't it give you that warm and fuzzy feeling all over?"

"Not particularly. If you know where they are, what are you doing on the phone with me? Waste them already. Those other suits are probably on their way to pick them up and when they do, I'm screwed. You, too, for that matter. If I'm going down, so are you."

Angel darted his eyes to the hallway again when he realized his voice had boomed.

"Pipe down. The beauty of all this is that I'm the one who answered the call. I gave only enough information to my superiors to satisfy them. Seems Santos and Ms. Lang had breakfast this morning at some truck stop on the highway. That's about as much as the Bureau knows. They're all chasing a pretty white rabbit that's already gone off to a new burrow."

Angel's laugh started slow and then grew to a full cackle. It was the first time today he actually felt good. "You know where they are."

"I've got it covered."

His voice hardened. "You had it covered the last time and you blew it."

"You just meet me where we agreed. It won't be long before we can put all this behind us."

Angel dropped the phone with a thud. So she was on the run again. Cassie Lang. He knew he'd seen her striking face before he'd seen the headlines. It had taken awhile to figure out where, but then he remembered the sleek picture on the back of one of his mother's shiny new paperbacks. His mother always kept a book or two in the living room, a few in the kitchen and the bedroom. There wasn't much to her life these days but her reading.

Walking to the living room, he glanced at the collection of books on the shelf above the television. One had Cassie Lang's name on it. Her face was there, too.

That face. A pretty thing like that wasn't something Angel was likely to forget again.

He reached for the new paperback still sitting neatly on the coffee table. His mother hadn't gotten around to reading this one yet. He leafed through it and found the picture on the back. She was wearing a bright white, high-collared shirt and her hair fell against it in shocking contrast. She was a looker with those big brown eyes and full red lips.

Cassie Lang.

121

"Bitch, you can run all you want. But with a face like that, there's no place you can hide that I won't find you. I will. And when I do, you'll die."

For the first time that day, Angel smiled.

* * *

Jake was outside behind the cabin when Cassie woke the next morning.

"You deserted me," she said.

"I thought I'd see if I could get this Jeep started. I found the keys on the hook in the pantry."

She planted her fists on her hips. "How's it going?"

"Battery is dead. But I expected it might be after sitting so long."

"There are a whole bunch of storage batteries in the supply room. Could you switch with one of those?"

"Probably not. They aren't the right size. But I can use one to juice this battery."

A slight stab of guilt pierced Cassie as she thought about Jake sleeping on the sofa last night. She'd wasted a perfectly good bed as she tossed and turned, thinking about Jake and the kiss they shared. And because she was awake, she'd heard every bit of his restlessness as well.

Cassie followed Jake to the supply room. "That sofa isn't the most comfortable place to sleep. Especially for someone your size."

"Last night it wouldn't have mattered. I could have slept upright in a chair and it would have been fine. I was so exhausted."

Cassie sighed at his lie. She knew it was only to ease her burden, but it gave no comfort.

"Still, I feel bad. The bed is very comfortable. Tonight, you should take it and I'll sleep on the sofa. I insist."

"You have a problem letting a man be chivalrous?"

Their gazes locked for a brief moment. She wondered if that was what he was being last night. "There's no need to be at a time like this. We've both been through hell."

"You've got that right. But it's not something we need to discuss right now."

"I'm not letting this go," she persisted.

He stopped what he was doing, and she caught a glint of amusement in his eyes. "I didn't think you would. But right now I'm hungry. And I want eggs."

"There are some powdered eggs in the pantry. I could go—"

Jake made a face that was almost comical. "No way! I want butter and grease and if I can manage a slab of steak, I'll get one of those, too."

She couldn't help but laugh. "Oh, your poor arteries. You were so paranoid about someone seeing us at the truck stop and now you want to go out for breakfast again?"

He heaved a sigh. "We don't really have a choice. We need to get some supplies if we're going to be staying here for any length of time. I'm not comfortable leaving you here by yourself until I get back."

"I'm a big girl."

"I know," he said with a gaze so potent it rooted her in place.

He recovered quickly. "The steak is just wishful thinking. You've been to this area before. Are there any small mom-and-pop stores around where we won't attract attention?"

Cassie couldn't help but laugh.

"What's so funny?" he said, stopping mid-motion as he hoisted up one of the batteries with one hand.

"Why would anyone be looking for us here?"

"Everyone is looking for you, Cassie. People are bound to recognize you," he said, his face dead serious.

"I'm not famous. Most people have never heard of Cassie Lang. You didn't even know who I was."

"Well, maybe not before. But now your name has been splashed across the headlines of one of the biggest newspapers in the country. Your face, too. If you weren't before, you can bet you're famous now."

Jake took two steps out of the supply closet, holding the

door open with the hand not clutching the battery. When she didn't readily follow, he poked his head in.

"What's wrong?"

"It's just...I've worked so hard to build my name as a serious author. Now something like this comes along and..."

His expression was sympathetic. "Come on."

Jake was right. Cassie Lang was famous now. Not for the eight years she'd worked hard becoming a bestselling crime novelist. She'd seen a murderer. And now that murderer wanted her dead.

* * *

"So much for not attracting attention?" Jake glanced at Cassie as they drove down the unplowed road toward the small town.

She looked at herself in the rear view mirror. "What do you mean?"

"Sunglasses, funky hat. All you need is a mustache and a trench coat instead of the long wool coat you're wearing."

"You think this is overkill?"

"When I said disguise yourself a little, I meant by wearing a big sweatshirt and ugly pants that don't show...so much of you. You need to blend in, not look so obvious. What you're wearing is like a neon sign that says 'Look at me!' You couldn't be any more conspicuous if you really had a neon sign over your head."

Cassie pulled off the hat she'd found stuffed on the shelf of Maureen's closet.

"I'm keeping the sunglasses on though. At least in the car. This snow is blinding. And the coat is warm."

Jake smiled and turned his attention to the narrow road.

"Maureen has quite a wardrobe up here for someone who comes so infrequently."

"Yeah, well, Maureen likes to shop. I've seen her in action and it's truly an art form. I doubt she even remembers half the clothes she buys, or misses this stuff."

"Just how big is Maureen? That coat looks huge on you," he said, seeming to be satisfied that was enough.

"It might not be hers at all. I don't think I've ever seen her

124

wear it before."

"Maybe it's her ex-husband's."

"Or Adam's."

Cassie knew next to nothing about Jake and yet she was already adept at reading his emotions. His hand gripped the steering wheel and his eyebrows were drawn together making a crease on his forehead.

He didn't trust Maureen like she did. And there was absolutely no reason he should. They hadn't built a relationship over the years, helping one another through not only the professional triumphs and tragedies, but the personal ones, too.

But even he had to know that Maureen had no power or means to cause a gas leak at the safe house.

"What are you mulling over in your head, Jake Santos?" she finally asked.

His hesitation seemed to wrap around her. "I need to check in with Kevin."

"If we make a phone call from the cabin, it'll be easy to trace us here. I lost my cell phone in the explosion."

"Me, too. But cell phones are just as traceable."

"What about prepaid cell phones? They're available at just about every corner grocery store."

"They could always trace the call to the cell tower that was used after the fact and zero in on our location. I'll need to use a pay phone. But we still have to be careful about call length and not let Kevin keep me on the phone too long."

"He doesn't believe I'm not involved."

Jake swept his eyes from the road to Cassie. "He never said that."

"He didn't have to. I'm a people watcher. I can read people very well. But you trust him?" She knew without hearing Jake's answer that he did.

"When you work side by side with someone the way I do with Kevin, you begin to develop a relationship that can't come close to anything else."

"Not even with a woman?"

Jake didn't look at her. He just shook his head. "You trust

your partner without even thinking."

"Jake, who were you talking with on the phone before we found the gas leak?"

"Kevin. Why?"

"Kevin was at the precinct that night. He could have leaked my name to the press."

He laughed, edgy and raw, and shook his head. "No way."

"Why not?"

"Because I know Kevin. He's just as concerned with your safety as I am."

"You had no trouble accusing Maureen and I believe in her completely. How's this different? We can't discount anyone."

"We're talking about a police officer, Cassie."

"Now look who's being naive. In all your years on the force, you've never heard of dirty officers? Besides, someone in the damned FBI was responsible for that gas leak. Agent Bellows couldn't have been the only one. Sure, he could have easily put something to prevent the doors from opening. But he didn't have time rig a gas leak in the time he had when we got there. Someone else from the FBI had to be involved too."

She had him there. Not that it made her feel good to put Jake in his place.

"We're talking about bond fraud and an FBI investigation that has gone on for years," she pressed. "You don't know who was involved in this. If the FBI had their hands it in, why not someone on the Providence PD?"

"It couldn't have been Kevin."

Cassie sighed. "Maybe not. But someone went to a lot of trouble to make sure we'd die in a very messy accident. Can we afford to rule out involvement by anyone yet?"

Jake was silent for longer than Cassie could handle. When she couldn't stand it anymore, she snapped at him.

"Don't shut me out of this. I need to know what you're thinking."

He quickly glanced at her, and then brought his eyes back to the road as they reached the main drag.

126

"Fagnelio was nothing but a small time hood with a few loyal members at his side. He had a rap sheet and paperwork on him that could fill my mother's hope chest starting from the time he was nine years old. He was way out of his league with Ritchie Trumbella, but he was in the organization."

"What was his connection to Ritchie?"

"The FBI had uncovered information about a bond fraud deal. Angel had made some noise about being cut in on a big deal Ritchie was putting together, but the word is Ritchie was going to squeeze out some people. Angel thought he was double-crossed and was mad as hell about it. He called me for a meeting to give me some details. Instead of a meeting, he shot up Rory's and everyone in it."

"What do you think happened?"

"Angel was probably only in the bond fraud as a runner to initiate himself into Trumbella's organization. It might have turned personal at some point. Novak had been working with Trumbella for two years. Angel never mentioned him by name, but maybe he was playing both Ritchie and Angel. That's the only way I can figure a connection between the shooting and the safe house explosion."

"But Agent Novak died in the shooting."

"And someone leaked your name to the press. Whoever it was is still alive. Bellows is in on it. I'm sure of it. No one else had access to the house the way he did. To think anything more would mean a major conspiracy in law enforcement. Too many people would have to be involved to keep it under wraps and that just seems too far-fetched to me."

"Who knew we were going to that safe house?"

"I don't know. The FBI was calling the shots. I don't know how under wraps Charley was keeping things. I don't even know if Captain Russo knew where we were going."

"Agent Bellows said the safe house was checked just before we arrived," Cassie said.

"Yeah. Someone could have easily rigged the house before we got there and then let Bellows finish it once we were securely inside. Or maybe he had it rigged all along and it was just his

127

doing. He was in Providence the night of the shooting."

"Do you really believe it was just him?"

Jake shrugged. "Charley hand-picked the team to baby-sit. They'd been expecting us."

"Realistically, we're talking about two people in the FBI, right? Agent Bellows and—"

"Charley," Jake said, his tone almost a groan.

Cassie cocked her head to one side. "Someone. There were a lot of agents in that room." When Jake didn't say anything, Cassie added, "What are you thinking?"

"I'm beginning to think maybe Ritchie Trumbella was the frosting on the cake."

"How do you mean?"

"Novak may have been getting too close. When you work undercover, some agents go underground for years. They get so lost in their new identity that they lose themselves. That's why it's important to have a connection with someone on the outside. Novak had to have been in contact with someone at the FBI, giving updates. Maybe he got too close to the truth. Maybe Novak was the real target all along."

Jake looked down the side street before pulling the wheel to make a left turn.

"Whoever leaked my name to the press knew I was at Rory's," Cassie said. "Knew my name was attached to the case."

"The Bureau had access to our files almost immediately. There were reporters crawling all over the streets outside the bar within a half hour of the shooting. Someone had to have recognized you."

"And now they know I identified Angel Fagnelio as the shooter."

"We don't have one iota of proof to eliminate anyone in this. I have to talk to Kevin."

Wordlessly, Jake downshifted spun into the parking lot of a small convenience store. He didn't have to say anything more for her to know what he was thinking. They weren't any closer to finding out the truth than they were the night of the shooting. But at least for now, they were safe.

CHAPTER TEN

Steak was truly wishful thinking. Jake was only slightly disappointed when he had to settle for bacon and a box of Corn Flakes to go with the eggs, and frozen hamburger patties they'd bought for dinner. The general store did have everything else they needed to hibernate for the next week or so. Since it was the *only* store within twenty miles of the cabin, that was a plus.

Jake gassed up the Jeep for the ride back to the cabin. They probably wouldn't need to go more than a total of a hundred miles while at the cabin, but it was good to be prepared. As safe as they were in this remote section of the mountains, Jake knew that safety could sometimes be an illusion.

But before they could head back to the secluded woods, Jake had one more errand that demanded his attention.

They stood in a phone booth located in the store's parking lot, Jake dialed the telephone number. Cassie stood just outside the booth's broken door, keeping it open. A ten-dollar watch with a second hand he'd just purchased at the store dangled from Cassie's fingers as she waited for the call to connect. The caller picked up after the first ring.

"Gordon."

As soon as Jake heard Kevin's voice, he nodded to Cassie. Her eyes flew to the second hand on the watch, keeping the time as he spoke.

"Kevin, it's me."

"Dammit, Jake, where the hell have you been? Russo's crawling all over and up my ass, flaming about you and Cassie."

"Cassie's with me. We're staying hidden for a while."

"Gotta tell you, buddy, I'm damned glad to hear your voice. The FBI has been very hush hush about what went down

L.A. MONDELLO

at that safe house. I don't know how you escaped that explosion, but..." He let his voice trail, paused before continuing. "I'm obligated to tell you that Captain Russo and Agent Tate have ordered you to bring Cassie back. Immediately."

"Are they standing over your shoulder or are they relying on a tap?"

Kevin sighed. "It was a given you'd call me first. And you know if Charley was standing over my shoulder she'd be holding the phone by now."

"I figured as much."

"She's been spitting fire. And as pretty as the woman is, it ain't a pretty sight. Ever since you took off from the safe house—"

"Like we had a choice! Bellows locked us in, Kev. No matter what Charley is telling you about what went down. It's an inside job. Someone in the FBI wanted us dead."

"What? Tate said it was a gas leak."

"It was. But that's all I can say right now. I'm going to bring Cassie back in, but only after Angel Fagnelio is behind bars and has been debriefed."

A heavy breath carried over the phone line, distorting the connection. "Is she really worth all this, Jake? You're killing your career doing it this way. You do know that, don't you?"

"Internal Affairs can strike me from their Christmas list. Get your end set up and I'll come in."

"Not a problem, just tell me how I can contact you."

"I'll call you."

"Jake, right now you're a suspect. There's been talk of you being in with Fagnelio from the start."

'Fuck. I walked right into this one. Charley all but stuck an apple in my mouth and put me on a spit as the scapegoat. Did you tell them about Debra Cantelli?"

"For all the good it did. Just tell me where you are, Jake," Kevin said. "I've got your back. You know that. You can't clear yourself if you're on the run."

"When you have Fagnelio. Then we'll come in. Not until then."

130

The sound of items crashing carried through the phone line. Jake could just picture Kevin pushing something across his desk in frustration. "Jake—"

Cassie reached through the phone booth door and cut the call.

"Time's up," she said. "Did he tell you anything?"

"They don't have Angel Fagnelio. There's nothing more I need to know."

Jake stood in the booth with his hand clutching the phone for a moment before either of them made a move.

"What if he lies? What if you call him next time and he tells you that Angel Fagnelio is behind bars and it isn't true?"

"I hate people who lie. And Kevin knows it. He wouldn't do that to me."

"Jake, you're not talking about *your friend*, Kevin," she said, her quick laugh dry. "He's a police officer who has the FBI breathing down his back. He may not have a choice."

"Let's get out of here," Jake said, stepping out of the phone booth and walking with Cassie back to the Jeep. It had begun to snow again while he'd made the phone call. Snow now clung to the back of Cassie's ridiculously large coat.

Deep down Jake refused to believe Kevin would betray the friendship they'd spent years nurturing. They'd been in tight spots together before. Some fueled by undercover work gone bad. Some dealing with dirty police politics in the precinct. In those years, they'd developed a connection, a sixth sense about each other. They knew by body movement and tone of voice when the other was holding back.

And they both despised liars. They had reason. And that reason began with Charlotte Tate.

Tate. Yeah, she was probably spitting fire right now. When the safe house blew sky high, Tate would have insisted on taking Cassie to God only knows where. She would have pulled Jake off the case immediately. From what Kevin just told him, he was being made the fall guy. Of course, he'd expected as much. The only way to make the truth go away was to blame him or kill him. Killing him hadn't worked twice. The only thing left was blame.

It all seemed too clean to him now, too convenient for the guilty party to frame him. There'd been no fuss at all with Cassie's simple request to have him be her bodyguard at the safe house.

Until Angel Fagnelio's conviction, the FBI and the federal prosecutors would want to make damned sure their star witness was safe. He wouldn't know where she'd gone or what had happened to her until the trial was over. He shouldn't care...but he did.

The thought of Cassie getting lost deep into a red-taped system, losing her identity, her family and everyone else she loved for months—maybe years—made his heart ache. He didn't want her to get lost. Not from him. Not when someone from the very agency who'd be protecting her so clearly wanted her not to testify against Angel Fagnelio. Even if it meant death.

Not when he couldn't figure out what this *thing* was building between them.

He shook off the thought. Cassie *would* eventually testify. There would come a day when they'd have to return to face Angel Fagnelio. The FBI would hide her away. *Away from him.*

A wave of nausea flooded his stomach and he pushed past the distressing thought. This case was so much more than just Angel Fagnelio. He had to find out who leaked Cassie's name to the press and who rigged the safe house to blow up.

"Do you think Kevin can help us?" Cassie asked, cutting into his thoughts.

He nodded, the conviction of it making him feel good for the first time in days. The one person he absolutely could trust was Kevin.

* * *

There was a good chance the fire had gone out in the ancient potbelly stove while they'd been gone. Jake drove the Jeep out to the back of the cabin where it was normally parked. The smoke that had been pluming out of the pipe chimney when they left was now only an occasional puff when the wind slammed against the cabin. The snow had picked up considerably on the drive. It wouldn't take long for the small rooms inside to turn into an icebox.

Ignoring the hunger pangs his stomach was screaming, he parked the Jeep next to a pile of split wood. He could easily get the stove going while Cassie started lunch.

Cassie shoved her door open and climbed out of the Jeep, pulling the collar of her coat together. Immediately upon closing her door, she opened the back door and lifted one of the four bags of groceries out of the back seat.

"I'm going to take in an armful of wood for the stove before I come out and get the rest of this stuff. It looks like the fire in the woodstove might have gone out."

"I can handle these while you get some wood," Cassie said. As she walked toward the cabin, she reached into her pocket with the hand that wasn't holding the grocery bag and dug around for the key.

Jake looked at the sky and tried to remember when he'd even noticed that it had begun to snow. When he'd called Kevin, he finally remembered. Since then, the snow had gotten heavier. It was just as well they'd gone out when they had.

His gaze darted from the house to the tree line on the far side of the property where another line of split cordwood was stacked neatly in a long row. Half of the row was covered by a sky-blue tarp. His eyes walked along the smooth satin of the untouched snow in the open area of the small field to the set of tiny prints, most likely made by a lone deer, to another set of deep marks in the snow. Up in these hills there had to be a lot of wildlife lurking about just beyond the tree line.

Jake reached down and plucked a few pieces of wood from the top of the pile that were already wet with snow and tossed them aside in favor of some drier wood underneath.

That's when he saw them. The deep marks next to the smaller ones in the snow, just beyond the longer woodpile by the tree line, looked innocent enough. But something told him those marks didn't come from a four-legged animal.

Jake couldn't remember if Cassie had gotten any wood this

morning while he was working on the Jeep, but quickly decided it didn't matter whether she had or not. They hadn't been gone all that long this morning, but it was snowing hard enough that the tracks he now saw leading to the house were too fresh to be from this morning.

Dropping the pile of wood he'd just picked up, he shoved his feet through the deeper snow toward the opposite side of the house, which was not visible from the driveway.

His heart slammed against his chest. The small bedroom window was shattered and slightly open as if someone had tried to close it, but didn't push down far enough. The bleached white curtain ruffled back and forth with each gust of wind. The opening wasn't all that big, but it was certainly big enough for someone of medium built to crawl through.

His adrenaline kicked in like a boot to the stomach. He went for the gun that was usually snug in his holster, but neither was there. It was automatic, something he'd done hundreds of times. There was a comfort in knowing his gun was secure against his ribs when he walked into imminent danger. But he'd lost the gun after the explosion at the safe house. Damn!

Cassie was in there. And he had nothing to protect her with.

With full force, Jake bolted to the woodpile and grabbed the small ax before heading toward the cabin, his feet moving with a will of their own. His pulse pounded in his ear as he tried to listen for sounds. A struggle. Voices. Anything. Dear God, if the perpetrator had used a silencer, he wouldn't have heard a thing.

Jake hugged the outer wall of the cabin, gripping the ax with both hands. There was no sound inside as he stood just outside the door. No rustle of groceries being pulled out of the bag. No footsteps on the smooth, knotty pine floors, or clanking of pots or pans on the stove.

"Cassie?" he called out, hoping and praying that the intruder was some local hell-bent on stealing goods from an unused rental property. Maybe they were long gone by now.

When no response came, fear gutted Jake, making his

breaths come out in shallow bursts. He closed his eyes for a second and tried not to think of Cassie lying dead on the floor in a pool of blood, but the image wouldn't fade from his brain.

With his left hand, he eased the cabin door open and walked into the darkness.

* * *

Pain pounded against Cassie's temple as she tried not to think about the gun pressed against her skull right above her left ear. She hadn't seen him come up behind her. She was too busy unloading packages from the bag she'd carried in from the Jeep. The scent of the intruder registered seconds before the feel of his hands against her mouth.

She'd been too terrified to scream even if he hadn't covered her mouth to muffle any warning sound she might make. His fingers bruised her cheeks and the barrel of the gun she'd yet to see dented her tender skin.

The raw scent of his sweat wasn't concealed by the heavy aftershave assaulting her nose, choking her. He reeked of the same fear Cassie felt deep in her bones. His body, hot and rigid, pressed against her back, making her skin crawl where there was forced contact.

She couldn't move. He crushed her hard against the counter, her stomach and pelvic bone pressed solidly against the edge.

"Stay quiet," her captor said against her ear, his threatening voice a harsh whisper.

Cassie flinched at his hot breath and closed her eyes against a wave of nausea that bubbled up her throat. He hadn't said the somewhat comforting words "and I won't hurt you" after demanding her silence. That surely made his intentions unmistakable. He wasn't there to hurt her. He was there to kill her.

Her chest rose and fell with each breath as she fought to focus and think of what to do. Somehow she needed to warn Jake that he was walking blindly into the tiger's pen. She'd gotten him into this by insisting he be her bodyguard. He didn't deserve to die. She wouldn't let him die. Especially not for her.

Still pressing his body against hers, pinning her in the corner of the small counter space, the stranger slowly released the hand gripping her mouth and whispered, "Not one word or I'll make sure this is slow and agonizing."

Quickly he pulled a knife in front of her view, just inches from her nose. The gun pressed tighter against her skull, reminding her that all it would take was the mere twitch of his finger to send a bullet passing through her brain, ending everything.

"What do you...what do you want?" she said, her voice shaky. She had no idea if this guy had already been in the house when they got back from the store or if he'd been waiting in the woods and saw her and Jake.

Jake. Oh, God, had this monster already killed him? She closed her eyes to the harsh image of the cold metal knife and the deadly harm this intruder intended.

"Don't worry your little head. I'm just going to take a little piece of you to remember you by when you're gone. We're going to take a nice picture of you and me. And then it'll be all over."

His voice didn't hold hate or malice or emotion of any kind. It was almost mechanical, as if this man had no feeling or conscience about what he was about to do.

"You stay still and this won't hurt a bit."

Her eyes flew open just as the knife disappeared from view. Cassie lost all breath in her lungs as the knife grazed the back of her head. She felt a small tug but no pain, and wondered if the terror of what was happening had numbed her senses.

He dangled a long strand of her hair in front of her.

"Hold this," he demanded.

She stared at her hair as he shook it in front of her. With trembling fingers, she gripped her hair. Seconds later he placed his cell phone in front of them.

"Smile pretty for the camera." He pressed his face against hers as she held the strand of hair in front of them.

A sob bubbled up her throat as he wrenched the strand of

hair from her.

"Touch a hair on her head and I'll kill you."

Relief and fear careened through Cassie with the sound of Jake's voice. His tone was lethal in a way she'd never heard before. To hear that kind of deadly emotion in any other man's voice would have Cassie trembling. But to hear Jake's voice at all filled her with relief so strong her knees weakened and threatened not to hold her any longer. Jake was alive. Thank you God, he hadn't been killed. But the relief was short-lived. Jake was unarmed.

"Too late."

Abruptly, the stranger wrapped his arm around Cassie's neck with the hand holding the knife and swung her around. Her head jerked back with the force of his blow. The gun discharged, the noise of it like an explosion in her ear. A scream ripped through her. She hadn't seen Jake behind them and when the gunman finally turned her around, using her body to shield himself, Jake was gone.

"Jake! Oh, God, no. You shot him!" she screamed.

"Shut up, bitch!"

Fury erupted, violent and blinding, from the depths of Cassie's core. With her left hand, she gripped the gunman's wrist like a vice, only marginally concerned with keeping the knife he held from slicing her skin. Flattening her right hand, tight and strong, Cassie delivered a quick thrust to his other hand, unleashing all her fury and sending the 45 caliber, that had only moments ago been pressed against her temple, flying out of the gunman's hand.

One small victory had her taking a quick breath, but the element of surprise was vital in survival and she knew the shock she'd given her attacker would quickly fade.

"Let her go!"

Jake's voice boomed and echoed against the walls of the cabin. To her great relief, Jake now held the gun out in front of him in both hands. An ax lay on the floor where he stood with his legs spread slightly apart.

Her attacker pressed the knife snug up against Cassie's

137

throat, the razor-sharp blade grazing her skin. Cassie sucked in a breath to keep the knife from pressing against her any further. One wrong move and the blade would go deep and cut her artery. She'd bleed to death all over the floor before any help could come.

"Shooting me isn't going to get you what you want, Santos," the man said. "Your bullet goes in me and the knife is going to come back with me, taking this pretty little head off with it."

Cassie heard the twisted smile in his voice. She zeroed in on Jake's face, his eyes focused on the man who seemed to be taking pleasure in her murder. There was hate there, something she'd yet to see in Jake. His square jaw was clenched tight, his body rigid but fully in control.

"Who sent you?"

"Who said anyone did?"

"You have Warlords written all over you," Jake bit back. "Fagnelio must be desperate, to send a rank amateur."

Jake's eyes never wavered from his target.

Those were clearly not words the man holding her wanted to hear. "Shut the fuck up! You know nothing! You're both dead whether you kill me or not."

His grip eased just a notch as his anger rose. The knife wobbled against her neck.

Cassie couldn't take it. Bloodshed was going to happen one way or another. It was just a matter of whose blood would be spilled. Too much was out of control.

"Don't tell me you drove all the way out here just for the clean air." Jake took a microscopic step toward them.

Cassie balled her fists and concentrated all her effort in keeping her right arm locked and rock solid. The blade held against her skin only needed to move an inch or so away in order to give her a window of opportunity.

"What do they make you for bringing home the prize?" Jake taunted, motioning to the strand of hair the man was still holding. "Their promises mean nothing. Fagnelio is in such deep shit he doesn't care who he's taking down with him. You do the deed and then they'll just kill you. That's how it works, you know. Did they tell you?"

The man's agitation grew by leaps. He took in a deep breath and his hand moved just enough for Cassie to slip her left hand up and grab the wrist holding the knife. She held on for dear life. A split second later, she rammed her right elbow square into the dirtbag's diaphragm, forcing him to hunch forward, throw his arms out, and loosen his hold as he lost all his breath.

Something instinctive took over her and had Cassie pivoting so she stood behind him. She delivered a punch to his gonads from behind and wound the hand still gripping his through his legs, making him hunch forward even more and teeter on his toes. One swift movement and she rammed him head first into the woodstove, knocking him unconscious.

Her heart still hammering, Cassie stepped back against the counter. It had all happened in seconds and now it was over. Jake rushed to the man sprawled out on the floor, checking for more weapons. He put a finger to his neck to check for a pulse.

With her hands covering her mouth, she glanced down at the pine floor where the knife had dropped. Her eyes fixed on the dark clump of hair. She'd seen him do it, watched him dangle it in front of her face as he snapped his evidence picture. But what he'd done finally sank in. It was her hair on the floor. Her body he'd touched. She shuddered with the memory.

Her hand went to the back of her head where she'd felt the tug earlier, searching for the spot where her hair had been cut away. She found it and twirled at the ends of freshly cut pieces of hair between her thumb and index finger.

Jake picked up the knife and the lock of hair, staring at it for a moment before turning to her.

"There might be more like him out there. We have to get out of here now."

Cassie looked at the hair in Jake's hand.

"That's mine," she said quietly.

Jake looked at her with eyes that mirrored the terror she felt inside. "I know."

Minutes later Jake drove the Jeep up a small rise in the road. Cassie didn't know if the wheels had left the ground or not, but she felt her body rise and then bounce down into the seat with the force as if they'd gone airborne. Her neck stung, hot and biting, where the knife had dug into her skin. Her body trembled violently as the magnitude of what had just transpired fully hit her.

Cassie had almost been killed. For the third time!

At the bar, Cassie had methodically gone over details with Jake, taking comfort in knowing that although she'd been at the wrong place at the wrong time, the violence she'd witnessed was not intended for her personally. The safe house was another story. Someone intended for her and Jake to die in that explosion, and it was by Jake's quick action and the grace of God that they'd made it out before the house disintegrated into a pile of ash and fiery rubble.

Today it was so much worse. She'd seen the burning death wish in the eyes of the man who wanted her dead.

"Jake, that wasn't an FBI agent," Cassie finally said weakly. They hadn't spoken for a few miles. Jake concentrated on the road and Cassie had retreated inside herself to find some of the peace she craved.

"I know." Jake glanced quickly at her before returning his eyes to the road. He turned the heat in the Jeep on full blast.

He'd brought the lock of hair with him, placing it out of view in the glove compartment. She didn't know why. It couldn't be reattached. Any evidence of that altercation with that man was in plain view on the cell phone he'd used to take her picture. But Jake had taken the strand of hair anyway and hidden it out of her view. Cassie knew it was there. She couldn't ignore it.

She looked down at herself and realized that in their haste she'd left that ridiculously big wool coat behind. She hadn't felt the cold when she climbed into the Jeep. She'd felt numb, unable to feel anything at all. But now the shock of what had happened was all too vivid.

Remembering the vileness of the man's eyes, she said, "He

was little more than a boy, Jake."

"Don't kid yourself. He may have been younger than you, but he'd have killed you and me without remorse. He nearly succeeded."

"But he didn't."

"No."

"Was he dead? Did I...kill him?" Her bottom lip wobbled uncontrollably and a sob bubbled up her throat.

"No," Jake said tightly and Cassie had the distinct feeling that Jake wished she had. He took his eyes off the road and looked at her, hard and resolute. "No, Cassie. You didn't kill him. But you had every right to. If you hadn't been able to get that gun out of his hand, most likely we'd both be dead right now. You did what you had to do. He'll probably come to in a little while and have one hell of an egg on his head for his efforts. I'd say he got off with more than he deserved."

Tears streamed down her cheeks. "He wasn't an agent."

"Angel sent him." Jake's expression was grim as he glanced at the glove compartment. "That lock of hair was meant as proof. The picture was proof, too."

"Proof of what?"

"That he'd been successful at his initiation. A lot of street gangs have their own signature. When a new recruit kills, he brings back a piece of his victim as proof."

"He could have cut a piece of hair from anyone."

"He could have, but if he presented it as proof to his leaders and they found out the truth, he'd be killed, too. To them it is honor, courage. It's a good thing he took it one step further and wanted a picture of you and his proof. He might have killed you before I found you."

"They have no respect for human life at all," she said quietly. "I can't figure out how he knew we were at the cabin."

Jake glanced at her, his blue-eyed gaze intense. "You have a face that is unforgettable, Cassie."

Jake's softly spoken words wrapped around her, easing her burden and igniting something deeper.

It wasn't just that she was recognizable. Her face was very

likely the first thing people had seen when they read the newspaper during their morning coffee. She hadn't been on the front page of the newspaper yesterday. She'd checked the vending machine at the truck stop when they'd stopped for breakfast. But that didn't mean anything.

She looked down at her trembling hands and saw blood staining them. She snapped her head up in alarm.

Jake reached out and clasped the hand closest to him. "You have blood on your shirt and on your neck. The knife most likely cut the outer skin during the struggle." He sighed heavily, dragged his hand over his head. "It could have killed you. Do you feel it."

Did she? Yes, her neck stung a little. She was too afraid to touch it for fear of what she might find. "I think it's just a surface cut."

"The blood is drying. It can't be a deep cut. But we'll have to clean that up when we get settled somewhere. You're not going to pass out, are you?"

Cassie shook her head. "We can't go anywhere, Jake. They'll find us. If they found me at Maureen's cabin, of all places, they'll find me anywhere."

He reached across the seat and slipped his wide hand, warm and reassuring, over hers. She wanted the comfort, but didn't think there was a chance in hell she'd ever feel comfort again.

CHAPTER ELEVEN

They'd driven little over an hour east and across the Massachusetts border until Jake found a little blink-of-an-eye town that had a motel on Main Street with a brightly lit neon sign that half spelled out the words "vacancies with kitchenette." It was set back from the road and had a parking lot in the back of the building. Satisfied that the Jeep wouldn't be seen from the road, he pulled into the parking lot and parked far enough away from the windows so the desk clerk couldn't see Cassie in the Jeep.

"I'll only be a minute," he said as he threw open the door. "If you see any cars at all, coming or going, I want you to hunch down."

Cassie nodded.

Jake hurried the registration along while trying not to clang any warning bells. He emptied his wallet of nearly all of its cash to pay for the room under an assumed name, being occupied only by him, and listed the license plate for his own car, not the Jeep's.

Cassie was staring straight ahead and didn't move as he climbed into the Jeep and fired up the engine to park it in the back.

They still had three bags of groceries they'd picked up earlier. He pulled them out of the back seat, looking around while Cassie unlocked the motel room door and switched on the light.

The low wattage bulb only slightly illuminated the room in a warm yellow glow. As advertised, a small kitchenette with compact refrigerator stood directly in front of them, next to the bathroom door. An ancient television on a flimsy stand stood next to the sharp-lined, ugly, muted green sofa that dominated the other wall. He looked beyond the room to a door that was slightly ajar.

"The bedroom must be back there. The clerk said the room had a separate bedroom." Jake dropped the grocery bags on the coffee table.

Cassie stood in the middle of the room, looking at all its drabness, hugging herself.

He moved past her to the bedroom door, flicked on the light, which seemed incredibly harsh compared to the barely glowing bulb in the first room, and stepped aside for her to see.

"Only one twin bed," she muttered, glancing in. "Did he mention that?"

Jake nodded. "I'll take the sofa."

Her head rose and her eyes flared.

"If you want to play fair, I'll flip you for it later."

Cassie seemed satisfied and reached for one of the grocery bags, pulling items out and setting them on top of the coffee table. When all three bags were empty, she frowned, picking up a package of hamburger buns.

"I think the frozen hamburger patties were in the bag I brought into the cabin."

"Given the circumstances, I think I can live without them." Jake wondered when Cassie's dam would finally break. He could feel the cracks widening in himself and couldn't fathom how Cassie was keeping herself together.

He reached for the ointment and gauze they'd bought for the scrape on Cassie's neck from the night before, during the explosion. Her white cotton shirt was now stained with crimson streaks and blotches. Jake tore the package of gauze open and laid it down on the coffee table.

"Here, sit down while I get a wet towel to clean these cuts."

Cassie did as she was told. Jake held his hand under the faucet, waiting for the cold tap water to turn warm, then doused a white terrycloth hand towel he'd pulled from the towel rack.

He knelt on the floor in front of her and pushed her long, dark hair back to expose her wounds. His mind raced to the lock of hair dangling from that dirtbag's hand when he walked into the cabin, and he grimaced.

"It's that bad?" Cassie's face flashed with alarm.

"No. Just a surface cut. Looks like the scab was torn off the scrape you got the other night too."

He opened the bottle of hydrogen peroxide and poured some on a gauze square. "This might sting."

She smiled weakly.

As he dabbed the soaking gauze pad against her neck and watched the bubbles flare, Jake found it hard to get the terrifying image of Cassie's attacker out of his brain. If he closed his eyes, it was if he were there again, seeing Cassie's head bent back with the force of the gun pressed tight against her temple.

"Where did you learn how to do those moves back there?" he asked.

"Maureen and I took a self-defense class a few years ago. It was all about empowerment and showing that no matter your size or your strength, a woman could defend herself from an attack. I always wondered if I'd remember what to do if it ever happened to me."

Jake forced a smile. "Now you know."

"Yes," Cassie said with a sigh.

Jake finished cleaning out her old wound and then dressed the area with gauze in silence as Cassie stared back at him. Her sable eyes bore into him in a way he couldn't ignore.

"You're all set," he said, getting to his feet.

"Are you hungry?"

His stomach was grumbling, mostly from the bag of potato chips they'd dug into in the Jeep. He glanced at the groceries, still strewn about on the coffee table.

"You sit back and relax," he said. "I can fix us something edible, I'm sure."

"You take good care of me, Jake." She leaned her body closer to him as she sat on the edge of the sofa. She planted her hands on her knees and pushed herself up until she stood right in front of him.

He held his breath, wanting just to bend his head and get a

145

fraction closer to her. He couldn't kiss her. He knew he shouldn't. That didn't mean he didn't want to with every ounce of his being.

"I make a mean chicken soup," he said softly, picking up one of the cans on the table.

"You don't have to cook for me to take care of me."

"No?"

She shook her head and licked her lips.

Good Lord, how Jake wanted to kiss her. What he wouldn't do to just forget all the reasons he couldn't and celebrate all the reasons he should cover her mouth with his. Forget his damned code of ethics. Forget Angel Fagnelio and all the scumbags of the world who inflicted pain for pleasure. All he wanted to do—no, needed to do—was kiss Cassie and feel her small body next to his. He needed it as much as he needed his next breath.

Jake gazed down at her, saw the moon and the stars shining in her warm brown eyes, felt the very earth beneath his feet shift.

"We keep playing this game, you and me, but we never take the next step." Her voice was like silk running over his skin, soft, feminine and enticing.

"Is that what you really want?"

She nodded without hesitation. With her deep sigh, her chest rose and stretched taut the stained cotton shirt she wore, defining the delicious swells of her breasts.

"It's your choice though," she said. "I've made my feelings perfectly clear."

"You have."

She nodded her head toward the open bedroom door. "I'm going to go in there now, pull this bloody shirt off me and leave you to think about what it is you really want."

For a lingering moment, their gazes locked. More was said in those few seconds than had been said the entire time they'd been together. With great strength, he held himself back from touching her. There was more than just lust flowing between them. Even he could see that. What they had was total explosive *emotion* that was rare.

Jake stood still in the center of the room, watching as Cassie walked to the bedroom. She didn't pause at the door this time, as she had last night. She just lifted her chin and gracefully moved away from him, never looking back.

Filling his lungs deeply with the stale air in the room, he ran his hand over his face, smelled the lingering scent of the ointment still clinging to his fingertips. He rolled the pad of his thumb and index finger together and closed his eyes, searching for an answer. Anything that would bring some sense to the insanity they'd been living these past few days.

He wanted Cassie. She'd made it more than clear she wanted him, too. He genuinely cared for her. He'd gone to bed with women for less than that before. But he wouldn't do that to Cassie.

She was special. More than special even. There was a rarity about Cassie that reached out and grabbed something deep inside, pulling him to her right from the start. She wasn't the kind of woman he could just have a simple fling with, then walk away. The truth was, he'd reached a point of no return where Cassie was concerned. He didn't know if he could walk away from her.

He'd been right about one thing from the start. Cassie Alvarez *was* lethal. But only to his heart. Her innocence and sass wrapped around him, making it hard to think about anything else but her. The very thought of waking up and not hearing her musical laughter broke him in two.

No one had a crystal ball to look into the future and see what tomorrow held, least of all him. He didn't know how this threat with Angel Fagnelio and the FBI would ultimately play out. And if he didn't have the answers to that, how could he think about moving forward toward any kind of future with Cassie beyond this case?

Except for one very real thing. Angel Fagnelio wasn't here. And more importantly, no one knew *they* were here. Of this much Jake could be certain. No one had followed them on the road leaving the cabin. He hadn't been distracted by

147

conversation as they drove because Cassie was virtually silent throughout the drive.

Fagnelio isn't here, Jake thought as he moved his feet toward the bedroom door. There was no threat that could destroy them. It was only him and Cassie. And right now, he wanted her.

Jake's pulse thrummed as he pushed off his boots. He was through debating about what he should and shouldn't do. Cassie wanted to make love with him, and he'd be damned if he wasn't going to give her exactly what they both admitted to wanting. What he now knew without a doubt he needed. *To hell with his code of ethics or self-imposed celibacy.*

The bedroom door was open. From the shadows playing on the wall, Jake knew Cassie was standing beside the twin bed. He paused at the threshold of the doorway, certain she hadn't heard him approach in his stocking feet.

Her back was to him. The fading daylight poked through the outdated brocade curtains and radiated around her in the dimming room. Although he couldn't see, with her head bent and by her movement Jake was sure she was unbuttoning her stained shirt.

"Do you want the door closed?" he asked, his voice rough and low, echoing an unanswered need he'd held back far too long.

Startled, she peered over her shoulder. Hesitating, she said, "That depends on which side of the door you want to be on."

With one long stride into the bedroom, he kicked the door shut, closing them both inside the tiny room. He heard her soft sigh of defeat, saw the slight sag of her shoulders, before she continued her task.

"Let me do that," he whispered.

Cassie swung around quickly, the flash of surprise in her eyes quickly changing to something different, something potent. A seductive smile tipped the corners of her full lips, hinting just a bit of her uncertainty.

"Okay."

As she dropped her hands to her side, her shirt fell open, revealing the soft, creamy flesh of her stomach and a hint of her dark nipples beneath her white lace bra.

Their gazes meshed and held for a quiet moment, saying so much more than words ever could.

He was standing in front of her before he could even fathom how his feet got him from point A to point B. His fingers grazed her silky soft skin, shooting a trail the likes of hot molten lava through his veins. As he fumbled with the buttons of her shirt, he trembled. *Good God, he was pathetic.* When was the last time he'd trembled undressing a woman? Had it really been that long?

No, it was all Cassie. Being this close to her, touching her velvety skin was enough to make him come undone.

He reached the last button and pushed her shirt open fully, sliding the fabric off her shoulders and allowing his fingers to linger on the smoothness of her skin.

She dipped her head, averting her gaze, hiding from him everything he wanted.

"Look at me," he rasped, tilting her chin up with the tips of his fingers.

Those sultry dark eyes, fringed with black lashes, had haunted him endlessly these past few nights. Now they were brimming with the burning desire she had just for him. He brushed his fingers across the silky smoothness of her cheeks and noticed they were the exotic color of rose petals.

Jake chuckled softly. "We're about to make love, and you're blushing?"

"Does that bother you?"

He shook his head. "I just don't want you to be embarrassed by anything we do."

Cassie quickly shook her head. "I'm not. I'm...it's been a long time for me."

Jake wanted to laugh, but decided Cassie wouldn't understand. How could she? "I haven't been with a woman in over three years, Cassie," he answered, realizing for the first time how infinitely long that seemed. "So I guess that makes us even."

Her doe-like eyes lifted to his with surprise.

"Really?"

He nodded.

"I don't want to disappoint you." Closing her eyes, Cassie chuckled lightly, concealing her face with her hand. "I don't know why I'm telling you this," she whispered.

"Have you changed your mind?" he asked, swallowing hard.

She shook her head. His heart pounded against his ribs.

Jake gently tugged her hand away from her face and kissed her lightly on the lips. Those lips, silky soft and moist. She tasted sweet, like the sugar she had with her coffee that morning. He wanted to drink her in, devour her as if he'd never had a meal, but he held himself back. After so long of going without he was now in danger of overload. Cupping her face between both hands, he gazed into her dark eyes, knowing he could easily drown there with no regrets.

He recalled what she'd said last night when they'd kissed at the cabin. How much he'd so brutally wanted her. How unsure she'd been, afraid he'd pulled away because she'd somehow done something wrong. He suddenly understood her hesitation.

"Someone, somewhere along the line fed you a great load of bull that you weren't any good as a lover, that you weren't desirable. The horrible crime is that you believed him."

Reaching up, she pulled his hand away and shrugged uncomfortably, averting her gaze. "What else could I believe when I...couldn't feel anything?"

"Look at me," Jake said, tilting her chin up with his fingers. "Haven't you seen the effect you have on me? I can't even be in the same room with you without losing my mind wanting you."

She swallowed visibly. "You didn't have any trouble resisting me last night. And I practically threw myself at your feet."

Closing his eyes, he laughed, his voice deep and rough with an aching need so strong he thought he'd self-combust.

"My God, Cassie, you're the most incredible woman I've ever met. I damn near died last night wanting you. I spent an hour on the front porch in the freezing cold trying to fan down the flames inside me after you closed that bedroom door."

Her eyes widened as she peered up at him. "I didn't know that."

He smiled and was rewarded in turn when the lips that had teased him for the past week tilted up to form a deliciously wide grin.

Brushing her dark hair away from her face, he rested his hand at the nape of her neck. He kissed her forehead, digging his fingers into her dark curls until he felt the spot where her hair had been cut. His body stiffened as the images of her being held back at the cabin assaulted him.

"What's wrong?" she asked.

"His hands. I can't get the image of him touching you, what he could have done to you, out of my mind. It's driving me crazy, Cassie."

"Ssh."

Cassie placed her index finger against his lips. His tongue darted out to taste her skin. With her other hand, she took his hand and placed it against the bare skin of her chest.

"This will help you wipe away those images."

His mouth came down crushingly hard upon hers. He was hungry for her in a way he didn't think would ever be satisfied. The images faded as he made a trail of kisses down the side of her cheek to the hollow of her neck where he'd bandaged the long scrape and cut marks from the knife. Even though they were now covered, the image of them, angry and raw, sprang up at him, a chilling reminder of what they'd gone through to get to this moment.

He fingered the gauzy area lightly.

"Does this hurt?"

"Not as much as it did."

"What about when I do this?" Bending his head, he dug his fingers in her wild hair and kissed her neck, giving the area around the bandage gentle, loving attention. He lingered there, greedily taking pleasure in the scent of her and the sweet and salty taste of her skin.

151

Cassie said nothing, but he could swear he'd heard her heart slam against the walls of her chest, giving answer to his question. Running her hands up his arms, to his shoulders, she let out a small whimper. As she laced her fingers behind his neck, her exposed skin pressed firmly against his shirt, and he was instantly annoyed by the barrier.

He wanted more. So much more. The fusion of hot flesh against hot flesh would only heighten his awareness of her, of what they were about to share.

Stretching up on her toes, she pressed her lips against his and grazed her tongue across the opening of his mouth to gain entrance. Jake quickly obliged and she seared him with a kiss so provocative, it set his whole body on fire, turning his mind into a complete nuclear meltdown.

She gasped for air as she pulled away from him, her fingers urgently digging into his shoulders. Running his hand down the side of her, he cupped her bottom, pressing her hard against him, taking pleasure as she squirmed against his arousal.

Cassie had never felt passion with anyone like she did now with Jake. She'd known right from the first time they'd met that he was different from any man she'd ever known. His magnetism drew her to him from the start. He was rugged and impossibly strong in body and will. At the same time, he was surprisingly gentle, stealing her breath away with the slightest thing he did.

And he gave her a feeling of empowerment she'd never known before in her life. She felt brave beyond her wildest dreams, strong against the powers holding her captive.

In one fell swoop, Jake lifted her in his arms as if she were light as air. Kissing her soundly, he gently placed her in the center of the absurdly tiny bed. He crushed her body with his own, making her sink deeply into the soft mattress.

When he pulled away from their kiss, Jake leaned back slightly and gazed down at her. "Tell me what you feel, Cassie," he commanded in a shaky whisper.

What could she say? That her body was on fire each time he touched her? Each time he looked at her the way he was right this second? That she ached to feel him moving inside her, feel his warm mouth on her naked body, and if he denied her that, she'd go insane with need?

Reaching up, she dug her fingers into his hair at the back of his head and pulled him down. She wanted his passion, wanted for him to lose control in it with her. He kissed her with a power that unearthed her, dipping well into the depths of her soul and turning her completely inside out. And when she couldn't take anymore, he gave her more.

Before she could comprehend how he'd managed to remove her bra, his mouth covered one of her nipples, sucking gently, while his thumb teased the other. His tongue was like exquisite torture, flicking her nipple to an aching erection, making her arch her back to be closer to his warm moist mouth. His hand cupped her breast with urgency and she heard herself moan. He switched sides, bathing her with attention until she bucked beneath him, unable to stand the pressure building inside her body. Liquid heat pooled inside her and flowed to her sensitive center.

"Too many clothes," she said breathlessly.

Jake made a trail of kisses down the center of her stomach, leaving a moist line that chilled her skin against the cool draft from the window. She grasped the button of her jeans to unclasp them, and he stilled her hand.

"Let me," he rasped. "I've waited a long time for this."

"So have I."

Cassie closed her eyes and allowed herself to be taken. She didn't need to be in control. Not here. She wanted to go wherever Jake wanted to take her and back again. She wanted to get as close to heaven as she could, and she knew without a doubt Jake would take her there.

He slipped his hands beneath the fabric of her jeans and pulled the denim down, leaving her with only her underwear. Vanity immediately invaded her mind for just a nanosecond, making her wish she'd worn some of the sexy lace panties she owned and hardly ever used. Instead, she wore her normal plain white cotton briefs that were comfortable and practical.

Opening her eyes, she peered up at Jake just as she heard the soft thud that was her blue jeans hitting the floor next to the bed. He leaned back on his knees, straddling her legs. The rise and fall of his chest grew more labored as his gaze roamed the length of her body, worshipping her as if she were a Greek Goddess.

He wanted her, plain white cotton briefs and all. And the very fact Jake was so completely turned on by her made Cassie toss away every ounce of uncertainty left inside her.

"Are you finished?" she teased, loving the way he made her feel so cherished.

A deep dimple appeared on Jake's left cheek as his lips stretched into a wide grin. Her heart melted.

"Not by a long shot."

"Good, because neither am I." Cassie sat up in bed and reached for his belt buckle, but he quickly stilled her hand.

"If it's all the same to you," he said, his voice tight. "I'm going to take care of these on my own. In the current state I'm in, getting these pants off may be more difficult a task to perform than taking off yours. This show will be over before anything happens."

Cassie giggled, but stopped when Jake's expression grew serious as he took off his pants and shirt.

They climbed beneath the blankets and were in each other arms, flesh melting against flesh, tongues dancing like fire-licked flames of the sun. It was more perfect than anything Cassie could have dreamed.

"Tell me what you feel, Cassie," she heard Jake rasp against her ear.

"I..." She couldn't breathe enough to say a word. He was torturing her with his fingers, delving deep inside her, bringing her higher and higher toward the threshold of release, until she thought she'd split in two.

"Tell me," he commanded, his breath hot and moist against her ear.

This was it, Cassie realized. A trust she'd never known. It was the very thing that had kept her heart in chains all these years. The reason all her relationships ended in failure. Never before had she been able to relinquish her sense of control to let anyone close enough to touch what mattered deep inside. Or to allow herself the freedom to succumb completely to love.

Love. Yes, this was the very real and wonderful difference. What she felt for Jake was an implicit trust that could only mean one thing. She was in love with Jake Santos. And that was something she'd never felt before, never allowed herself to experience.

He could lead her anywhere and she would go willingly, give herself up to the power of that love, to that trust she'd bestowed him, body and soul.

"I...I want you inside me."

She lay beneath him, unable to think beyond the pleasure and tension building in her with each passing second. With Jake's hard thighs cradled against her softness, Cassie tightly gripped his hips and moved against him in an urgent plea.

And he answered her, entering her slowly, deliberately, until she fell into the rhythm he set. She wrapped her legs around his waist, locking him to her as they rode the white-hot wave of fire threatening to disintegrate her senses, until she tumbled over the edge to the other side. Seconds later, when the world around her finally came back into view, she felt Jake's body harden, and his whole body shuddered in her arms.

He lay on top of her for a few moments while his labored breathing eased. Rolling to his side, he pulled her against him. His skin was hot and slick with sweat from their lovemaking. They lay quietly for a long while with nothing but the steady rhythm of their breathing breaking the silence. Jake stroked her hair as she buried her face against his warm chest, listening to his powerful heartbeat.

"Tell me, Cassie," Jake said softly, a hint of mischief in his voice. "Did you feel anything or are we going to have to keep at this until we get it right?"

She couldn't help it. Cassie tossed her head back and laughed hard. She felt so good, so alive for the first time in days.

"You know what they say, practice makes perfect."

They made love again as the light died in the room. Wrapping a blanket around himself, Jake tiptoed into the other room only long enough to grab a block of cheese and crackers to satisfy the grumbling of their bellies. And then they made love again, slow and languorous in the darkness of the night as if the world outside their door didn't exist.

CHAPTER TWELVE

It was cold when Jake woke the next morning. Frost had grown spider web lines on the windowpane, clearly visible between the opening of the curtains. With the bedroom door closed, none of the heat from the other room could filter into the small bedroom. The walls of this drab hotel room were paper-thin and the wind pounding against the outer wall seeped inside and lifted the curtain with every gust.

He burrowed deeply under the blanket, closer to the warmth of Cassie's naked body and the memories of what they'd shared last night.

In her sleep, Cassie responded by curling up until her lovely nakedness was spoon fashion against his body. The bed was way too small for the two of them, but they'd made due.

Jake listened to her rhythmic breathing, tracing the delicate features of her face with his eyes. He liked watching her sleep. The way her lips were slightly parted and moved as if she were talking in her dreams. The way her wild, dark curls fanned out like peacock feathers across her pillow and spilled over her smooth bare shoulders.

And he liked the way she felt in his arms. All woman, soft and warm, seductive and hot. There was something incredibly comforting about lying in bed with a woman and not having the slightest itch to leave. Certainly a first for him, Jake thought with a satisfied sigh.

They'd have to climb out of bed eventually. They couldn't afford to pretend that the world outside didn't exist. It did. And it would come crashing down around them soon enough.

He and Cassie had made love several times during the night and still he couldn't believe how much he wanted her again. He'd always thought he knew what it was like to really

157

make love. But unpleasantness soon followed when the woman he was with wanted more of a relationship after the pleasure of sex had given him a release.

There was a time after the shooting five years ago when he thought he had something to prove. Something that had nothing to do with feelings or emotions or even the act of sex itself. *Sex with a vengeance.* A direct result of the shooting, the precinct psychologist had said. Jake needed to feel alive, needed to prove that although he was shot, he hadn't been killed. Tyler hadn't been killed either. They'd survived.

He couldn't say the same for that lost woman who'd stopped to ask for directions. Debra Cantelli and her unborn child had been the victims of bad circumstances. Being in the wrong place at the wrong time. They were dead and he was alive.

Guilt ate at Jake even though there wasn't a thing he could have done to prevent their deaths. He hadn't known about Debra Cantelli's connection to Angel Fagnelio back then. It had to have been eating at Angel all this time, multiplying over the years, to have had him lie so still during their meetings, waiting for the perfect moment to strike back.

Jake had sat through his share of mandatory sessions with the house shrink, been deemed fit for duty, and went on. Tyler hadn't. He'd left the force and no amount of convincing by anyone could change his mind. For him, life had begun again.

For Jake, there was more guilt, more women, and more unpleasantness until one morning he woke up next to a stranger and just felt numb.

That's when it ended and he finally opened his eyes to his own self-destruction. The worried stares of his parents, Beth's constant pleas to give up law enforcement, the litany of lectures from his sisters hadn't penetrated that thick layer of blame he'd poured around himself.

The feeling of being totally alone after making love to a woman whose name he couldn't even remember had. At that moment he knew it had to stop. And he vowed to stay detached from romantic entanglements to keep himself focused.

He ran his finger across Cassie's brow. *Way to stay detached, Santos.*

But even as he silently admonished himself, he knew that Cassie was different than all the others. There was no unpleasantness now. Only a contentment he'd never shared with another woman. He wanted more of Cassie, more from their relationship than just simple sexual gratification to wash away guilt. He wanted her in his life.

Now he knew with absolute certainty that this was the first time he'd ever truly made love to a woman. And Jake wasn't going to let that go.

Which was part of the problem he dwelled on as he lay there with Cassie tucked protectively against to him. What kind of a life could they possibly have with so much still unresolved? Cassie deserved security and the love of a man who'd be able to give her some semblance of stability.

Angel Fagnelio and Lord only knew who else from the FBI are still out there hunting them down. And because of that fact, she didn't have security.

Jake rolled on his back, propped his free arm behind his head, and blankly stared up at the paneled ceiling above them. He had to get moving. He needed word from Kevin. As much as he wanted to hold Cassie all to his own, they needed resolution. Cassie needed it.

"You're not supposed to have such a serious face the morning after we make love."

Jake peered down into Cassie's dark eyes at the sound of her sleepy voice, breathed in the warm scent of her skin mixed with the lingering scent of sex. Burrowing deeper under the blanket, he pushed away the dark thoughts that were plaguing him.

"Is that so."

She nodded once.

"I didn't realize you'd woken up." He kissed her lips and let himself linger there, to dwell on the memories of their lovemaking.

"You're thinking about Angel Fagnelio again, aren't you?

You only look like that when you're thinking about him."

"I don't want to," he admitted.

"Neither do I, but I've made a decision."

"Oh, you have, have you?" he said, trying to hang on to the lighthearted feeling he'd had before reality crashed in on them.

One look at Cassie and he knew she was serious, too. Draping the blanket across her breasts with one hand and sitting up to face him, she pushed her wildly tangled hair away from her face.

"I've had enough. I'm through running from Angel Fagnelio and whatever he has in store."

"What are you saying?"

"Simply that I'm tired of hiding out like a scared child afraid to be hit. If Angel Fagnelio wants to find me, then I'll make it easy for him."

"No way!" he ground out, fear crashing in on him completely.

She lay back down again, pressing her warm, soft body against his, and tenderly stroked her fingertips across the course hairs on his chest.

"I can't be afraid anymore, Jake. I want to be in control of my life again. But I can't be if I make whoever is responsible for all this madness believe he's won by driving me away. We can't beat them at their game, but we can turn the tables on them."

Jake shook his head. "You can't play with these people at all, Cassie. You saw what happened at Rory's. What happened yesterday at the cabin. You were damn near killed. They won't think twice about wasting whoever or whatever gets in their way."

"I can't go back if Fagnelio isn't in custody. And he won't come out of hiding unless I show myself to him. So I'll just give him what he wants."

"Absolutely not! I refuse to let you use yourself as bait." Jake was sitting up in bed now, forcing the sudden rage and fear down. What the hell was she thinking?

"I don't intend to." Cassie sighed, shaking her head. "Jake, listen to me. When your sister Jenna was attacked by that mugger, it wasn't the money she was fighting for. She didn't give a damn about that. It was just a symbol of something bigger being stolen from inside her. It would have been smarter—safer—for Jenna to just let that thug run off with her purse and all her money. I'm sure she knew that. But she couldn't do it because the cost to her sense of safety was worth so much more.

"That's just how I feel now. Angel Fagnelio is stealing everything I am from me. Everything I've fought so long and hard to get back after Emilio was killed. I can't just hide out and let him have that. I'll fight till the end if I have to, but he's not going to win."

"It's bigger than just Fagnelio. More complicated."

"Maybe so, but we're not getting any closer to figuring out what it is being here. All we're doing is running scared. We need to face him. And as soon as Angel shows his face, you know the rest will follow."

She was right, of course, as much as Jake didn't want to admit it. Still, he couldn't hold back the dread that it would all fall apart for them when they returned.

"I'm not going to put you out on display just to catch Fagnelio," he said, pushing both hands over his disheveled hair.

Cassie reach out and took his hand. "I'm not asking you to."

Shaking his head, Jake chuckled wryly. "Someone from the Bureau is in on this. We can't trust them until we know who that person is."

Cassie let out a heavy sigh and nibbled on her bottom lip. "No, but you trust Kevin."

"He's not FBI."

"But he's on our side. That counts for something."

In Jake's book, it counted for a whole hell of a lot. But as soon as they stepped one boot back into the precinct, that trust would mean squat.

"I believe Kevin is probably the one person in this whole mess we can trust. So we call him, tell him we're coming back.

161

I'll call Maureen and tell her, too. I'm already suspected of leaking my own name for publicity and compromising this case. Whoever is involved from the FBI wouldn't dare try something in front of a group of reporters with cameras—"

Awareness of her plan suddenly dawned on him. "To record their every move."

"Exactly. Once Fagnelio knows I'm back, he'll make some attempt to do his dirty work and be caught."

Jake thought about it a minute. "It might work."

They lay quietly beside each other, two bodies molded together as if they were one being as the morning light crept into the room. He didn't want the light to invade them here. But it would. And when it did, would darkness of another kind steal the light once again?

As much as Jake wanted to hold Cassie in his arms like this forever, keep her safely tucked away in a place where the Angel Fagnelios of the world couldn't harm her, he knew this was no life for them. And the realization that he definitely wanted a life with Cassie was as earth shattering as the danger they'd been forced to face.

He'd never looked beyond the morning light before. But now he was thinking about a long string of sunrises and sunsets that he and Cassie could have together, and a family of their own to go along with it.

Maybe his sisters had been right. Bertie, Carolyn, Beth, Susan, and Jenna had always said all it would take was one special woman to bowl him over, and he'd be a family man.

But even that dream was a long way off. Before he and Cassie could have the kind of life she deserved, they had to go back and face the demon.

"You're an amazingly strong woman, Cassie," he whispered, tenderly stroking his fingers across her forehead. He let his fingers get lost in the silky softness of her wild hair as he bent his head to kiss the tip of her nose.

She smiled up at him and his heart flipped. "Yeah, well, this is all new to me. Tricking the bad guys is CJ's forte, not mine."

Jake chuckled softly, but his admiration for her strength was enough to level him. "You're a lot more like CJ than you realize."

"You think so?"

"What do you think?"

Her face was suddenly serious and she let out a long, slow breath that hinted of regret. "Much as I hate to, I think we need to get out of bed and make some phone calls."

CHAPTER THIRTEEN

Snow fell like crystal confetti from the sky, pasting itself to the windshield of the Jeep. Cassie sat in the front seat and pulled Jake's leather jacket tighter around her body, breathing in the cold, crisp air, and watching as Jake stood in the phone booth. Their nightmare would be over soon. Life would get back to normal. *She couldn't wait.*

Her earlier conviction to beat Angel Fagnelio was wavering. Cassie knew they needed to go back to the city or nothing would be resolved. And she needed resolution, needed to feel her life was on steady ground again, more than anything. Her only fear was the price she and Jake would both pay to get it.

Anything could go wrong. *Everything could.* That was the problem.

Oh, what she wouldn't do to stay buried under the blankets, making love to Jake Santos for the rest of her days. It was a wonderful dream that became a reality last night. He'd been more than she'd expected. Certainly more than she'd ever known or felt.

Pushing the sleeve of the leather jacket up her arm, she ran her bare fingers against the cold glass window, wiping away the condensation building there. Jake was still talking on the phone, rocking back and forth on his feet in an effort to ward off the cold from this morning's drop in temperature. An omen? Cassie didn't want to think so. She glanced down at herself and groaned. She should have at least given him his own coat since he was the one standing outside.

Jake suddenly stood stiffly. From the cold? Nerves? Maybe a little of both. She felt it, too. Her stomach lurched. Something had happened, that much was evident by the harsh look on

Jake's face.

Through the cloudy window, Cassie watched him drop the phone into the cradle and make his way back to the Jeep with long quick strides. A rush of cold air swept into the vehicle when he opened the door.

"How'd it go?"

"I talked Ty. I knew Kevin would call him first to see if I'd called him too. I was counting on it. Kevin contacted Ty about an hour ago with an update."

Jake's expression was grim, his lips drew into a thin line as he buckled his seatbelt.

"What did Tyler say?"

"They have him," Jake said, punching the key into the ignition and firing the engine.

Confused and a little taken aback by Jake's reaction, she asked, "This is good news then. When did they catch him?"

"Sometime last night. Charley set up some kind of sting thinking she could ferret out the mole in the Bureau. Agent Bellows took the bait with Fagnelio by his side. They caught Fagnelio, but Bellows was killed during the raid."

Cassie closed her eyes, a slow breath of air seeping through her lips. So much bloodshed and death.

As the Jeep began to move, she looked over at Jake. "Angel must have found out the person he sent to the cabin hadn't succeeded in killing us."

"Apparently."

Cassie's pulse thrummed strong against her temple. She placed her fingers against the ache to steady it. *Control.* "What kind of raid?"

"At your place."

"My apartment?" She heard the shock in her own voice and took a quick breath to calm down before continuing. "They killed Bellows in my home?"

Jake's expression was sympathetic. "You won't be going back there for a few days anyway and since the crime scene is now secured—"

Goosebumps raised on her arm and quickly raced crawled

all over her body. *He'd come after her in her own home.*

"After sending someone to kill me yesterday, I can't imagine why Fagnelio would think I'd feel safe enough to just go back to my own apartment."

"My thoughts exactly. But it wouldn't be the first time a rat sniffed out a piece of cheese only to get caught in his own trap. Tyler only gave me the basics. He said Kevin would fill me in on the rest when we get back. But the FBI is insisting Bellows set up the explosion at the safe house and tipped off the papers about you being their material witness."

She eyed him skeptically. "And you believe it?"

"They caught him with Fagnelio. He was in the city the night of the shooting at Rory's. He was there at the safe house when it exploded."

She sank against the back of the seat and slipped her seat belt on as if on autopilot. "What if this is all a ruse to get me back to the city?"

Jake shook his head, shifting the Jeep into gear as it accelerated along the road. "This is the real thing."

Once they were out on the road, Jake switched on the wipers, then reached over and grasped Cassie's hand. He squeezed it with just the right amount of pressure to help steady her trembling hand and give her some comfort.

"At least we can feel safe knowing that Fagnelio is behind bars where he belongs," he said easy enough, but something was still turning around in Jake's mind. She heard it in his voice. In what he was saying and what he *wasn't* saying. Cassie glanced at his face, saw the tightness in his jaw and the faint crimp in his brow that remained as he spoke the words.

"So now that they're sure the leak was Agent Bellows and Fagnelio is behind bars, it's all over, right? There's no more threat to my life?" *Please, God, she hoped so.*

Jake gave his answer in the gentle squeeze of her hand. Cassie knew he was trying to comfort her and to some extent, it did. But in the end, she got none of the peace she craved. She swallowed back the bile in her mouth and closed her eyes before snatching her hand from Jake's grasp.

"Don't do that," she said, straightening her posture.

Jake glanced at her, startled. "You don't want me to touch you?"

"Not like that. I don't want you to lie to me."

Jake took his eyes off the road for a fraction of moment to look at her. He cursed under his breath. "Dammit, Cassie. I haven't lied to you yet, have I?"

She shook her head slowly.

"And I never will. Especially about Fagnelio."

"I'm not talking about Fagnelio. He may be behind bars, but there's no guarantee he'll stay there. That is what you're thinking, right? That's what you're afraid of. And even if he does stay in jail, someone might still come after me before the trial."

Jake gripped the wheel tighter. "Charley sent Bellows down to the safe house ahead of us. He'd worked in Virginia for years, knew the layout of safe house and the staff. That's why Charley put him on the team with Agent Radcowski. Bellows could easily have rigged the gas line in the house. Now Bellows is dead and Fagnelio is in custody. I just don't know. It all seems so…neat, too clean to have fallen into place so nicely."

A chill shot up Cassie's spine. "Shooting someone in cold blood in my apartment doesn't sound very neat to me."

"No, it's not."

"But now that Fagnelio is behind bars this will all be over as soon as I testify, right?"

Jake glanced at Cassie and sighed. "I know it's been hard on you."

"Yeah, I want my life back. Don't you? I don't want to have to worry about strange packages coming in the mail or looking over my shoulder when you're not around."

A smile tipped the corners of his mouth and made her pulse quicken. She remembered that smile looking down at her last night as they made love. "You still want me around when all this is over?"

"Yes," she said without hesitation. It felt good to make that affirmation. "But not like this. Not if it means always being afraid."

She turned in her seat and plunged her hands deep into the pocket of the leather jacket. Her heart ached with the emptiness of not having Jake's hand firmly clasping hers. She wanted his comfort, but the sudden weight of leaving the safety of what they'd shared last night left her feeling utterly exposed.

Jake pulled over to the shoulder of the road and parked the Jeep, keeping it idling.

"I'm sorry. I keep forgetting you're not just the normal average citizen who swallows every line that's fed to them."

"Is that what you do to people? You tell them things they want to hear, feed them some fairy tale and take them to bed?"

She'd gone too far and instantly regretted her words. A dark shadow clouded Jake's features, making the lines on his face deepen.

"You really think I made love to you as some way to trick you into believing you weren't in any danger?"

"No," she said, regret filling her. "I don't believe that at all. The fact is, I'm having a hard time believing much of anything lately."

"Cassie, I have to bring you in to testify in front of a grand jury in just two days. Over these next two days, the federal prosecutor is going to hold you and occupy every waking moment of your time to shape your testimony so their case against Angel Fagnelio is ironclad. In the meantime, I'll be sitting back at the station taking it for all it's worth from Captain Russo for not bringing you in sooner. Not to mention how Charley will rip me to shreds and I *still* don't know who to trust."

Jake slammed his palm against the steering wheel and they sat silently for an agonizingly long time. Her fear made her lash out at Jake when she knew damn well this whole situation was eating him up inside the same way it was destroying her.

An eighteen-wheel truck whizzed past them, rocking the Jeep with its momentum and spraying it with a mass of dirt and slush from the road.

"I don't know if the threat is gone," Jake said, staring at the truck as it sped down the road ahead of them. "I don't know if Bellows was working alone, or if there is someone else. With all this upset in Ritchie Trumbella's organization, someone could still be worried about Fagnelio running his mouth. They might just hang him out to dry and rot in a federal prison. There's so much spinning around in my head and so much has happened I don't know what to think.

"The only thing I know for sure is how I feel, Cassie. The idea of bringing you back is eating at me." He reached across the seat and brushed his fingers against her cheek. "I just want to hold you and make love to you again. Not because I'm trying to feed you a line of bull. But because I need it, Cassie. I need to have you close to me. I don't like what we're going back to face. But we have no choice. We're out of time."

"No," she said softly, reaching up and holding his hand to her cheek. "We at least have time for this."

She reached over and wrapped her arms around him. Lacing her fingers behind his neck, she kissed him. He pulled her hard against him, kissing her back with all the raging fear that threatened to eat at every bit of control they had.

"If nothing else, we have time for this," she whispered against his lips.

Jake jammed the car back into gear and punched the gas. Skidding back onto the highway, the Jeep left a spray of mud and gravel in its wake.

They stayed in the motel longer than Cassie knew they should. Daylight was slipping away when they finally headed back on the road toward the city.

Jake held her hand as they drove in silence, the pad of his thumb rubbing against her skin. The rumbling of the tires on the pavement invaded the quiet compartment, chipping into Cassie's thoughts. But she didn't want to think about what was ahead of them.

Along the way Jake periodically reassured her that everything would be okay. It would be—as long as she was with Jake. How could she have come to depend on his strength in such a short period of time?

It had only been a few days since they'd met and this

169

whole nightmare began. They'd come a long way since then. She wasn't just an ordinary citizen that Jake was assigned to protect. And Jake was no ordinary man.

Three years ago, she'd broken her engagement because she couldn't feel anything for her fiancé. Dennis had tried to be patient but in the end, his frustration had him lashing out at her, calling her bitter names that still brought pain in remembrance.

She thought she had loved Dennis, but now she wasn't so sure. She'd genuinely cared for him, but she never felt about Dennis the way she did for Jake. She never melted in his arms with his touch.

Maybe Jake was right. It wasn't that she was all wrong for romance. She just hadn't been with the right man.

The short time they'd been together felt like a lifetime, but the circumstances were unusual. Outside the little world she and Jake had been thrust into, they hardly knew anything about each other.

When this was all over, things would be different. They'd have time. She could only hope that she wouldn't wake up the morning after and find out all these powerful emotions pulling her and Jake together like a magnet were just an illusion.

She couldn't let her fear of the past destroy what could be between her and Jake. Dennis and his bitter names were no longer part of her life. Jake was here and now, and as soon as they got through the trial and Angel Fagnelio was locked away for life, she and Jake would have all the time in the world to discover all there was to know about each other.

It was only a few more days of waiting. If what Jake said was true, the federal prosecutor was not going to let her out of his sight for the next forty-eight hours. She'd go over and over her statement to the police. They'd drill her on how to answer, what to reveal, so that Angel Fagnelio's lawyer didn't stand a chance.

Cassie had been through this before when she testified in her cousin's murder. It would be no different this time. And when it was over, her life would be her own again.

Until then she'd just have to accept the fact that she was

the FBI's one and only witness to place Angel Fagnelio at the scene of the crime. The only one who'd seen him lean out the car window and blast the life out of Rory's and all the people inside. He didn't care who he'd hit. He didn't care that he'd taken another person's life. Just like with the man who sneered at her after killing Emilio's, Cassie would do her part and make sure Angel Fagnelio cared each and every day he sat in prison.

As they drew closer to the city, Cassie noticed the deep lines etched at the corners of Jake's mouth. *Serious and intense.* She knew that well. Kevin claimed Jake was born serious and intense. But Jake was much more. Cassie had seen firsthand the tender side of him when he touched her, the vulnerable side when he spoke of his sisters, right alongside the rough-edged exterior he held out for the rest of the world to see.

She'd seen it all and wanted it, wanted Jake Santos in her life. It was the only thing about this nightmare that was bearable.

* * *

"You've got to be kidding," Jake raged, bolting out of his chair in Russo's office.

Captain Russo waved him back in his seat. "Calm down."

"An accident? That's what you're blaming that inferno on?"

"That's the official word. The FBI hasn't uncovered any evidence that the system was tampered with."

Jake turned to Charley, who was sitting on the edge of the credenza. "We were locked inside. If we hadn't been able to escape from the window we would have blown up with the house. That's no damned accident, Charley."

"Though our investigation is still open, all evidence is leading toward an accident," Charley said coolly.

"How about the evidence I saw with my own damned eyes."

"Unfortunately you weren't around until today to give that bit information to our investigators. It might have helped."

"Someone had to keep your star witness alive."

Kevin had been leaning back, balancing his chair on the

back two legs. He pushed forward and the chair hit the floor with a thud. "He's been a little busy," he said, his witty sarcasm seeming to grate on Charley's nerves.

"So I gathered." She folded her arms across her chest and glared at him in his corner seat. She released a quick sigh. "Write it up in your statement, Santos, and I'll include that information in the final report. If there was any tampering, we'll uncover the evidence eventually. I'm expecting Agent Radcowski in any time now with the preliminary report. I sent him down to Virginia to oversee the investigation. In the meantime, I need to deal with why you decided to take matters into your own hands and flee with the FBI's material witness."

"You handpicked Bellows and sent him down to the safe house."

She was standing now, face to face with Jake. "I've worked with him for three years and have never had any reason to believe he'd betray me. I've trusted him with my life more times than I can count."

"And you trusted him with Cassie's."

"That's right!"

It was at precisely that moment that Agent Radcowski blew into Captain Russo's office with barely a knock on the door. He gave a casual nod to Charley.

"Did I come at a bad time?" he said, taking in the mood of the room.

"No," Charley answered. "Is that the report, David?"

Agent Radcowski nodded and handed it to her. Charley grabbed the report and quickly opened the file.

"Nice of you to show your face, Santos," Radcowski said. "What the hell took you so long?"

With so many people in Russo's office, Radcowski took it upon himself to sit on the edge of the captain's desk.

The glare Russo pierced Radcowski with was foreboding. His eyes crawled from the agent's face, to the toppled over pictures now face down on the desk, back to Radcowski's face. Never once did the intensity of his glare wane.

Radcowski merely smiled.

A few seconds passed and Russo finally said, "Would you mind getting your big carcass off my son's picture?"

Radcowski glanced down at the desk, seemingly aware for the first time of what he'd disrupted, but not of how strongly it affected Captain Russo. He moved slowly and they all waited for him to arrange the pictures back into place.

"Agent Tate tells us you were in charge of the investigation at the safe house. Your boys are talking gas leak. Is that right?" Russo said, cutting to the chase.

Radcowski glanced at Charley.

"One of my men almost died in that explosion," Russo said sharply. "Don't give me the run around."

Charley nodded her head and Radcowski shrugged.

"See for yourself. They found some fragments that might indicate the system had been tampered with. But until they can do further forensics, they can't rule on whether the damage was done before or caused by the explosion."

"They were only in the house a short while. It wasn't long enough to build up enough fumes to cause the kind of explosion that took place. " Charley said.

"The fire investigator thinks the source of the spark was in the system itself."

"In other words, instead of a little explosion, they wanted the big bang," Kevin called out from the corner of the room.

"I'll say," Jake said. "The house went up like a bomb. Someone definitely wanted us very much dead," he added sarcastically. Yet even as he said the words, the totality of what did happen made him shudder.

Radcowski shrugged again. "It would appear that way. I've asked that once the two doors are identified in the rubble, if they didn't burn to ash, they be checked thoroughly."

"And there were no signs of this when your men cleaned house before the guests arrived? Seems to me someone flunked the white glove test," Kevin added.

Radcowski scowled at Kevin before turning his attention to Jake. "That safe house has been quiet for months. It was thoroughly checked, and there wasn't any reason to suspect

173

security had been compromised. Bellows was with Cassie and Jake. But that doesn't mean he didn't have opportunity to tamper with something."

Charley pulled her attention from the report she'd been reading. "Our experts are still sifting through fragments of the rubble. Some traces of suspect chemicals were found. Whatever it was, it'll eventually show itself when the full investigation has been completed." She snapped the folder closed. "Until then, we have other pressing matters to deal with."

"Such as?" the captain asked.

"The security of our witness."

Russo sighed. "She's in protective custody until the grand jury trial. There isn't much more that can be done until then."

"We need to put things in place for after the grand jury trial. This case has become too high profile and unfortunately, so has our witness."

Jake knew where this was going. "We've already had a taste of what protective custody is to the Bureau. Cassie wants her life back."

Charley shook her head. "Yeah, well, I'd love to see the Beatles do a reunion concert but that's not going to happen in this lifetime."

"She wants her life back, Charley," he repeated.

After a short pause Charley said, "I know that. But it's not going to happen and deep down, if you listen to your gut instinct, you know it, too. Don't you, Jake?"

She was right. It had nagged at him ever since the phone call with Tyler. Initial relief quickly changed to dread. He knew Cassie had sensed it, even though he'd tried his damnedest to keep his feelings to himself.

"She's not getting lost, Charley."

"You can't watch her 24/7."

"You said Bellows was working with Fagnelio."

"Unfortunately, he was."

"And Fagnelio's not talking."

"There's no guarantee it will stay that way."

Jake's voice rose above Charley's. "Just tell me what you're afraid of."

Her voice matched his. "You know damn well what I'm afraid of. Someone from Ritchie Trumbella's family might have something to prove. It's a very volatile time with Ritchie out of the picture. It's a bad break, but I don't think Cassie can go back to the life she had. Ever."

"Cassie's no threat to Ritchie Trumbella's organization. Only Fagnelio is, and you have him in custody."

Kevin's voice broke into the tension between Jake and Charley. "You're going to lose Cassie in the system?" Kevin blurted out.

Charley rolled her eyes. "I'm not the heartless bitch you both think I am. I'm sorry for what Cassie has to go through. But this situation is out of control."

"I'll protect her," Jake said resolutely.

"Listen to yourself, Jake." Russo abruptly stood and leaned his weight on his fists, now firmly planted on the coffee stains and doodles of his desk blotter. His face wore a haggard expression filled with understanding. "No one man can do it all. God knows we try, but as soon as we turn our back for one second, you have dirtbags like Fagnelio invading your home with drugs and God knows what else."

Charley let out a slow breath and unfolded her arms in front of her. "Tell me, Jake, just how far are you willing to go for this woman?"

It grated on Jake more than he could think how Charley could refer to a woman as special as Cassie as "this woman."

When he didn't answer right away, Charley continued. "Say you give up your job here and guard her at a safe house for six months, a year. Then what?"

Jake cast her a hard look. "I gave her my word. To some people that still means something."

Charley ignored his jibe. "I understand you have a big family. Very close-knit. Are you willing to give them up to be with Cassie no matter how this turns out?"

"What they hell does that have to do with anything?" he charged.

At the same time, Charley's voice rose above his. "Because that is what this is going to take."

"Bellows didn't leak Cassie's name to the papers, Jake," Kevin said, cutting into his awareness.

Jake swung around to look at his partner, looked directly into his eyes and knew Kevin believed what he'd said was true. His gut bunched until he thought he'd keel over.

"What are you talking about? Of course it was Bellows." *It had to be Bellows.*

Kevin shook his head.

Jake's mind raced to thoughts of Cassie, trapped in that hotel room swarming with federal agents and prosecutors drilling her endlessly. He knew her well enough to know she was looking for the light at the end of the tunnel, the light where she'd be free to come and go as she chose, without worry that someone was waiting behind every doorway. That would get her through the next few days. Without that light, she'd crumbled and fade to dust.

"She can't live in a hole forever. It'll kill her."

"No, she can't," Charley said in a tone that Jake thought held genuine sympathy. It was more than he'd ever expected from Charlotte Tate. "There are other ways."

He gave a hard laugh that held no humor. "Not witness protection."

"Unfortunately, I think it may need to be a bit more than just witness protection. Whether Cassie wants it or not, this case is about to make her a household name. And it has nothing to do with her writing career. The publicity her publishing company could cash in on with the press will send her sales skyrocketing. I'm not sure there's any place she could hide that people won't recognize Cassie Lang's face or know her name. She may have to leave the country. And even then she'll be recognized. But it's the only way to ensure she won't be reached."

"No, it would kill her."

"I can't see it any other way."

Russo sat back down hard, his chair groaning and

squeaking under the weight. "I'm afraid I have to agree, Jake. This has gotten too far out of hand. Until this is over—"

"Bellows was the mole in the Bureau. You caught him last night. He must have leaked Cassie's name to the media so that—"

"He wasn't the leak, Jake," Russo said, his voice grave.

"He had to be," Jake insisted. *Had to be?* Jake wondered, waging war with himself. To think anything else would mean only one thing—Cassie would be gone.

"Bellows requested a transfer up to the New York office a little over a year ago," Radcowski said. "That's about the time we figured the bond fraud scheme started. He was in the city the night of the shooting."

Charley continued. "We were about to bust Trumbella's organization wide open. During our investigation, we were able to plant an agent deep undercover, who then fed us information about the organization and the bond fraud deal. They'd been working with a Colombian company called The Aztec Corporation. The agent was able to tell us that he suspected a mole in the Bureau was working closely with Ritchie to help him stay one step ahead of us."

Radcowski plucked the file folder Charley had dropped on Russo's desk. "Since Bellows walked right into Charley's sting with Fagnelio by his side, it pretty much makes him number one suspect. Unfortunately, he's dead and we can't ask him. But he never leaked Ms. Alvarez's name to the media."

"What makes you so sure?"

Charley cleared her throat and looked at Jake directly. "Because Agent Bellows had an ironclad alibi the night of the shooting at Rory's. He was with me. The entire night."

The air in the room was thick, almost enough to choke every bit of breath from Jake's lungs.

Dammit, it was exactly what he'd dreaded. *Too neat.* There was someone else out there.

Jake's jaw tightened. "Where are you taking Cassie?"

Charley shook her head. "That information is not being released."

"And that's it? You're just going to take her away until Fagnelio decides to roll?"

"On the contrary, Detective," Charley said as she nodded to Agent Radcowski. "The more evidence we can gather against the Trumbella clan and Angel Fagnelio the less pressure will be on Cassie. I've asked John to work with me on special assignment. I'm also asking you."

Frowning, he asked. "Why me?"

"I need people on my team I can trust." Charley gave a dry laugh. "These days they've become few and far between. But the way I see it, you have a vested interest in finding out the truth. If you feel the way I think you do about Cassie, then I'm betting you're my best shot at digging up the evidence on Fagnelio. If you do, we can keep Cassie from having to testify, take the heat off her with Trumbella's organization. It's the only chance Cassie has at getting her life back. Are you willing to work on my team?"

"Fagnelio was after me too because of my involvement in his sister's death five years ago."

"I know that. I think we can use that to our advantage."

Jake tossed the idea around in his head a minute. He couldn't do a damned thing to help Cassie if he was locked up with her for the next who-knows-how-many months. If he was out on the street, now that was a different story.

But it could take months if not years to find the kind of information needed to secure a conviction without Cassie's testimony. They didn't have years. *Someone else was out there.*

"Who shot Bellows, Charley?" he asked.

Kevin ran his hand over his face. "Jeez, Jake does it really matter?"

"Was it you?" he asked his partner.

Kevin turned his eyes toward the floor. *Not a good sign.*

"Are you willing to be part of this team or not, Jake? I need to know," Charley pressed.

"Answer the damned question!"

"You're either in or out?"

"Who shot him, Charley?"

"I did!"

Jake stared at Charley for a long moment, saw the tears that welled up in her eyes and the tightness in her stand as she held herself together. She kept her composure and he had to admit he admired that about her.

He once believed there was nothing but ice flowing through Charlotte Tate's veins. She was woman with an agenda who didn't care who she stepped on to get where she was going. Looking at her now...

No one broke the silence.

"I'm in," Jake finally said.

And he walked out the door.

CHAPTER FOURTEEN

I'm getting a cat, Maureen, Cassie typed on her brand spankin' new laptop, courtesy of the FBI. Or rather, FBI Agent Charlotte Tate. Cassie had the feeling it was more of a personal gift than one made by the United States government. The new hairstyle too. Charlotte had taken one look at the chunk of hair missing from the back of Cassie's head and an hour later a hair stylist was being frisked at the hotel room door.

Both gifts were very much appreciated. Especially the laptop. Cassie felt more at home with her fingers clicking on a keyboard while she stared at a computer screen than she did most anywhere else. Especially here in the hotel room with a half dozen chattering agents just outside her bedroom door.

And I'm getting real houseplants, Cassie continued typing. *None of those plastic things. I'm going to learn how to take care of something real and live for once in my life. Something that will miss me if I'm gone. If this mess has taught me anything it's that I could leave for six whole months and no one would be the wiser. I'm moving out of the city, too, getting a cat, and maybe a dog. Well, maybe I won't be that ambitious just yet. I'll start with a cat. They can pretty much take care of themselves, right? All I have to do is feed it and snuggle with it once in a while and it will be happy. I can already hear you snickering about* that *sounding just like a man.*

Cassie's fingers paused on the keyboard as she re-read what she'd just written. She had that, too, she thought wickedly, thinking about Jake. But she wouldn't elaborate further on her relationship with Jake until she had a chance to introduce them face to face.

She continued typing. *Yeah, I'll stick with the cat and live plants for now. If all goes well tomorrow, you'll be seeing me in a few days. I can't wait. I'll fill you in on the scoop then.*

Cassie signed her email and punched the send button.

She'd been strictly advised not to make any calls until after tomorrow's trial. But what harm could a simple email from her own on-line account do? Especially since Maureen probably wouldn't get around to reading it until tomorrow anyway. By that time the trial would be over and it wouldn't matter.

Despite the suggestion that she should just lay low, she'd given Maureen the message to call her parents and let them know she was okay. Surely by now they'd know the danger she'd been in and have seen all the news coverage of the shooting at her apartment. They must be worried sick, and rightly so.

As much as Cassie knew she was being a coward by having Maureen make the call, she couldn't help it. With all that had gone on, she couldn't deal with her father's disapproval. He wouldn't have to say anything, but Emilio's death and the subsequent trial would hang between them again. Old memories would invade that quiet security they'd all fought so hard for.

She couldn't think of that now. Once she testified and Fagnelio was put behind bars for good, it would all be over and she could get back to her life. She'd worry about mending fences with her father then.

After folding down the laptop screen, Cassie stretched to pull the stiffness out of her muscles. For the first time in the last few days, she breathed a sigh of relief and couldn't help but smile. A real honest-to-goodness, feel-it-from-your-toes-to-your-hairline smile. *Normalcy.* Who'd ever have thought something as simple as sending an email to her editor would make her feel so happy, so *grounded.*

She'd been holed up in one of the most luxurious hotel rooms just outside the city, been fed wonderful food by the best chef and she didn't give a damn. All she wanted was to go home to her own apartment and curl up on her sofa with Jake.

Jake. She hadn't seen him since the moment they'd returned. One step into the station and all hell broke loose. It was just as Jake had warned. The federal prosecutor, Aaron Savage, immediately whisked her away to seclusion. They'd gone over the case countless times. While she sat in a chair in the middle of the room, she repeated her testimony, giving in detail what she'd seen the night of the shooting at Rory's.

Both the prosecutor and his assistant took turns pitching questions of all kinds at her, to see if she would trip up. Each time her testimony never wavered. They seemed pleased both with that and with their chances of convincing the judge there was enough solid evidence to warrant bringing Angel Fagnelio to trial for the multiple murders.

Everyone was happy.

Except her.

Cassie wanted to see Jake. She wanted to be home. And since she couldn't have that, she wanted Jake. She knew he'd be buried in a mountain of paperwork. She also knew by the brash comments the new agents in charge of guarding her let slip, that neither Captain Russo nor Agent Tate held Jake high on their list of favorite people right now.

When Jake walked through the door some hours later, she launched herself into his arms, relief filling her.

"What took you so long?"

He didn't say a word for a minute. Charley Tate had followed him into the hotel room and gave him a strong look. Although she'd been nice enough on the few times Cassie had to deal with her, it was obvious there was no love lost between her and Jake. Obviously, something had gone on between them to draw such a hard line.

She pulled him into the bedroom of her suite, not caring that the other agents were still in the main suite. The queen-sized bed was made and what few clothes she'd been able to get access to were folded neatly and piled on top of the dresser. She absolutely refused to put them in the drawers. She wasn't staying here any longer than she had to so there was no need to settle in.

As Jake glanced at the bed, a frown crinkled his brow.

"You have something on your mind, Detective?" she teased, snaking her arms beneath his leather jacket. The familiar scent of leather and man welcomed her. Oh, what she wouldn't do to take a tumble on that big bed with Jake after the day she'd had.

He shrugged lazily. "More than you know."

Smiling up at him, she said, "I can think of a good way to ease a little tension."

As he enfolded her in his arms, Cassie couldn't help but revel in how good he felt. It had been two long days, too long to do without something she'd all but thought would never exist in her life.

"Tomorrow is a big day," he said, his voice filled with regret. "It'll be exhausting."

"I know."

"If we go anywhere near that bed you know we won't get any sleep tonight."

"You're probably right. But the good news is tomorrow it will all be over. I suppose I can survive one more night without being in your arms."

Still smiling, she leaned against the wall of his solid chest, found the comfort she craved there. Jake hesitated just a fraction of a second before tightening his hold. It was just enough for Cassie to notice her smile hadn't had the effect it usually had on him.

Finally, after too long a time, Jake kissed her deeply, then pulled her into a wing chair in the corner of the room so she sat sideways in his lap. He felt so right. Being in his arms made sense out of so many things tangling her sanity.

He'd asked her if she still wanted him in her life when this whole mess was over. And she did. After years of holding her emotions in a box, it felt good to finally free them. And with Jake she could. They just had one more day to get through.

Cassie burrowed her face into the crook of Jake's neck and inhaled deeply. He smelled fresh and clean, his skin smooth, as if he'd just showered and shaved before he'd come over to see her.

"Did you get everything worked out at the station?" she whispered.

"Most everything. I have to meet with Charley and Kevin a little later to go over some things."

"What things?"

"Nothing you need to concern yourself with now."

Laughter from the other room broke through the closed door, invading their quiet place. Cassie recognized Agent Tate's voice and wondered if she and Jake planned to leave together. She didn't want to feel insecure about it, but she realized with certainty that she did.

Jake's arms tightened around her and she didn't want to delve into what that meant. He had gone *somewhere*.

It was amazing. He was holding her close enough for her to hear his heartbeat, smell his skin and drink in his warmth. He was here, but he'd gone someplace else in his mind.

"What's with you and Agent Tate?" she finally asked, cursing herself silently for doing it.

"Me and Charley?"

Her cheeks flamed and she pulled away from his arms. "There's been a lot of talk, not that I want to listen."

Jake stared directly at her, his gaze so intense she had to look away.

"A lot has happened. There's going to be a lot of talk until the whole truth comes out, Cassie."

"I don't mean about the case."

Finally, she lifted her eyes to meet his, saw the crease form in a knot in the center of his forehead. Serious and intense. She'd smile at how utterly adorable he looked if she didn't feel so insecure.

"Charlotte is a very beautiful woman...and I know she was seriously involved with a police officer a few years ago—"

Awareness seemed to take hold of Jake and he suddenly flashed one of those make-your-knees-weak smiles of his. Cassie's cheeks burned so strong it made her want to sink through the floor.

"And you think it was me?"

Cassie lifted herself from his lap, but Jake immediately reeled her back in, crushing her against him. She needed that comfort. She didn't know if this insecurity was because of the trial or idle chatter from agents who had too much time on their hands. Or something more.

She was being ridiculous. Jake was a man of integrity. What had happened in Jake's life before they'd come together didn't matter. It didn't change what was happening between them now.

"I'm sorry I mentioned it. It's none of my business."

"I'm making it your business," he said, his face still filled with a tinge of amusement.

Damn, he actually liked that she was jealous!

Jake tilted her chin up so she was forced to look at him. "But it wasn't me. It was Tyler."

A sudden feeling of giddy relief rushed through her. *It had to be insanity.*

"I don't understand why you and Charlotte are always at each other's throats then."

"Too much bad blood, I guess."

"I can understand that of Tyler, if they were lovers and it didn't work out."

"It was more than that. Tyler was...crazy in love with Charley. I'd never seen anything like it before."

"What happened?"

"Tyler had an informant who had a lot of information on a case the FBI was working on. Their investigation had stalled and since this informant only trusted Ty, they needed him to get the information they wanted. He and Charley hit it off from the word go."

Jake's face changed, became vacant and haunted. The hard lines around the corners of his mouth deepened. But Cassie didn't press him further. She waited until he was ready to come back from wherever he'd gone.

"There was going to be a major shipment of cocaine. Ty had the information, passed it on to the FBI. A bust this big is what makes careers. It all could have been Tyler's for the asking for his part."

"But he quit."

"Yeah, he quit," Jake said tightly. "After being ambushed in an alley on the opposite side of town, he spent a month in the hospital. Charley, on the other hand, took all the glory of the bust."

"But I thought they were working together."

"They were, but at the last minute, she sent him on a wild goose chase. Told him his informant called and needed to see him immediately. I was his partner so we both went."

"Tyler's informant shot him?"

Jake shook his head, a flash of bitterness shadowing his features. "It was a lie. Tyler's informant *had* called. But to tell him they'd moved up the shipment two days early and to a new location because they suspected the raid. Charley took the call and never told Tyler."

"So when you got to the place you thought you were supposed to meet his informant—"

"He never showed, of course. We waited around until…"

Jake's whole body tensed as he spoke, as if he was having a hard time reliving what had happened. Cassie understood that feeling too well.

"She was in the wrong place at the wrong time. We'd been waiting for over a half hour when we figured maybe we got it wrong. It was late. We radioed back to the station that it was a no show. That's when we found out the FBI had raided the cocaine shipment. Tyler was furious."

"I can't say I blame him."

Jake's laugh was harsh and he shook his head. "It was a lousy time to be lost in the dark, but there was this woman, Debra Cantelli, who'd pulled up beside us asking for directions as we were ready to leave. Said she got lost trying to find her Lamaze class. I remember thinking at the time she looked just like my sister, Beth, who was also pregnant. Out of nowhere a bunch of punks decided to use the alley as a shooting gallery."

Cassie gasped. "You were shot?"

"I took a few bullets to the vest. Both Tyler and I were wearing Kevlar. Ty was a stickler for it when we were out on the street. He was a damned good cop. I learned a lot from him."

"Were you both hurt?"

Jake shrugged. "All things considered, I fared pretty well. The vest took the bullets but the impact broke two ribs, which pierced my lung, causing it to collapse. I couldn't breathe. I remember lying on the ground..."

Jake closed his eyes tight. He hadn't allowed himself to visit those dark memories in a long time. So much destruction happened in those short seconds. He opened his eyes again in the dim hotel room and could still see Tyler bleeding on the ground, still hear the last gasp come from Debra Cantelli, who's life, along with that of her unborn child, had ended in that moment.

Of course, Jake hadn't learned her name until much later. Not until he was in intensive care and heard her husband in the next room saying good-bye to his wife. One minute you're racing from a board meeting that had gone too late, the next you're holding your dead wife and child for the last time.

"Debra Cantelli was Angel Fagnelio's half-sister."

Cassie's eyes widened in surprise.

"I didn't know about the connection between them until just the other day. My guess is Angel knew all along when I was undercover and one of those bullets he blew into Rory's was meant for me."

Jake drew in a breath, good and deep, like he couldn't do back then, as if to remind himself once again that he was alive. He'd survived.

He glanced down at Cassie's ghostly face, saw the same raw fear he'd seen the night of the shooting at Rory's.

"Hey, I'm here," he said, giving her a gentle squeeze. "I was the lucky one. One of the bullets that hit Ty skimmed his vest and hit a major artery. Kevin had just heard us radio in when a call came in about shots fired at our location. He was in the vicinity. When he got there, he knew there was nothing anyone could do for Debra Cantelli, although I don't think Angel sees it quite like that. Kevin did save Tyler though. If Kevin hadn't gotten there, Ty would have bled to death."

"Like Emilio," she whispered.

Jake cursed under his breath. "God, Cassie, I'm sorry."

She swallowed hard and he realized she was trembling. "It's okay."

"It's not okay. I didn't mean to have you relive what you went through with your cousin. It's bad enough you've had to do that all day today and then again tomorrow."

"It'll all be over soon," she said, settling back against his chest.

He should tell her. Everything in him screamed that he should tell her the truth. Cassie deserved to hear the truth. She deserved to hear it from him. But he couldn't. After all she'd been through, how could she make it through tomorrow knowing her life was about to change forever? How could he take one night of peace away from her? From them?

And what if he did tell her? She could always refuse to testify. Having her life back was pretty strong motivation not to. And then she'd be out on her own and no matter how hard he tried, he couldn't protect her.

"Jake?"

"Hmm?"

"Are you afraid? I mean of seeing Angel Fagnelio face to face."

"No. He's exactly where he should be, behind bars. He can't hurt anyone else now."

And that's where he was going to stay. *He definitely couldn't tell Cassie tonight,* Jake decided.

Cassie played with the collar of his shirt. The gravity of tomorrow's events would crash down on them sooner or later. But Jake didn't really want to think about it now, didn't want Cassie to have to carry that burden. Not when she was in his arms like this, where he knew he could keep her safe. Tomorrow was a different story.

After a moment, she said, "Did you ever think that maybe Charlotte lied because she was afraid if Tyler went to that raid he'd be killed?"

"She was the one who sent him—"

"I know. She sent him to that alley. But what happened there was just the crazy randomness of life. What were the odds that something like that could happen, huh? A million to one?"

Jake didn't want to think about it. Not because it wasn't a

possibility, but because he'd been second guessing himself where Charlotte Tate was concerned ever since their meeting at the station earlier.

She'd shot and killed her own lover. Good Lord, that had to mess up your head in ways he didn't want to explore. He squeezed Cassie tighter and felt his heartbeat race, just thinking about what had to be going through Charley's mind when she pulled that trigger.

Charlotte Tate afraid? Of course, there was a very distinct possibility that Jake had been wrong all these years about Charley's motives for lying to them. His anger made him assume it was greed on her part. But maybe it had been as Cassie suggested. None of them were immune to fear.

He thought about those long weeks of recovery after the shooting. Charley had been by Tyler's side while he lay unconscious in a hospital bed. Jake was too angry to see anything other than what he'd wanted to see. He had his own demons to fight. Maybe he'd been unfair.

Maybe not. Charley had been involved with John Bellows and *he* had wanted Cassie dead. That wasn't something Jake was likely to forget. Had Charley had some knowledge that Bellows was working with Fagnelio? They only had her word that she'd been with John Bellows the night of the shooting at Rory's.

Jake just didn't know. All he knew was that sticking close to Charlotte Tate and her cohorts was the best chance he had to help Cassie. Even if it meant he had to leave her for a while.

He stayed just long enough for Cassie to fall asleep. In those quiet moments just before sleep claimed her, she asked if everything was going to be all right. As if she knew the truth.

As Jake closed her bedroom door, prepared to meet with Kevin and Charley, guilt tore at his soul. He'd done the one thing he had sworn he'd never do to her. He'd lied.

CHAPTER FIFTEEN

Getting out of bed proved surprisingly easy given how little sleep Cassie managed to seize. She'd woken several times in the darkness, caught between fatigue and the dark thoughts invading her mind. Nightmares of gunfire, of running, and of Emilio.

She'd reached across the bed for something and realized all too quickly it was Jake she was searching for. But Jake wasn't here with her in the hotel. It amazed her how much she'd come to depend on his strength these last few days.

She remembered these dreams well. She'd had them for months after Emilio's death, so much that she'd needed sleeping pills to get her through the night. She'd gone through that nightmare alone. Now new dreams intermingled with old ones. But this time, she wasn't completely alone. She had Jake. At least she had that comfort.

The sooner the trial was over, the sooner life for both of them would get back to normal. Cassie was banking on it.

Jake arrived at the hotel a little while after she'd showered and dressed. U.S. marshals were lavishing great attention on the breakfast ordered up from the hotel kitchen. The thought of eggs sitting in her stomach all morning was revolting. Instead of getting her fill, she sat across from Jake in silence and picked at her toast. She welcomed the silence from the agents as well.

The plan was that Jake and Kevin would escort her to the courthouse in an unmarked car, something less conspicuous than arriving with an entourage of agents and U.S. marshals for the press to feed on. Agents Tate and Radcowski would be in a decoy car in front of them to throw off the press.

When it was finally time to go, they stepped out the back door of the hotel into a heavy downpour. A flood of memories washed over her as the rain fell hard, pelting the roof of Kevin's sport utility truck in an ominous cadence.

Jake sat in the back seat next to her and squeezed her hand. She jumped at his touch as the door slammed shut.

Keeping his hand protectively over hers, he said, "It's just rain."

She nodded and leaned into him, needing his warmth and strength. "It was raining during Emilio's trial, too. Ironic, huh?"

Jake answered in concern by letting go of her hand and wrapping his arm around her instead. Compassion filled his smoky blue eyes and made her heart squeeze. With his lips on her forehead, he whispered, "I've missed you."

Unshed tears clung to her eyelashes as she gazed up at him. "Me, too."

"The trial shouldn't take too long."

They approached the Federal Courthouse and as they'd suspected, the torrential downpour hadn't deterred any of the reporters hungry to get their story. Camera crews were lined along the sidewalk in front, waiting for "the news" to arrive. Scaffolding and news vans littered downtown Main Street. The torrent of people and the decreased visibility caused by the rain would make it hard to spot anyone...

Anyone who was still out to kill her?

Cassie had tried not to think about that being a possibility, but it had always been *there*. She clenched her fists and tried to breathe evenly. Jake was by her side. She had a fleet of FBI agents surrounding the building and strategically located across the street. Nothing was going to happen.

But even as Cassie told herself that, she wondered what would happen if there was still danger lurking about. In the past week Jake had used his body to shield her. Would he do it again? If bullets started flying, would he put his life in danger to save hers?

She snaked her arm under his jacket and squeezed. Her heart plummeted. *No Kevlar vest.*

She couldn't deal with losing Jake. Not now. Not ever. What was he thinking not wearing any protective clothing?

Jake leaned forward to talk to Kevin over the sound of the rain on the roof. "When Radcowski stops the car out front, they're going to wait a few minutes before opening the door. As soon as they stop, take us around back," he said.

"They always take prisoners in through the back, don't they?" Cassie asked, flitting a glance to Kevin's reflection in the rear view mirror and then to Jake.

Kevin's face peered at her from the tiny glass. "We're never going to get you through this crowd, Cassie."

Jake sat back next to her. "You're not even going to see Fagnelio. If the wagon's there, then we know he's inside already. There's nothing to be afraid of."

Cassie nodded, turning in her seat to watch the throng of reporters engulf the car that Agents Tate and Radcowski were driving. The tinted windows of the car and the moisture on the window made it impossible for anyone to see inside.

"You're the boss," she said, chuckling nervously as she turned back in her seat.

Jake gave a slight chuckle. "Since when?"

The SUV rolled to a stop as close to the back door of the courthouse as Kevin could maneuver. Almost immediately, Kevin bolted into the rain and ran to the side door to talk to who Cassie perceived to be another FBI agent. As he jogged back to the truck, he popped open a black umbrella.

Jake shoved open the door. Bile rose up strong from Cassie's stomach, threatening to choke her. Brushing her fingers across her cheek, she wondered if her skin looked as pale and clammy as she felt. As Jake stepped out into the rain, she clutched her stomach, hoping to God she wouldn't get violently sick right there in the car.

From where she was sitting, Cassie could see the paddy wagon parked alongside the truck. The doors were closed.

Jake reached a hand inside to help her out of the car.

"You ready for this?"

"About as ready as I'll ever be," Cassie said.

She stepped out into the rain.

The trial went off without a hitch, much to Jake's relief. The judge denied all motions for bail and set the date for the criminal trial to be held in six months.

Six whole months being separated from Cassie. He'd have to tell her the truth.

Cassie had only been in his life a short time, but the thought of living without her for six whole months was unthinkable. He couldn't figure out how she'd done it, but she'd gotten under his skin. And it wasn't likely that was going to change. Yeah, Jake knew the moment he saw her all decked out in that slinky red spandex dress and that ridiculous makeup, Cassie had stolen his heart. He'd tried to keep himself detached. And he'd failed. Now he knew with absolute certainty that he was in love with Cassie Alvarez and all her aliases. There was no going back.

She was Cassie Alvarez, the tender, innocent woman who longed to take control of her life. Cassie Lang, the infamous crime novelist with a wild imagination. And she was CJ Carmen, no matter how much she didn't believe it. Steam, sass and innocence all rolled up to make one hell of a woman. And he was helplessly in love with every inch of her.

They convened in a conference room at the courthouse soon after the motion for trial. Cassie was sitting next to the federal prosecutor, Aaron Savage. A look of pure relief smoothed the worried creases he'd seen on her face earlier. He was glad for the reprieve. But he knew it wouldn't last.

Charley came up behind Jake as he stood in the doorway. She pulled him back into the corridor by the arm.

"I have to tell her," Jake said.

"It might be easier if I do it," she said sympathetically.

His chuckle was wry. "It's not going to be easy any way she gets it."

Charley shrugged. "At least she'll hate me instead of you."

"That's awfully big of you."

"Hey, I do my best to puff out as big as you boys."

Jake strode into the conference room with Charley following behind.

Agents filed out of the conference room as he approached Cassie. "Could I have a moment with her?" he asked Aaron Savage. The prosecutor ignored Jake.

Charley tapped her foot on the tile floor, cutting into his silence as they waited for a response.

"Maybe you want to go get a soda or something, Savage?" Kevin ground out from the doorway. "We could all go over the details of the transfer."

"You'll be filled in with whatever you need to know when the time comes, Detective Gordon. As for you," Aaron said pointedly to Jake. "What makes you think I'm going to let you be alone with my witness after the stunt you pulled?"

"Enough already," Charley said. "We have a few minutes before we have to leave. I suggest we put it to good use."

"What's going on here?" Cassie asked, her expression one of pure bewilderment. "What transfer are you talking about?"

Cassie's questioning eyes darted back and forth from the prosecutor to Jake, then to Kevin, to Charley and then back to Jake. Kevin turned his head and looked out to the hall. Jake couldn't do that. He *wouldn't* do that to Cassie.

"For cripes sake, Savage," Charley said. "We have about fifty police officers and federal agents roaming this hallway alone. I'll stick one or ten of them at the door. Trust me, he's not going to fly with her anywhere without us taking notice."

Jake smiled dryly at the burly man. "I promise to behave myself."

"Don't smart mouth me, Santos. You're lucky to even be here at all." Savage snapped his briefcase closed and flipped his wrist to check his watch. "No more than two minutes. I don't want Ms. Alvarez hanging around the courthouse any longer than she has to. And the door stays open with you and Gordon guarding it." He glanced sharply at Kevin. "And just so you don't get it in your head to try anything *heroic*, I'll be watching *you*. Two minutes." Without another glance, he strode heavy-footed from the room.

Kevin leaned against the doorjamb with his back to Jake and Cassie, his arms knotted across his chest. It didn't afford them much privacy, but it was the best they had at the moment.

"Guess I'm the last one to know about the party. Mind filling me in on the details?" Cassie said the words lightly, but even the slight lilt in her voice didn't mask the fear that had tumbled back. "Jake? What's going on?"

There was no easy way to do it. So Jake didn't even bother to try. Cassie was familiar with how the system worked. So was he. But even in knowing it, sometimes things fell apart. Like now. And there was nothing either of them could do to change the inevitable.

Jake did the only thing he *could* do. He pulled Cassie's small body into his arms and held her for a long, lingering moment, trying to breathe in the fragrant scent of her shampoo and the smell that was uniquely her. She was soft and warm and belonged there in his arms. A piece of himself he didn't even know he was missing.

He closed his eyes, and drank her in. Every detail flowed through his mind and his senses. He had to remember this feeling. It was all he had until this nightmare was over.

"You're a material witness," he finally said in a voice that sounded far away to his ears. "They want you to go with them, Cassie."

Even in his arms, Jake felt Cassie sway. He held her tighter.

"But I testified. I thought this was over."

"Charley thinks otherwise. She wants you in protective custody. She's afraid of repercussions."

"Fagnelio is behind bars. He's in jail!" Cassie insisted.

"We still don't know who leaked your name to the press, Cassie. Until we know who it was—"

"You said it was Agent Bellows."

"I was wrong."

She let the words sink in. Jake could see her turning something over in her mind as he peered into her sable eyes.

Tears brimmed the corners of her eyes, but she pushed out her chin and held them back. A trooper. It was what he loved about her.

"Did you know about this last night?"

On some level, Jake had expected Cassie to ask that question. But hearing it from her lips, he realized he hadn't been prepared for the depth of betrayal behind the words.

"Yes."

She nodded.

"You won't be coming with me then."

It was a conclusion, not a question, he noticed with dread. Whatever feelings of deception she had, she hid them well. It didn't relieve him from feeling like a son-of-a-bitch for not telling her the truth sooner.

He cupped her face with both his hands and kissed her. Her lips were just as soft as he remembered and just as sweet. "I want to. Believe me when I say that."

She pulled from his grasp, leaving him cold. From the vacant look on her face, Jake knew she didn't believe him.

"The FBI thinks Fagnelio is going to talk to save himself. Maybe cop a deal to give information about the breach within the FBI. They don't take kindly to treason within their own organization. If that happens—"

"Then whoever leaked my name to the papers will want me dead to prevent Fagnelio the trouble of saving his own hide," she said evenly. Jake knew that inside she was anything but.

"Exactly. But there is a lot of turmoil in Trumbella's organization—"

"So even if Fagnelio doesn't talk, there'll always be the threat that he will one day reveal information about their organization that may lead to an indictment."

His eyebrows furrowed into a tight knot. She was too...calm. "Yes, that's right."

She laughed cynically. "Don't look so surprised, Jake. I told you when we first met that I research my books thoroughly. I know how this system works. I just never dreamed one day I'd be living the nightmare I created in my own novels."

The room seemed enormous as she stepped away from him. Moving toward the huge conference table, she picked up a piece of paper and then calmly placed it back down on the polished surface without glancing at him. Without showing any emotion at all.

"Any way you look at it I'm the final piece of a series of ugly puzzles. Eliminating me is the one thing that will keep peace in Trumbella's clan and keep the dirty secrets of a rogue FBI agent quiet. I'm never going to get my life back, am I, Jake?"

Her sultry dark eyes lifted to meet his. He caught the slight tremble of her full lips.

"Cassie, someone needs to uncover enough information about Trumbella's organization to keep you from having to testify. That's the only way the heat will be taken off you."

"Answer me," she said with a small laugh that hinted of her inner hysteria.

"Maybe not," he said quietly.

"And you knew that all along?"

He cleared his throat and looked directly at her. "I knew as soon as I heard Bellows was killed that something wasn't right."

He lifted his arms and stepped toward Cassie, but she abruptly pushed back.

"No, Jake. It's okay."

He cursed loudly, didn't care who was there to hear. "Cassie, I'm sorry—"

"It's okay," she insisted. "You did what you had to do. You went one step further and even managed to do what the FBI couldn't do themselves. You saved my life."

"You saved mine," he reminded her quietly.

Her eyes drifted to his and she cocked her head to one side, offering him a weak smile.

"Then I guess we're even. No strings for either of us."

"What the hell is that supposed to mean?"

She caught her bottom lip between her teeth for a moment before speaking. "I'm giving you the opportunity for a clean break. Giving you...your out."

He jammed his fingers through his thick crop of hair and rested his hand at the nape of his neck. "What?"

"This break may have been forced by circumstance, but it was bound to happen eventually."

When Jake didn't immediately understand, she continued.

"I had a lot of time in the hotel to hear the stories about Jake Santos and his women. You don't have to feel obligated to me now because I took things too seriously. That's my fault. I'll always be grateful for everything you did to save my life."

Cassie's words were harder than a kick to the gut. "You think I'm blowing you off? After everything we've been through, that's what you really believe?"

Her shoulders slumped with the weight of her sigh. "Let's call it what it is, a natural end…to a difficult situation. A clean break."

"And you're making it easy on me by letting me off the hook. Is that it?"

"Pretty much. I think that's the best way."

"I think it sucks!"

Her determined expression faltered slightly. He had to admit he admired her for what she was trying to do. Still, he wanted no part of it.

"Don't make this any harder than it has to be." Reaching up, Cassie kissed him softly on the lips. It wasn't the kind of kiss he'd expected or come to know from her. It surely wasn't what he wanted either. She didn't sink against him and mold into his arms or give up her heart and soul to him. This kiss was restrained, as if she'd shut herself off completely. As he put his arms around her to draw her ever closer, she slipped away from his embrace.

Jake grabbed at the tightness in his chest that threatened to choke the life out of him. He thought he'd die. Good Lord, what was happening to them?

"You listen to me, Cassie. No matter what happens, I want you to know that…" He swallowed hard. What could he say to her?

He hadn't said the words. He loved this woman with every beat of his heart, and he hadn't told her. He needed more time. *They* needed more time.

"Good-bye, Jake."

The sting of her abrupt change left Jake shell shocked. Other women? Cassie wasn't just some other woman. She was special, incredible, like no one he'd ever met before in his life. She was Cassie, dammit, and he didn't want to be let off the hook.

"Cassie, I'm going to find the evidence—"

But she was gone already, quickly striding through the opening in the doorway Kevin had given her. His partner turned to him with a look of sympathy in his expression. Jake loathed his pity.

The walk into the corridor seemed surreal. Agents in blue pinstriped suits lined the hallway. Police, both in uniform and undercover, stood in their own groupings.

He searched the hallway, through the throng of people standing and moving about, for some sign of Cassie. There was none.

"She ran into the ladies room," Charley said, placing her hand on his shoulder. He glanced at Charley and saw compassion in her eyes. "I take it she didn't take the news well."

"Not particularly," he ground out, heading toward the restroom, ready to plow through the U.S. marshal parked at the door.

"Jake, you can't go into the ladies room."

"Want to see me?"

A stronger hand held him back, forcing him to swing around. Captain Russo gripped Jake hard by the upper arm. "Give her some space, Jake. She'll come around."

He stared at the closed door Cassie had just fled behind. "She thinks I sold her out."

"She needs some time," Charley said. "I'll talk to her when we get to the safe house."

It was like the air had been sucked out of the hallway. "*You'll* talk to her?"

"That's right."

Confusion and anger whirled into one. "What about this team you're supposed to be heading up to investigate Angel

Fagnelio and his cohorts? What about the Trumbella organization?"

Charley lifted her chin. "That will go on unabated, but with Agent Radcowski heading up the team instead of me."

"I didn't sign on with Radcowski."

"There's been a change of plans."

"Since last night?"

She didn't answer his question, Jake noticed. In true Charlotte Tate form the ice woman forged on with the subject at hand.

"I thought it best if I guard Cassie until the trial. No one will know her whereabouts but me."

"The only reason I agreed to let her out of my sight—"

"She'll still have the protection she needs, Detective."

Captain Russo's hand was gripping Jake's arm again. "Don't be stupid, Jake. It won't help Cassie to cause a scene. Come with me and we'll talk things through."

Charley scanned the hall, then glanced at the door to the ladies room. "I think that's a good idea. I'm going to check on Cassie."

"What the hell is going on here?" Jake roared, throwing his hands up in the air and charging toward the restroom door only to be held back by the captain.

"Knock it off, Jake," Russo seethed. "Don't make me have to arrest you."

Charley gave a hard look to Russo, then to Jake. "Great idea. Cuff him."

* * *

Cassie splashed cold water on her face and glanced at her torn expression in the mirror. She needed the shock of the frigid water. She wouldn't cry. She refused to cry over Jake.

He wasn't coming with her. *Good Lord, she was truly alone.* And what was worse, Cassie couldn't even go home to her own haven to lick her wounds. She was being forced back into hiding for God only knew how long. Maybe forever.

She closed her eyes so she wouldn't see the tears that

refused to hide themselves from her reflection in the mirror.

He didn't love her. She'd always known Jake was an honorable man, a knight in black leather armor when she'd needed him. He was a good cop, and, she thought with an ache in her heart, an incredible lover who'd awakened senses she never dreamed existed in her.

But he didn't love her. What did she expect? They'd only known each other a handful of days. This was her nightmare, not his. No one was telling him he couldn't walk out the door and go home. It wasn't fair for her to expect Jake to leave his family and friends to live in hiding with her.

What she'd shared with Jake had been real, special. For her anyway. And maybe on some level it had been real and special for Jake, too. Cassie wanted to believe that.

She wasn't the same woman she'd been before she met Jake. And now nothing would ever be the same again.

A dry laugh escaped her lips as she pulled a paper towel from the dispenser and brusquely wiped the water and tears from her face. The towel was abrasive against her cheek, but at least she could feel *something* other than the pain in her heart.

She thought of the irony. Before she'd met Jake, she tried so hard to keep her life in her control. It had made her dead inside to the point of ruining her relationship with other men.

Jake had changed all that. He'd opened her up, touched the marrow of her soul and made her feel again.

And she learned the one thing she couldn't control was her feelings. She loved Jake. And right now loving him hurt like hell.

A gust of wind blew into the confines of the small restroom as the door swung open. Agent Tate stood in the doorway in her navy pantsuit and flat-heeled boots.

"It's time, Cassie," she said.

Cassie could hardly find her voice. "Where am I going?"

Charlotte closed the door and with surety in her step, walked over to the sink where Cassie was standing. She leaned a hip against the gold-flecked vanity before crossing her arms across her chest.

"I'm not quite sure yet," she answered. "I haven't worked

201

out all the details. But I'll make sure you're as comfortable as you can possibly be outside of your own environment."

Charlotte's honesty was laudable. Cassie needed honesty more than anything right now. Still she needed more. Everything she'd fought so hard for when Emilio died was disintegrating before her very eyes. Tossing the crumpled paper towel into the garbage pail, she straightened her spine and looked squarely at Charlotte.

"I want the truth. Is this nightmare ever going to be over?"

To her surprise, Charlotte's lips lifted to a genuine smile. "Yes, Cassie, it will. I have a feeling this will all be over very soon."

CHAPTER SIXTEEN

"It should be me going with her. She thinks I've sold her out." Jake peered over his shoulder as Captain Russo led him toward the stairwell.

He was numb. Cassie was gone. Or she would be as soon as Charley got hold of her. And that would be the end of it.

"Once things cool down, she'll understand." Jake was barely aware of Russo's voice as he spoke.

Things never cool down with the mob. Cassie had said those words to him when this nightmare started. And she was right. Would she ever forgive him?

It didn't matter. Somehow he'd failed her. He should be the one hearing her voice every night and seeing her sunshine smile each and every morning. But it wasn't going to be him.

As they reached the door to the stairwell, Jake peered at the flurry of agents in the hallway. Kevin came running through the swarm of people. Jake ground himself to a stop to keep from going any further.

"Something doesn't feel right about all this, Kevin. Where's Radcowski?"

"I don't know. He brought Fagnelio to the bus but it's just sitting there."

"Why are all these agents still here? I thought Charley wanted to keep Cassie's transfer low profile?"

"Probably afraid of another screw up." Russo shook his head impatiently. "It doesn't matter. It's out of our hands. Come on, Santos."

Just as Jake was about to turn toward the doorway again, Cassie stepped out of the ladies room. His heart leaped. Her eyes were red and puffy as if she'd had a good cry. Her gaze locked with his and she smiled weakly, as if she'd forgiven him for failing her. He'd never forgive himself.

She walked up to them, seemingly unaware that his hands were bound behind his back. A flurry of U.S. marshal's motioned to each other and began to gather around.

"I'm ready," she said. She was talking to Charley, but looking at Jake.

"I'll walk with you to the car," Jake said. His arms ached to reach for her, to hold her and never let go. But he couldn't move them in the confines of the handcuffs binding his wrists.

Charley held up a hand and stepped between them, eyeing her warningly. "I'm afraid that's not possible." She turned to Kevin after taking a quick glance up and down the hallway. "I thought Agent Radcowski was with you?"

"He said he wanted to see Fagnelio off, but the paddy wagon hasn't left yet."

She darted a glance to Cassie. "I don't like hanging around in the hall like this. Let's go."

Cassie didn't cry aloud as she turned away. Jake knew she'd wait until no one was looking.

"What the hell is this all about?" Kevin asked, noticing the handcuffs for the first time.

"Go with her, Kev," Jake pleaded. There wasn't anything he could do. He hadn't felt so powerless since the day he and Tyler had been ambushed in that alley. Fear crawled under his skin as he tried to pull his hands free of their restraints, already knowing they wouldn't budge without the key.

Kevin just nodded. "I'll make sure she makes it off okay with Charley." He headed toward the back door where they were leading Cassie.

To his credit, Captain Russo actually looked sympathetic. "I know it stinks, but you have to listen to me."

But Jake wasn't listening. Instead, he stood paralyzed as Cassie took each step down the corridor. The back door opened to a heavy downpour, mirroring what he felt in his heart.

Someone popped an umbrella open and Cassie stepped out into the rain. Even through the downpour, Jake could see a hoard of reports rush forward to get their shot at their headlining news. A band of police officers forced them back. Flash bulbs went off furiously.

"Cassie." He breathed her name more than said it. But now she was gone.

He hadn't been aware of how he'd been pushing forward against police officers and Captain Russo as they held him back. He was vaguely aware of being shoved into the stairwell and slammed against the cold hard wall. As his face connected with concrete, a stabbing pain shot up his jaw and cheek and blurred his vision for a moment. It took a second for his head to clear and the sharp pain in his face to ebb to a steady throb.

Cassie was gone. Good God Almighty, they'd taken her!

"Quit acting like an idiot, Jake," Russo seethed. "Whatever you're thinking you know, you're wrong."

Jake blinked, trying to swing around to face the Captain, but Russo's full weight pinned him against the wall. A second kick of adrenaline surged through him like a raging river.

"Charley was with Bellows the night of the shooting. Charley shot Bellows at Cassie's apartment. Now she's leaving with Cassie. Charley has to be the leak!"

"No."

"Take off the cuffs, dammit!"

"Listen."

"Not until you get me free."

Russo slammed Jake against the concrete wall again and grabbed him by the upper shirt, holding him under his weight. The cold metal handcuffs bit into his wrists.

"Charley isn't the leak."

"Why else would she have—"

"He killed my son, Jake. My boy. I had no choice."

The raw emotion in the Paul Russo's voice was unmistakable, heartbreaking. It matched the strength of his force against Jake. He couldn't break free with the handicap of having his hands restrained behind his back.

"Who? What are you talking about?"

"Paulie might have taken those drugs that ended his life, but that dirtbag Fagnelio was responsible. He sold the drugs to

Paulie. It was because of him my son had that monkey on his back all those years and no matter how hard he tried, he couldn't get it off. I tried so hard—"

"What does this have to do with Cassie?"

"I saw him the night of the shooting at Rory's. I watched Fagnelio get into that car and drive off. You told me you were going to meet him that night and I wanted to make damned sure he went."

"You set me up?!"

"No! How could you think that? I wanted that slippery bastard to pay. Every time he'd been arrested, I thought he'd get his due for what he'd done to my boy and so many others. But he always managed to get away. Always. He was never going to pay for what he did to Paulie."

"So you were tailing him?"

"I couldn't sleep at night thinking of what he did, so I watched him. Waiting for him to slip up. He's going to pay, Jake. He's going to pay!"

Russo's voice broke and his grip eased a fraction. It was enough for Jake to pull free from the wall and swing around. The captain's face was haunted, taking on a new degree of anger, one born of grief and revenge. Jake understood the kind of mad passion that had driven him. The same kind of grief and anger that had Angel Fagnelio hating Jake all these years. He'd make sure whoever hurt Cassie would pay for the rest of their lives.

"He'll pay. But not if we don't find out who leaked Cassie's name to the press first."

"This is what I'm trying to tell you, dammit. I did it. I'm the leak!"

* * *

Cassie was blinded by flashbulbs firing out of control as she stepped out into the rain. She didn't remember them being here when she'd arrived earlier and wasn't sure why they'd positioned themselves here now.

Kevin gripped her arm and moved her forward toward the waiting car that would take her to her holding cell. Oh, she knew the new location would be luxurious, as the last one had been. But it would imprison her just the same. She fought wave after wave of nausea, trying desperately to keep herself from breaking down.

Not now.

For a moment when they were inside, Cassie actually thought Jake would tell her the words she wanted to hear. That he was helplessly in love with her.

What a fool!

How could she think that after such a short time together, Jake would risk his career just to be with her? Just because she knew without a doubt that she loved Jake Santos, that the thought of never being in his arms again was like a slow death, didn't mean he felt the same way. For the next six months, the memory of his hands on her skin, his mouth on her would haunt her every waking moment.

Another flashbulb went off and then another as a flurry of reporters began running toward another back door. More flashbulbs... *Pop, pop, pop.*

"Get down!" Pure horror clouded Kevin's face. He slammed Cassie to the rough pavement with insurmountable force. Her face hit the wet tar, and his strong hand kept her still while his body hovered over her.

"Get her to the car," Charley yelled.

Firecrackers...screams...the rain beating her down to the ground and splattering her face, sucking the life out of her.

"Get off me," she screamed, fighting Kevin as he pinned her in place.

The unmistakable and deadly sound of gunfire exploded near her ear. She pushed Kevin off her, horrified to find his gun was drawn, and he'd been the one to fire.

People were scrambling for cover. Ignoring the orders of the agents screeching orders back and forth between gunfire, Kevin gripped Cassie by the upper arm and dragged her behind a guardrail. It was feeble cover from flying bullets, but that's all they had at the moment without putting them directly in the line of fire. Even the run to the row of cars where Agent Radcowski was crouched would put them in direct line of fire.

Kevin cursed and frantically looked back and forth, searching the vicinity and the roof of the building. "Where the hell are they shooting from?"

Thank God Jake was inside. Cassie glanced in the direction they'd just come and saw the door to the courthouse was closed. In the middle of pandemonium, at least she had the comfort of knowing Jake was out of the path of flying bullets.

She'd thought he was bulletproof. At least that's the way she felt when Jake covered her with his body of armor. But he was a mere mortal man. She knew all too well that bullets killed, and Cassie didn't want Jake dying because of her.

A bullet splintered the wood rail just above her head.

"For God sake, Cassie, get low to the ground," Kevin ground out.

The realization that she was going to die suddenly flooded her. She was going to die right there in the middle of a puddle and she had never told Jake she loved him. She was going to die. But at least Jake was safe.

* * *

Jake could hardly believe what he'd just heard. Anger surged through him at bullet speed, winding every muscle in his body into a tight knot.

"You sacrificed Cassie's life—"

"It was the only way, Jake. He was going to walk again and you know it! I never thought it would go this far. Believe me. Fagnelio has gotten away with murder long before this. But there's more, and we don't have much time."

"If anything happens to Cassie—"

"It won't. There's still time."

"Take off the cuffs," Jake demanded, trying to keep his emotions in check, trying to clear his mind enough to keep from unleashing all his fear and pent up frustration out on the Captain.

Russo uncuffed him and took a wide step back as if waiting for Jake to take all his anger, all his energy and swing at him. "I saw the driver of the car, Jake."

Whatever thoughts of retribution Jake had at that moment ended with that statement. *The elusive driver.* Cassie couldn't remember his face the night of the shooting. No one was talking.

"Was it Charley?"

Russo shook his head.

"Bellows?"

"It was Agent Radcowski. I knew it the moment he sat his arrogant ass in the chair in my office that he was behind—"

"Why didn't you say something before now?"

"I needed him to bring Fagnelio in. He was the only one who could do it. That's why I wanted you to get away. I didn't know how deep this went into the FBI. I thought you'd be safe out—"

The Captain halted with the sound of popping, mixed in with torrential rain outside. Popping? No, gunfire!

"Cassie!"

* * *

An eerie silence hung in the air for a few seconds. The heavy downpour had ebbed with the gunfire as if the sky had chosen to give them a break. Those few seconds dragged on endlessly as another sheet of rain blew across the parking lot and pelted down on top of Cassie.

Kevin's eyes were ominously bright as he scanned the area around them. Water poured down his face. He blinked it away and opened his eyes wide, making him look more ferocious than the happy-go-lucky guy she'd been introduced to.

He didn't trust her. But he'd given Jake his word, so here he was protecting her.

"Jake." She said his name softly and as if by sheer will the back door to the courthouse flew open. Three uniformed cops scrambled out the door and took cover behind the paddy wagon.

Jake stepped out into the downpour, the dark metal of his gun bleeding in with the color of his rain soaked hands and his shirt. By his stance, she knew he held a gun. And she knew he *wasn't* wearing a bulletproof vest.

A clap of thunder and a flare of lightning zigzagged across the black sky. Cassie heard another pop, pop, pop from behind her.

"I'm taking her to the car!" Agent Radcowski yelled from just beyond a row of cars.

She lifted up on her hands and heard someone screaming. Then in a split second, she realized it was her.

"Get down, Cassie!" Jake screamed, lifting his Glock into position. In his face, she saw both fear and hatred.

Agent Radcowski gripped her by the upper arm and dragged her away from Kevin.

"What the hell is Santos doing?" she heard Charley yell from right by her side.

"He's aiming at us!" Agent Radcowski scowled. "I told you he was trying to kill the girl all along."

"No," Cassie breathed. What were they saying? Radcowski lifted his gun into position, aiming it directly at Jake. To Cassie's horror, Charley did the same.

"Drop the weapon, Santos!" Charley yelled. As Charley lifted her gun into position, a surge of adrenaline raced through Cassie.

When she lifted her head and turned back, she had a sudden sense of déjà-vu. There was something about Agent Radcowski. Maybe it was the dark clouds, or the scowl on his face. He turned his head a fraction toward Jake, who was now charging in their direction, and it flashed in her mind. Darkness. Windows exploding. The face of the person sitting behind the wheel of the getaway car. The face of the man standing with her.

She looked at Agent Radcowski. It was him! He was the one involved with Fagnelio all along. He helped kill all those people. *And he wanted* her *dead.*

"Shoot him," Radcowski scowled.

"No!" Cassie tried to break free, but Charley held her back.

Bursting forward, Cassie tackled Charley to the ground, rolling with her until they were out in the open, prime target for anyone to take aim.

"Stay down!" Charley demanded.

Cassie was done being a victim. Someone had wanted her dead and now she knew that without a doubt that person was Agent Radcowski. Too many people had already died at the hands of this monster.

"Charlotte, it was Agent Radcowski!" Cassie pleaded.

It took a second for that bit of information to register in the wake of all the confusion.

Before Agent Tate could make another move, a white spark of light spit from the barrel of Agent Radcowski's gun, followed by the sound of gunpowder igniting. Kevin rose to his feet in front of Cassie, shielding her view of Jake. Another mighty clap of thunder coupled with a torrent of pistol fire rang out in the dark sky. Kevin flew back against the guardrail, gasping, his eyes wide open. And then she finally saw Jake.

An eerie silence blanketed them for a moment. She lifted to her knees and saw Jake running full force toward her now. Agents encircled her. People were screaming. Before she could clear her mind among the confusion, she'd lost sight of Jake.

"Jake?" she called out.

Where had he gone?

"Let me go," she screamed at a U.S. marshal who was pulling her away toward an open car door.

"Let go of her." Jake appeared by her side at that instant, crushing her wet body against him, and kissing her.

She looked at him, touched his face, his chest. "Thank God, you weren't hurt. I thought you'd be killed," she said, unable to hold back her tears.

"You might be letting me off the hook, but let me tell you lady, I'm not letting *you* off the hook."

New tears sprang to her eyes. "Thank God," she whispered.

"I was so afraid I'd never get a chance to tell you how much I love you."

She let the cold rain and hot tears roll helplessly down her cheeks. Agents and uniformed cops were screaming orders around them, trying to sort through the crowd and attend to the injured.

"You love me?"

Through the rain, she saw his tears. "More than I ever thought I could."

Not even the bright flashbulbs that went off distracted him from her. The press had now emerged again, despite the police officers' attempts at holding them back, and were hot to get their story. Oblivious, Jake just gazed down at her, the rain dripping off his wet hair and face. She saw the love shining in his eyes and written all over his face.

"I love you, too," she said, reaching up and wrapping her arms around him. "I don't want to be without you."

"I don't think that's a problem anymore," she heard Kevin say from behind them.

"Oh, Kevin," she gasped. She'd seen him go down during the last round of gunfire.

They both turned and saw Charlotte crouched by Kevin's side, helping him to his feet. The small hole in the center of his shirt was unmistakable.

"You okay, buddy?" Jake asked.

Kevin nodded.

"Hurts like a bastard, huh?" Jake said, reaching a hand out to his partner, a look of relief and gratitude filled his expression.

"Knocked the damn air right out of my lungs."

"You really okay?"

Kevin nodded, opening his wet shirt, which revealed a bulletproof vest. He'd taken a bullet meant for Jake, and for that she was eternally grateful. Jake wasn't wearing any armor to protect him. She knew he would have taken the bullet for her, with or without a vest. It both filled her heart with love and with colossal fear.

In the moments that passed, the rain subsided, the ambulances arrived, and the story of what had happened unfolded.

In an attempt to cover his involvement in the bond fraud, Agent Radcowski orchestrated an escape attempt during Cassie's transfer to cause confusion in the hopes that either Fagnelio or Cassie, the one star witness who could prove instrumental in tracing his partnership with Ritchie Trumbella back to him, would be killed.

Captain Russo, suspecting Radcowski would make his move but not having any evidence to prove otherwise, orchestrated a media mob to keep Radcowski from getting away with murder again.

Agent Radcowski had killed Angel Fagnelio and later confessed to being the real strong arm, along with Agent Bellows, in the bond fraud. Charlotte Tate had unknowingly been a source of information for Bellows and knew nothing about the other agents' involvement.

Three weeks later, Cassie had come to terms with the outcome and had submerged herself back into her work and real estate ads for houses outside the city. Jake spent every night at her apartment, coming in late with an apologetic look on his face.

It was no different this night.

Jake crept into her dark bedroom and sank down on the bed next to Cassie.

"Did I wake you?" he asked, when he realized she was watching him.

"No, I just got into bed myself."

He smiled weakly, pulling off his boots.

Cassie sat up in bed. "Stop doing that."

"Doing what?"

She sputtered. "Don't give me that, Santos. You've been coming here for the past three weeks with this gloomy look like you think I'm going to toss you out the window for being late."

He shrugged sheepishly. "I'm sorry."

"For what? Coming home late? That's your job."

"That doesn't bother you?"

"Not as much as thinking about you chasing bad guys."

His eyebrows furrowed, darkening his expression. "That's about what I do. Is that something you can live with? I mean, day in and day out?"

213

"I'm getting used to it. If there is one thing I've learned these past few weeks, life doesn't give you any guarantees. What we went through, most people can't even fathom. I want what we have for as long as we are blessed to have it. I can be happy with that."

"It's not going to make you mad to eat dinner alone half the time?"

She smirked. "Speaking of dinner, I burned it tonight."

Jake cursed under his breath. Cassie chuckled and shook him teasingly.

"I was writing, silly. I forgot all about the roast because I had to get this one scene written. By the time I remembered dinner, it had petrified in the oven. I'm saving it to use as a doorstop."

The rich sound of Jake's laugh lifted her heart and filled it beyond capacity.

"You didn't get mad at me when you woke up and found me at my computer last week, did you?"

He shook his head. "But what does that have to do with anything?"

"Everything. You chase bad guys and I write about them. Both of us run on a moment's notice." She snaked her arms around him and nuzzled her face in his neck. "Don't you see, we're perfect together?"

She heard his laughter bubble up from his chest.

"I guess you're right."

"I know I'm right. So what are you going to do about it, Detective?"

He gave her a teasing sidelong glance. "Are you getting bossy with me again, CJ?"

She laughed at Jake's reference to CJ. He'd come to calling her that whenever she asserted herself. And she had to admit, she rather liked playing the heroine. He rolled her onto her back and covered her body with his as he kissed her with a wild passion she'd come to know and love.

"You know, CJ Carmen has fallen in love."

Jake's eyebrows knitted. "Oh, really?"

"Yes, she found a man who is quite a lot like you."

"Is she going to finally settle down and marry the guy?"

Cassie heaved an exaggerated sigh and dramatically propped the back of her hand over her forehead. "Alas, he hasn't asked her yet."

Jake tsked and shook his head. "Damn fool. We're going to have to change that. What do you say we rewrite that scene? Together this time. Until we get it right."

She gazed up that the most extraordinary man she'd ever met. She couldn't have written his character any better if she tried. "I'd say that's perfect."

THE END

Dear Reader:

Thank you so much for reading MATERIAL WITNESS. *This book was written over 10 years ago and was supposed to be the first in a series I did for Love Inspired Suspense. I ended up writing book 2 and publishing* Yuletide Protector – Harlequin Love Inspired Suspense *as a Love Inspired Suspense book in 2009. So if you'd like to see more of Jake Santos and Kevin Gordon, check out* Yuletide Protector – Harlequin Love Inspired Suspense, *available as an e-book.*

I plan on continuing the three series I currently have available: Fate with a Helping Hand, Texas Hearts, and this new one, which at this point has no title. Hmm, if you can think of a good series name, email me at LisaMondello@aol.com. I love hearing from readers.

Please check out my other books published as Lisa Mondello, as well as a new Young Adult book, co-written with my daughter, entitled NO STRINGS ATTACHED. NO STRINGS ATTACHED *will be published in late summer or early fall 2012. Check back on my blog for news and upcoming books at http://www.lisamondello.blogspot.com.*

If you HAVE *checked my blog before or have read any of the numerous interviews I've done online, then you may have heard me mention that I used to manage a Boston/Worcester Rock Band. Those were very special days for me. Tragically, one of the members of that band, a dear friend of mine who I'd known for 30 years, died on April 5, 2012. Scott Ricciuti was, and will always be in my eyes, a rock star! He was passionate about music, and his family and friends. I hope you take the opportunity to check out his music at http://www.ScottRicciuti.com or check Youtube for one of his many performances in the Boston/Worcester area. Through his music you'll get a small glimpse of the man so many of us loved. Keep the music alive…*

Many thanks,

Lisa Mondello

EBooks available by Lisa Mondello

The Marriage Contract

All I Want for Christmas is You

The Knight and Maggie's Baby

Her Heart for the Asking ++

His Heart for the Trusting++

The More I See++

Nothing but Trouble

Cradle of Secrets – Harlequin Love Inspired Suspense**

Her Only Protector – Harlequin Love Inspired Suspense**

Yuletide Protector – Harlequin Love Inspired Suspense

Fresh-Start Family – Harlequin Love Inspired Romance

In a Doctor's Arms – Harlequin Love Inspired Romance

Fate with a Helping Hand (Massachusetts) Series
+ + **Texas Hearts Series**
** **Cradle** Series

PREVIEWS

HER HEART FOR THE ASKING – Book 1

Mandy Morgan swore she'd never step foot in Texas again after Beau Gentry left her for life on the rodeo circuit eight years before. But now her uncle's heart is failing and she has to convince him that surgery will save his life. She never dreamed the first thing she'd see when she stepped off the plane would be her biggest nightmare...the one man she'd never stopped loving.

Beau Gentry had the fever for two things: the rodeo and Mandy Morgan. But for Beau, loving Mandy was complicated by his father's vendetta against her uncle. This led him to make the hardest decision of his life and he can still see the bitterness and hurt on Mandy's face. All these years it has killed him to think Mandy had forgotten him and moved as far away as possible from him. But now they're back in Texas, and he's going to do all he can to win back her love.

Excerpt of Her Heart for the Asking –Book 1

"What are you doing here?" Mandy Morgan asked, dropping her too-heavy overnight case on the sun-roasted tarmac. After a grueling forty-eight hour work stint and a five-hour flight from Philadelphia, she stood wilting under the brutal Texas sun, facing her biggest nightmare.Beau Gentry.

She groaned inwardly, drinking Beau in with her eyes as if she hadn't had a drop of water in months. Eight years was more like it. If she were eight years smarter, she would be moving her aching feet as fast as she could in the opposite direction. But all she could do was stare at eyes so bright they rivaled the blazing sun. At lips so kissable she'd spent the better part of her adult life trying to wipe the memory clean from her mind.

She had expected Beau would have aged some. When she allowed herself to think about him at all, she reminded herself. The faint lines etched in the corners of his sleepy gray-blue eyes gave a hint of maturity, but most probably caused by long days in the cruel sun.

She fought the urge to take a closer look at his ruggedly handsome features, but failed. How could he have gotten better looking after being abused by every bronc-busting horse on the rodeo circuit? His angular jaw, strong and determined, was shaded with beard growth that was probably a day old, maybe more. Mandy suspected if Beau grew a full beard, it would grow in thick and be the smooth texture of his almost black head of hair. She forced aside past memories that gave her such knowledge with renewed irritation.

The man didn't even have the decency to have a crooked nose. What should have been bent and awkward from being broken a few too many times was instead long and straight, shaped perfectly between high cheek bones most women would swoon over, or kill to have themselves. But on Beau Gentry, it was just one thousand percent robust cowboy.

Damn him.

"I'm your ride out to the Double T," Beau said, gripping the edge of his white straw cowboy hat and tipping it in a cordial gesture.

She ground the heels of her low pumps into the soft tar to contain her growing irritation. Did he think she was an idiot? "No way."

"'Fraid so," he said, his expression slightly askew.

"Hank didn't mention anything about you coming to get me when I spoke to him on the phone."

"I suspect he thought you would have found some excuse not to come if you knew I was picking you up."

"He would have been right. Why didn't one of the hands come get me?"

Settling his hand at the base of his neck, Beau replied, "You're looking at him. As of three weeks ago I am one of the ranch hands at the Double T."

HIS HEART FOR THE TRUSTING – Book 2

Ever since Mitch Broader set foot in Texas, he dreamed of owning his own ranch. Now that he's bought a share in the Double T Ranch, he's one step closer to the dream. Then his past greets him in the form of a baby basket, complete with infant and birth certificate naming him as the father. He can't change diapers and work toward his dream at the same time.

When Sara Lightfoot, "Miss Hollywood" in Mitch's eyes, rescues him with her particular knack for handling his precocious son, he hires her on the spot as a temporary nanny. No matter how much Sara's dark eyes and warm heart make this bachelor think of settling down and making their arrangement permanent, she's made it perfectly clear she has other plans that don't include him or his dreams.

Sara Lightfoot never thought she'd return to her home on the reservation. Now she plans to reclaim the life she left by going back to the reservation as a Native American storyteller, teaching the Apache children stories of their culture. She didn't expect Mitch Broader's sexy smile or job offer as a live-in nanny to derail those plans. After all she's been through to come home, can she open up her heart once again to love?

THE KNIGHT AND MAGGIE'S BABY

"The secondary characters were amazing...a very good book." *Cocktails and Books*."...had me in tears because it was so beautiful. Such a lovely story of two people falling in love against the odds." *Crystal @ Snowdrops Dreams of Books*

Sometimes fate needs a little help...

Jonah Wallace knows what it's like to grow up without love. Despite having more money than the Queen of England, his childhood was cold and stale as he grew up in boarding schools. He's dedicated his life to helping homeless and displaced children find the love and support they need by creating the Haven House Foundation, work that resulted in him being Knighted by the Queen.

Now that he's living in America, his work is going along just fine...until his grandfather gives fate a little nudge by insisting he take a wife before he can inherit.

Coffee shop owner Maggie Bonelli is pregnant, and the baby's dad has gone AWOL. She knows too well the pain of growing up without a daddy. So when Jonah Wallace comes into her shop proposing marriage for a year, she takes him up on his offer, even if it's only for a year. Live in a mansion and give her baby a name and a daddy to call his/her own. But can they keep their perfect arraignment strictly business...or will fate's helping hand bring them love at last?

THE MARRIAGE CONTRACT

"Hilariously funny!" "Delightful!" 4 STARS Romantic Times Magazine

What would you do to get a second chance at love? Sometimes fate needs a little helping hand...

When Ruthie Carvalho finds an old birthday card with a marriage proposal scribbled on the back, she figures she's hit pay dirt and is destined to get her 35-year-old daughter married.

The trouble is, Ruthie can't stand Cara's boyfriend, and Cara is just stubborn enough to push in the opposite direction of what her mother wants.

When Devin Michaels gets a phone call from his old friend's mom, he knows Ruthie is up to something. But he's at a crossroad. It's been 17 years since he's seen Cara and memories of their soulful talks and walks on the beach make him long to reconnect.

Going back to the seaside town of Westport, Massachusetts, to reconnect with Cara seems like just the thing to do. One look at Cara and the years seem to melt away. With a little help and "creative" planning from Ruthie, can these old friends become lovers and have a second chance at happiness?

CPSIA information can be obtained at www.ICGtesting.com
Printed in the USA
LVOW041815041212

310079LV00002B/192/P